Remember the Past

...Only as it gives you Pleasure

Maria Grace

White Soup Press

Published by: White Soup Press

Remember the Past
Copyright © 2014 Maria Grace

For information, address
author.MariaGrace@gmail.com

ISBN-10: 0692263179
ISBN-13: 978-0692263174 (White Soup Press)

Author's Website: RandomBitsofFaascination.com
Email address: **Author.MariaGrace@gmail.com**

Dedication

For my husband and sons.
You have always believed in me.

❧Chapter 1

Everyone has a past. Oftentimes it behooves one to think of the past only as its remembrance gives one pleasure.

"I DO NOT SEE HOW you can disagree. Truly, I do not." Lady Catherine's features settled into the familiar expression of a school mistress who knew best: lips pressed tight, eyes narrowed and staring down her nose. She perched on the overstuffed chair and folded her hands in her lap.

Fitzwilliam Darcy opened his mouth to comment but shut it before the words escaped. When his mother-in-law wore that expression, only a fool considered arguing. The dear woman possessed the Fitzwilliams' hallmark stubbornness in far greater measure than her petite stature implied.

"If my Anne were still with us, she would agree—"

"With what would she agree?" Richard Fitzwilliam poked his head in the doorway.

Darcy jumped and twisted around in his seat. "I swear you will drive me barking mad!"

"How so?" Fitzwilliam sauntered in. His heavy boots barely whispered against the carpet.

"Sneaking up on me! One day I will—" Darcy rose and shook a pointing finger.

"Balderdash! You would do no such thing, and even if you did, you would stand no chance—"

"Yes, yes, I know, against a retired colonel of His Majesty's army. I know. You say it often enough."

Fitzwilliam chuckled and dropped onto the settee. His long legs stretched into the center of the room, perfectly situated to trip the unsuspecting. "You are merely unhappy George and David have learned from their uncle, the hero. What have they done this time?"

"Ask the butler who is cleaning the ink spilled on my desk, and coat, and breeches."

Lady Catherine leaned forward. "Really, Fitzwilliam, retired colonel or not, I am not sure you should be teaching my grandsons—"

"They are boys, madam, and if I have anything to say on the matter, they will be permitted to act like boys."

"Your dear mother, Lady Matlock, never allowed—"

"No, she did not, and I vowed never to see the same inflicted upon any boy in my influence. In fact, it is high time I taught them to fence." Fitzwilliam brandished an invisible foil.

"They are full young for that." She groaned and pinched her temples.

Fitzwilliam grinned his maddening cocksure smile. "So then, Aunt, on what do you insist Anne would agree with you?"

Darcy grumbled and sank into his chair.

She smoothed her skirt over her lap. "I am sure you will agree. It only stands to reason that—"

"No, madam, it does not." Darcy pressed his eyes with thumb and forefinger.

"What stands to reason?" Fitzwilliam asked.

"A widower in possession of children and an estate—"

"And a good fortune," Darcy muttered.

"Naturally, a good fortune, that goes without saying."

"What about such a gentleman?" Fitzwilliam enjoyed this far too much.

"Why, he must be in want of a wife, of course." She sprang to her feet and wandered across the room, stopping in front of the large picture window. "A retired admiral of the White, Thomas Bennet, a widower with four children, two daughters and two sons—"

"And five thousand a year." Darcy rolled his eyes.

Lady Catherine shot him a look certain to sour milk. "He purchased Alston Hall and will move in this week."

"Ah, that explains the to-do on the road today," Fitzwilliam said.

"You saw him?" Lady Catherine brightened.

"Indeed, spoke with him myself. Seems a most amiable gentleman, for a sailor." Fitzwilliam winked. "Though I understand you do not approve of the navy, Darce, something about it bringing people of obscure birth into positions they do not deserve."

Darcy drummed his fingers along his jaw. Fitzwilliam never forgot any comment he could later use out of context.

"What a fine thing for our family." She clapped her hands. "You must visit him, of course, as soon as may be arranged."

"How is this a fine thing for our family?"

"You must consider the boys and Georgiana. Your sister pines for the company of other young women, and you yourself complain the parish lacks fitting companions for her. Here this Bennet fellow has two daughters. Your boys desperately need playmates of their own age to do … well, boy-things with, and now two are come into the neighborhood."

"And precisely how, madam," Darcy clutched the arms of his chair until the fabric threatened to give way, "have you ascertained any of this family are fitting company? For all you know, this admiral could be a shopkeeper's son with tawdry morals and a mouth like … like a sailor."

"What has come over you? You are simply impossible! Go and visit our new neighbor, or I promise you, I will do so myself without you." She harrumphed and stomped out.

Silence lingered in her wake as they both watched the door. Darcy held his breath, a little trepidatious of her return.

"She was right about one thing," Fitzwilliam said. "What has come over you?"

Darcy let his head fall back against the chair. "I already met the man."

"When? How?"

"Shortly after you encountered him. George and I went riding and came upon one of their coaches stuck in the mud. We helped them free it and suggested an alternative road."

"And?"

"And I found him an amiable gentleman with well-mannered sons who will make excellent playmates for George and David."

"So, why the row you created?" Fitzwilliam pointed his chin toward the doorway.

"He still grieves an esteemed wife, lost only last winter, and does not deserve match-making machinations."

"And his daughters? Are they pretty? What of their dowries?"

"They remained in the carriage." Darcy rubbed the back of his neck. "I do not believe, 'Hello, pleased to meet you. Are your daughters suitably attractive, or do their fortunes offer sufficient compensation for their facial deformities?' is considered a polite introduction, even in the wilds of Derbyshire."

Fitzwilliam snickered.

"You will be able to judge for yourself soon enough."

"You are going to visit them?"

"No." Darcy pushed to his feet and laced his hands behind his head. "Alston Hall will require a full staff working two weeks complete, probably more, to make the place livable. They brought only a half dozen long-time servants with them."

"So?"

"So, I invited them to stay at Pemberley. Mrs. Reynolds can help them hire a proper staff."

"You did what?" Fitzwilliam slapped the settee.

"They did not immediately accept the invitation. However, after they visit Alston Hall, I am certain they will."

"Do I comprehend you correctly? You invited them to stay? Here? A stranger—and a sailor no less?

What are you thinking? You are no lover of company, particularly that of strangers."

"We have both read of his exploits often enough. His connections and his reputation are common knowledge. To call him a stranger is hardly fitting. I regard it an honor to host a man of his standing." Darcy looked away and shrugged. "Besides, he reminded me of Father."

Fitzwilliam slapped Darcy's shoulder harder than necessary. "I'll be damned. I shall not tell Aunt Catherine, though. She likes surprises."

"Are we almost there?" Francis Bennet clambered over his father's lap and smashed his nose against the side glass. "You said we would arrive before supper. I'm hungry."

Elizabeth stretched across the coach to grab his arm, but he squirmed out of her reach. It was high time Francis learned not to speak every thought that crossed his mind.

"No 'Lisbet! I want to see!" He bounced on his father's knee.

Admiral Thomas Bennet grimaced and seized him around the ribs, lifting him off his lap.

"Come here." Jane caught his elbow and pulled him toward her. "You know Papa's leg pains him."

He bowed his head and scraped his feet. "I am sorry, Papa."

Papa lost his officer's glare and ruffled the boy's hair.

Francis lurched toward Jane, stumbled and fell into his identical twin's shoulder. "Oh, oh! I see it, I see it!"

"Look, Papa." Philip tapped the glass. "See the gables and look—look, there's the turret, just as you described. Might that room be ours, Papa?"

"We shall see." He kneaded his thigh.

Philip flattened himself against his father's side, making room for Francis near the side glass. "It is just as grand as Papa said. Isn't it, Jane?"

"Why not sit beside Jane so you can get a better view?" Papa gave Philip a gentle push toward the opposite seat.

Jane settled him beside her and draped her arm around him.

"I think it horrid." Francis tossed his curls and stamped. "Why did we have to leave Longbourn? I liked it there. You said we would not have to move again." He stuck out his bottom lip.

"That is enough!" Elizabeth hissed.

Papa's brows knotted, and he ground his teeth.

One day Francis would learn the meaning of that expression and be far more careful about provoking it.

"We left because my nip farthing, ninnyhammer brother, Collins, insisted on installing his worthless son and his French wife-in-water-colors there."

"He wanted to bring a painting to Longbourn?" Philip huddled close to Jane. Papa's ire always upset him, poor boy. "Mightn't we have stayed and let him hang the painting?"

"It is a little more complicated than that, dear," Jane said.

"Bloody, rank, white livered …"

Elizabeth caught his eye. Philip would soon ask what all those words meant and she was not about to explain mistresses and other manly things to him.

Papa could have that conversation all to himself.

Papa wrinkled his nose. "An honorable man would have given us more than a month to vacate."

Elizabeth laid her hand on his arm. "Let it go. You always say a man should be captain of his own ship. Now that Alston Hall is yours, you are master. You were never happy at Longbourn with the specter of our uncle looming over you."

"My voice of reason." He patted her hand, scowl softening. "Using my own words against me, no less, clever lass."

"I still think—"

"Francis!" Jane and Elizabeth cried.

The coach slowed as it trundled up the gravel lane. The looming, dark windows in the pale stone elevation dared them to approach.

"Let us see if she floats." Admiral Bennet pushed the door open before the coach came to a complete stop.

He jumped down, grimaced and clutched his knee. The boys bounded after him. Jane and Elizabeth waited for the coach to come to a proper halt. By that time though, Papa was long gone. After so protracted a journey, one could by no means expect patience from him.

Papa's man, Piper, shambled over from the other coach and handed them out. Frightening scars puckered the old sailor-come-valet's face and his eye patch lent him a menacing air, one he cultivated at every opportunity. All the Bennets knew better, though. He had been with Admiral Bennet for as long as the girls could remember. The two men had saved each other's lives so many times neither kept count.

Mrs. Hill, their longtime housekeeper, and Miss

Iola Wexley, the boys' long-suffering governess, joined them at the front door.

"Permission to come aboard, Cap'n?" Piper saluted and squeezed his good eye shut, drawing his cheek and lip into something resembling a snarl.

The boys saluted. "Permission, Papa?"

"Permission granted." Papa twisted the key in the lock and wrenched the doorknob. The hinges squealed their protests and the door inched open. He took his sons' hands and stepped over the threshold. The rest followed.

Elizabeth sniffed the stale air, musty and dusty as a well-traveled sea chest. Jane sneezed. Twice.

"At least they kept the furniture properly covered," Mrs. Hill muttered. "I best go find the kitchen." She trundled off.

Elizabeth bit back a giggle. Only Mrs. Hill dared wander away without awaiting the Admiral's orders. He gave her a wider berth than even Piper. Not even he had cheek enough to raise the sturdy woman's ire.

"Miss Wexley, survey the servants' rooms." He turned to Piper. "Take the boys and reconnoiter the east wing. Perhaps you can find a school room and nursery."

The twins moaned and sputtered incomplete protests that they dare not give full voice lest Papa find it necessary to correct their attitudes.

"Yes, sir." Piper saluted.

Francis and Philip mimicked him and followed him upstairs.

Elizabeth cleared her throat.

"Ah, Lizzy, do not say it. Go look through the house first. You and Jane take the west wing whilst I survey downstairs. I am certain you will yet find the manor meets your standards."

"Yes, Papa." Elizabeth trudged toward the stairs, Jane at her side.

"It is a lovely house, is it not?" Jane whispered.

"The architecture is beautiful, I fully grant you." Elizabeth clutched the banister in one hand and her skirts in the other. "Mahogany and paper hangings are lovely, dust and disrepair are not."

"The roof and the windows appear sound," Jane offered in her plucky, trying-to-make-the-best-of-it-voice.

"A fine beginning, indeed." Elizabeth landed her foot on the final step a little harder than strictly necessary. "If you are correct, I am grateful. Still, I hope for more than just roof and windows."

The hall stretched on and on and disappeared into the horizon. A chill wind whistled and moaned past them.

"My goodness." Jane rubbed her arms. "This is a grand place, indeed."

Elizabeth shrugged and yanked the first door. "These look like family quarters." She pulled the dusty sheets off the press and jerked open a drawer. A moth flew out as she tugged out a crumpled sheet. "Badly folded and musty." Her nose wrinkled and she fought not to sneeze. "Everything must be washed before it can be used. Much will need mending too."

Jane jerked back the bed's dust covers to reveal an elegantly carved frame. "How lovely." She sat down.

The mattress caved in and swallowed her.

Elizabeth wrestled her away from the hungry featherbed. "That needs work, too."

"Perhaps we should rig some hammocks from the bed posts." Jane held the musty sheet between the bedposts.

"No doubt Piper still sleeps in one." Elizabeth beckoned Jane to the next room.

Half an hour later they met Papa in the foyer.

"I found neither coal nor firewood," Mrs. Hill screwed her lips into her smile-so-she-did-not-frown expression that Elizabeth assiduously avoided, "and if you be askin' me, it be far too early in the spring to be without the option of a good fire. Not to mention, I expect you will be demanding proper meals from time to time, and fire be required for that effort, too."

"No bedroom is fit to sleep in right now." Elizabeth crossed her arms and leveled a stern gaze at Papa. "We must take Mr. Darcy up on his offer—"

"No, I will arrange rooms at the Bull in Lambton where I stayed when I came to see the place in—"

"What of the fire? Mr. Darcy said repairs to the inn were not complete." Jane tapped her foot softly on the dusty marble floor.

"I do not like it."

"You do not have to." Elizabeth set her jaw.

He harrumphed. "I suppose we have little choice but to impose on our neighbor's hospitality. I will send Piper to warn them."

"It is good of you to do so, but I have no doubt we are already expected," Elizabeth murmured.

Happily, Papa did not appear to have heard.

A quarter hour later, two carriages trundled toward Pemberley.

Darcy and Fitzwilliam waited at the top of the steps.

"What do you know? He left the caravan of

wagons at Alston Hall." Fitzwilliam squinted and shaded his eyes with his hand. "What would possess a man to carry so much furniture along? Especially when none of it equals the appointments of Alston."

"I daresay you shall not rest until you have pried the information out of some member of their household." Darcy tugged his coat sleeves and straightened his cravat. "Do wait until morning before you begin interrogations. I prefer them to believe us civilized for at least one evening."

"On my honor, I shall not torture their servants until morning."

"That is good of you."

The first carriage pulled up to the house.

The door opened before the driver could dismount. Admiral Bennet emerged, two young boys in his wake.

Darcy bowed. "Welcome to Pemberley."

The admiral bowed from his shoulders, a stiff, awkward motion that spoke to many long hours confined in travel. "Thank you for your invitation, sir. I regret imposing upon you so early in our acquaintance."

"Nonsense, you and your family are most esteemed company."

Bennet glanced at his boys. "I fear these scamps may change your mind in short order. My sons, Francis and Philip."

The boys bowed clumsily but in tandem. The two lads did more than merely favor each other. They were mirror images of one another. Oh, the trouble that could lead to! Thankfully, his own boys were not similarly endowed or Mrs. Reynolds would have surely retired by now.

Fitzwilliam hunkered down on one knee. "You look like fine young men, both of you. So which of you is the eldest?"

"Me." Francis pointed his thumb at his chest.

"Only by five minutes."

"Doesn't matter, I am still the oldest." Francis tossed his head but pulled up short when his father's eyes turned stormy.

"Do enlighten me. How does one tell you apart?" Fitzwilliam asked.

"It took our governess ever so long to sort it out." Francis clapped his hands over his mouth and chortled. "She still calls me Philip often enough."

Philip made a small bow. "If you please, sir, I am right handed. Francis uses his left."

"But Papa won't make me switch owing to that it will make me a more formidabab ... formida ... a more better swordsman." Francis grinned.

"So he is teaching you the sword already?" Fitzwilliam raised his eyebrows.

"Indeed, sir. We have wooden ones for practice now—"

"We brought them in our trunk ... do you want to see?"

"Papa says when I turn eleven, he shall—"

George and David tumbled through the front door.

"See, there! The two identical boys I told you about!" George shouted and pulled his younger brother down the stairs. "David would not believe me that you were just alike. I was right!"

Darcy caught George's shoulder. "May I present my sons, George and David."

The four boys bowed to one another, nearly

knocking their heads together. Laughing, they attempted to shake hands only to have the greeting end in a tangle of arms.

Both fathers reached in to sort the jumble of limbs.

"Papa," George peeked up, "may we go to the barn and show them the colts?"

"My grooms are in the barns and will supervise them closely," Darcy said.

The twins stood stone still, their hands tightly clasped before them. They all but quivered with the effort to maintain a posture of silent attention, or at least a boyish semblance of it.

Bennet stroked his chin. "A good run is just the thing they need. Now mind yourselves, gentlemen. You know how to conduct yourselves in company and around horses. Do not allow me to hear you have done otherwise."

"Yes, sir. Thank you, sir." They saluted their father and ran off behind their new playmates.

Fitzwilliam stood and cocked his head at Bennet.

"No, I do not make them salute. My man, Piper, did so for many years at sea and cannot seem to shake the practice. They picked it up from him."

A young woman appeared behind Bennet. "Papa?"

"Ah, yes, forgive me, girls. Gentlemen, may I present my daughters, Jane and Elizabeth. Mr. Darcy and Col. Fitzwilliam."

"We appreciate your hospitality, sir." Miss Elizabeth curtsied.

What an arresting creature. Not conventionally beautiful but stunning, nonetheless, with eyes full of curious intelligence, a musical voice, and a beguiling curve of her lips that held him too powerfully for escape. An unmistakable air of confidence and strength draped about her shoulders, unlike any other woman he had encountered.

Her brow knotted.

Botheration, he was staring! Where had his manners gone? He blinked and shook his head. "You are most welcome. Please come inside."

Fitzwilliam ushered them in.

A flurry of feathers and taffeta breezed into the foyer. "Welcome to Pemberley." Aunt Catherine beamed with her broadest good-hostess smile.

"May I present my aunt, Lady Catherine de Bourgh. Aunt, these are our guests and newest neighbors, Admiral Bennet and his daughters, Miss Jane Bennet and Miss Elizabeth Bennet."

The admiral bowed over her proffered hand. "Thank you for your gracious invitation to my family."

"We are delighted to have you as our guests." Aunt Catherine possessed particular skill in making guests feel at ease and glowed with the opportunity to exercise it. "I have a light luncheon served in the parlor. Please—"

"I am sure they would prefer to refresh themselves after their travels," Darcy said.

"Nonsense," Bennet waved him down. "We would be most pleased to join her for refreshments." He gestured to his daughters who mumbled amiable syllables.

Weary creases lined Bennet's forehead and dust smudged his otherwise lovely daughters' cheeks. Darcy swallowed a sigh. Sailor or not, Bennet's manners were impeccable.

Aunt Catherine batted her eyes at Darcy. What joy,

she would be insufferable now. "Come then, this way."

They fell into step behind her.

Georgiana met them within the parlor, hovering over the fully laden sideboard.

"May I present my sister, Miss Darcy?"

The ladies curtsied. The men bowed and made introductions all around.

"A lovely spread and on such short notice, thank you." Bennet gestured toward the sideboard and sat.

"Please help yourselves whilst I make tea." Aunt Catherine took a seat beside him.

George burst in, the three younger boys hard on his heels. "Ha! I told you I was fastest!"

"That was not fair!" Francis—or was it Philip—grabbed at George's coattail.

Darcy and Bennet sprang to their feet. "Boys!"

The youngsters stumbled and stopped before their fathers. They clasped their hands behind their backs, still panting, trickles of sweat and dirt trailing down the sides of their faces.

Two young women appeared at the doorway, strands of hair plastered to their cheeks, bonnets askance.

Darcy looked from them to Bennet. "Your governess, sir?"

"Yes, Miss Wexley." Bennet cocked an eyebrow at his sons.

The boys lowered their faces and studied the floor. Clearly, they understood his expression well.

"Miss Mallory, take the children and Miss Wexley to the kitchen. I am sure Mrs. Reynolds can arrange refreshment for them. Then you may show them upstairs."

"Papa, please, can they stay in the nursery with us? We have plenty of room." George clapped softly.

"Please?" David edged closer to his new friends.

"May we, Papa?" Philip—or was it Francis—asked, wide-eyed.

Fitzwilliam slapped his thigh. "You'll not keep them apart, I fear. Best make it official, lest they creep about the house in the middle of the night."

Darcy grumbled. "They do not need you giving them new ideas."

"That idea is hardly new. I seem to remember—"

"If Mr. Darcy approves, then you may." Bennet rubbed his eyes. "Consider their request carefully, though. I daresay the amount of mischief …"

"We will be good, Papa. We promise, sir." Francis—or perhaps Philip—stepped a little closer to his father. His expression shifted subtly, and he straightened his shoulders. "You have my word."

That was definitely Philip. He had far more decorum than his brother.

Bennet's severe mien broke, and he ruffled his son's unruly curls.

"Can their appeal be accommodated, Miss Mallory?" Darcy asked.

To the weary woman's credit she did not give voice to the sigh she surely would rather have uttered. "Yes sir, I believe so."

"I suppose it is decided. Now, out with you. The next time I see you, I expect you to be cleaned up and behaving as proper young gentlemen."

"Yes, Father," George and David said.

"Yes, sir!" Francis and Philip saluted smartly and followed the governesses out.

"I shall have to add something to Miss Wexley's

pay this quarter. Lizzy, you must remind me—"

"You say that every quarter." Miss Elizabeth's eyes sparkled.

Did the admiral approve such levity?

Georgiana hid a tiny giggle in her hand.

He blinked, but no, nothing changed. Georgiana still smiled and her eyes twinkled. What had he just seen? She rarely showed even that much participation in a conversation with those outside the family. Remarkable.

Aunt Catherine's brows rose. She noticed too. "How did you find Alston Hall?"

"Dusty." Miss Bennet sniffled.

Georgiana and Miss Elizabeth shared a silent conversation and tittered softly. Quite remarkable.

"I fear the rooms have not been aired in some time." Miss Elizabeth arranged her hands in her lap. "But the furnishings appear lovely."

Aunt Catherine smoothed her skirts. "I hope you do not find the tired styling disappointing."

"It will not signify." Miss Bennet winked at her sister. "It is appointed far more comfortably than a number of our previous houses."

"Have you lived many places?" Fitzwilliam stared, no, gawked at Miss Bennet.

She wore the same mantle as her younger sister though her beauty was of a more conventional form. Still, Darcy's attention wandered toward Miss Elizabeth.

Admiral Bennet fixed on Fitzwilliam. "I always kept my family as close to me as possible. Both my dear wives set up housekeeping in whatever port was nearest."

"They must have been extraordinary women."

Fitzwilliam balanced his chin on his fist.

"Indeed, they were." Bennet touched the black ribbon encircling his sleeve.

The sort of silence that Darcy dreaded most filtered into the room—the awkward suffocating feeling when one was all too apt to say exactly the wrong thing.

"In what ports did you make your home?" Aunt Catherine asked.

"Naples, Gibraltar, Bombay and Jamaica. We visited several other places as well." Miss Bennet's voice trailed off.

"An astonishing list for young women like yourselves. What did you think of your adventures?" Fitzwilliam really must stop staring.

Miss Bennet turned to her father with eyes so full of warmth, the heat in Darcy's cheeks rose. What kind of man inspired such devotion?

"I liked them very well. Sometimes though, having spent so much time abroad, I find the *ton* difficult to understand," Miss Bennet said.

Aunt Catherine snapped her fan open and fluttered it. "If you like, I can make introductions for you in town during the Season. I assume you will be going to London then?"

"Your offer is most kind, Lady Catherine." Bennet pulled himself up a little straighter. "You will, of course, understand when I assure you, my daughters are in no need of introductions. I served under Prince William for years and count him among my friends. He saw to their sponsorship himself when they were presented at court. Even so, we prefer to live away from the crush."

Aunt Catherine gasped, and Fitzwilliam's eyes

widened.

Bennet's cup clinked against its saucer. "If you do not mind—"

"Of course, your rooms are prepared so you may rest before dinner. My housekeeper will show you to your rooms." Darcy rang for Mrs. Reynolds who appeared a moment later.

The Bennets followed her out.

"Prince William?" Fitzwilliam whistled through his teeth. "Our neighbors keep illustrious company."

"What an excellent thing, indeed. There are surely no better companions for our dear Georgiana." Aunt Catherine flicked her fan closed.

Georgiana blushed, and she huddled into her tightly clasped hands.

"When we next go to town, they might be able to put her in the way of some very worthy gentlemen."

Darcy let his head drop back and counted ceiling roses. Aunt Catherine always managed to find a ray of sunshine in everything.

Elizabeth sat on the bed, taking in the glories of Pemberley's guest room. What luxury! The elegant oak furnishings, softened by rich silks and velvets did not compare to the greatest indulgence–a room to herself! Whilst traveling, she shared with Jane and sometimes even her brothers.

Luxurious, but lonely. She invited Jane for a sisterly *tête-à-tête* before retiring.

Jane lounged against mountains of bed pillows on a soft feather bed and brushed Elizabeth's hair. Lady Catherine had offered the services of her lady's maid, but tonight even a servant's presence was more than

Elizabeth could bear. The balm her soul required resided in Jane's serenity—and company.

"I expect we shall not experience scenes beyond Derbyshire for quite some time." Jane slid Lady Ellen's silver brush through Elizabeth's locks.

"You are probably right. Fortunately, the county is lovely, and I do not expect restless to overtake me any time soon." She surrendered to Jane's strokes, the hairbrush drawing her tension away.

"I think—no, I am determined—I shall like living here very much."

"Because the landscape is so attractive—or the neighbors?"

"Lizzy!"

Elizabeth looked over her shoulder. Jane's expression was just as she expected: a mix of shock and approval only Jane could achieve. "You do not disagree?"

"I ... what ... what would you have me say?"

"Col. Fitzwilliam spent a great deal of time staring at you. He is a well-looking man, though perhaps a bit too much like Francis for your liking."

"Francis?"

Elizabeth tucked her knees under her chin. "Did you not recognize the mischief in his eyes? He bore an uncanny resemblance to our brother."

"I perceived nothing of the sort, though I did notice the attentions Mr. Darcy cast your way."

"You may stop noticing that immediately." Elizabeth turned her back.

"Scoot closer so I can plait your hair." Jane's sure fingers worked through Elizabeth's tresses. "Mr. Darcy is very well-looking, too."

"I had not observed." If Jane did not see her face,

she might well get away with this tiny falsehood.

"Yes, you did. You also discerned his well-formed opinions, his excellent taste and his faultless manners, all on display from dining to drawing room."

"I grant you, he is a gracious host but nothing more." Also untrue. He was a doting father, attentive brother and kind, devoted nephew.

"Hand me the ribbon." Jane plucked it from Elizabeth's palm. "I fail to comprehend why—"

"No, please." Elizabeth slid off the bed and put several steps between her and Jane's suffocating words.

"Derbyshire is not London."

"No, but people are still people. They change little with location."

"The *ton* is very different—"

"How do you know?" Elizabeth edged back. The window bench halted her retreat.

"Why do you insist—"

"How do you expect me to forget what happened? You do not, cannot understand." She veiled herself with the curtains. Jane must not see her face, not now.

"You must allow not all men are like him," Jane whispered near her shoulder.

"Perhaps not." She sat on the window bench. "How is one to tell for certain?"

Jane knelt beside the bench and leaned her head in Elizabeth's lap. "How might one ever be certain? Consider though, his family does much to recommend him."

"Perhaps." The denizens of Pemberley did, on first acquaintance at least, seem agreeable. More than agreeable, they were ... at ease with one another and entirely unpretentious.

Sweet Jane's assumptions might be utterly correct. But even if Mr. Darcy fulfilled every one of Jane's expectations, did that not make it all the more likely he would find Elizabeth as lacking as the *ton* had? Derbyshire might be different from London, but their move had not altered her.

Then again, Mr. Darcy did seem very dissimilar to other gentlemen who bore the distinction in name only. His demeanor, even with the high spirits of the youngsters, was respectful and courteous, accepting their natures as they were, not critical and dismissive. And the way he looked at them—was not that the truest measure of his character?

Perhaps it was possible. He might be worth a chance.

Chapter 2

ELIZABETH HAD NEARLY FORGOTTEN what it was like to wake in the same bed two nights together. What a glorious feeling! Two days of Pemberley's comfortable beds, attentive staff, and excellent victuals did much to assuage the stiff muscles and short tempers birthed out of weeks confined in travel. Papa's smile returned, though in brief spells and most often in Lady Catherine's company. The tiny tense lines that accented Jane's eyes eased with the semblance of normal life.

A vagabond's existence did not agree with any of them. After losing Longbourn, dare she hope Alston Hall would provide the sense of stability for which they all longed? Maybe … In the meantime, wisdom demanded she not set her expectations too high, especially with so much work ahead of them.

The morning room's windows captured the

sunbeams and made them dance. Coffee and scones offered a fragrant accompaniment for their steps. An appealing backdrop for what promised to be an unappealing conversation. Nothing regarding their move had been simple or without conflict. Why should smooth sailing begin now?

She sat down and served herself a plate and coffee. "Papa, you cannot be serious."

"When have I ever joked about such a thing? Staffing a house is not coordinating an armada."

She clutched her temples. "Why do you still insist running a household is no different from managing a ship, or the entire Navy?"

"Your stepmother—"

"Papa, I miss her as much as you do and possibly even more."

His eyes glimmered but he blinked it away.

"You have no idea what she did to keep the household running according to your standards. Servants cannot be drilled like seamen."

"Why not?"

Best she leave that unanswered. "It will take weeks to hire them and months to train them thereafter."

"Preposterous!" He slapped the table.

China rattled.

Boyish laughter and pounding footsteps filled the air. Papa harrumphed and marched into the hall. She followed close behind.

"Gentlemen!"

Francis and Philip skidded to a stop along the slick tile and came to a halt in front of him. George and David stumbled as they tried not to run into the others.

"You will be respectful of our host's home." Papa

paced before the boys, hands clasped behind his back.

"Yes sir," all four intoned in unison, voices quivery.

"Have you ever been permitted to race through the halls of my house?"

"No, sir." They scuffed their feet.

"I will accept no more of this unruly behavior. You know better." He leaned forward just enough to tower over the twins.

Though he did not address the Darcy boys, they squirmed in his shadow.

"If you must run, do so outside where you will find an entire estate fit for the activity."

"Yes, sir."

"If this happens again, you will be confined to the nursery for a week complete."

The governesses pelted down the stairs. Miss Mallory struggled to tie her apron.

"Sir!" Miss Wexley shoved wayward strands of hair behind her ears and tucked in loose hairpins. "I am sorry, sir. They—"

"No need to explain. We will have no repetition of this episode. Will we, gentlemen?" He emphasized each syllable of the last word.

"No, sir!" Francis and Philip saluted.

George, then David, attempted to mimic the gesture. George nearly poked himself in the eye.

Elizabeth caught her giggle just before it escaped, at the cost of a well-bitten cheek.

"Go to the nursery and wait until your governesses are ready to escort you downstairs."

"But, Papa! The scones smell so good." Francis licked his lips.

"Do you think your behavior should be rewarded

with scones?"

Francis hung his head and scuffed his toes against the marble floor. "No, sir."

"Nor do I. You will not starve to death in the course of a single morning. Perhaps a few hunger pangs will give you pause the next time you are tempted to escape your governess."

"Thank you, sir." Miss Wexley urged the boys toward the stairs.

Miss Mallory took her charges by the hand and led them away.

Slow applause filled the hall.

Mr. Darcy sauntered around the corner. "I may begin taking notes. My scamps saluted you as well."

How well he looked, his easy manner unaffected and eyes full of good cheer.

"I do not mean to usurp your authority, sir." Papa dipped his head slightly.

"No, not at all. I would have said much the same thing had I encountered them first." Mr. Darcy gestured toward the morning room. "You were a step ahead of me this morning."

Papa returned to the table. "I made a point of that in the navy. Found it rather useful for keeping alive in those days."

"I can well imagine. Good morning, Miss Elizabeth."

"Good morning, Mr. Darcy." She sat down.

"Perhaps you will help us settle a minor dispute between my daughter and I." Papa leaned back and crossed his ankles.

Elizabeth sniffed. Why bring Mr. Darcy into this discussion? What did he know of Papa's exacting standards and expectations for his household?

"I am pleased to offer what assistance I may."

"Not to be ungrateful, but I would rather not impose upon your generous hospitality any longer than absolutely necessary. My daughter," Papa cleared his throat, "believes it will take several weeks to hire a staff and more after that to train them—six weeks to two months for the manor to be readied for occupancy. I cannot see it taking over a week to sign them on and a few days beyond that to arrange the house. What say you?"

"If you are prepared to string hammocks from the rafters in the attic, let us forego this discussion and move in immediately. Perhaps Piper has spares among his kit." She flashed a fleeting, tight smile, the one that sent her brothers scurrying for cover. Perhaps it would work on Mr. Darcy, too. He was certainly no ally in this skirmish. "However, short of that, I maintain my original estimate."

Darcy's gaze shifted from father to daughter and lingered. "Forgive me, Miss Elizabeth. I am loath to contradict you in any way."

She held her breath. He was about to say something astoundingly stupid. A gracious guest must not react to even the most outlandish of statements— or so her stepmother had schooled her. Though it might kill her, she would honor the beloved woman's memory.

"I find myself agreeing with your father. Hiring a staff is not as complicated a task as you make it out to be."

There. He had done it. At least he did not attempt to be condescending as well. Little help that. "I see. You gentlemen surely know what you are about. I will stay out of the way and submit to your greater expertise in this matter. Pray excuse me." She rose, curtsied and escaped their company.

Elizabeth forced herself to walk slowly, shoulders square, back straight. Stomping away in a huff only agitated Papa. She counted her steps down the corridor, footfalls echoing on the tile. One, two, three, four …

Walk like a lady, not a sailor. Her vision blurred and a tear strayed down her cheek. If only Lady Ellen were here. She had managed Papa so skillfully that he never knew he had been managed. Elizabeth sank into one of the hall chairs.

Jane was the patient one. Thou shalt not covet thy neighbor's property, but what about her temperament? Was that a sin as well?

Why would Papa choose now to be so utterly maddening? Surely he had some good reason—

"Miss Elizabeth?" Lady Catherine stood several feet away and scrutinized her with an expression very much like Lady Ellen's. "Are you well? Might I do something for you?"

"I doubt it. I just spoke with Papa."

Lady Catherine sat beside her. "I dread to ask what he said, but I must. Was it colossally stupid?"

"Papa expects the entire staff to be hired and trained in a matter of a se'nnight and the house readied just a few days thereafter."

"The end of the fortnight? You are not serious."

"I tried to convince them both—"

"No! Tell me he did not interfere!" She clapped her hand over her mouth.

Elizabeth wrinkled her nose and twitched her head in a gesture only another woman would understand.

"Let me offer apologies for him, please. He knows

little of household matters beyond, of course, the appearance of ease with which they are accomplished."

"Apparently he and Papa are of similar minds. Even Mrs. Hill will despair of achieving his current expectations. She may very well quit the household when I tell her."

The edges of Lady Catherine's eyes crinkled up like the pleats of a fan. "They both need to recognize their limits." She rose and shook out her skirts. "Come, my dear, help me gather my books."

Elizabeth followed her to the housekeeper's office and accepted two heavy, handwritten ledgers. Lady Catherine gathered several more and marched to the morning room.

Papa and Mr. Darcy jumped to their feet and attempted to greet them.

"Here." Lady Catherine dropped her books on the table and motioned for Elizabeth to do the same. Cups and saucers clattered.

"What, may I ask, are these, and why have they landed on my breakfast table?" Mr. Darcy's face darkened, every feature tightening as though in preparation for a storm.

What a fearsome expression, rivaling even Papa's glower.

"Since you both deem yourselves experts in the womanly arts of household management, I assume you intend to take over what has been delegated into my obviously incapable hands. Here you have my guides—penned by my own humble quill—containing my modest instructions on the hiring, management, and training of servants; the receipts necessary for any number of household chores as well as the direction for their use—or perhaps you already know how to make a breeches ball and how to remove oils stains from the floors; directions for the gardens, both kitchen and flowers; guidelines for the poultry and dairy; and whatever else is needed to accomplish all you expect within your hallowed walls. There—" Her quivering hand pointed to the stack Elizabeth dropped. "—are the household accounts. You may use them to extrapolate the proper quantities of goods to order; the periodicity of those orders; the appropriate vendor from whom to purchase; and how you should allocate the budget for such ends. Go on, pick them up, look."

They each picked up a book.

"Sit, sit, you have a long morning ahead of you." She pointed at the chairs with her fan.

They obeyed.

Apparently, at least in her home, Lady Catherine outranked a Rear Admiral of the White. Lady Ellen would have been impressed.

"Enjoy yourselves. We are going out." She looped her arm in Elizabeth's.

"Where are you going?" Mr. Darcy asked, eyes not leaving the ledger.

"We shall take Miss Bennet and Georgiana to Lambton for some shopping. I feel a distinct need to call upon the confectioner." She snapped her fan shut and led Elizabeth out.

They returned to Pemberley in the late afternoon, weary from a most successful trip to Lambton. Not only did they meet the shopkeepers and visit the best shops, Lady Catherine introduced them to several local ladies pleased to make their acquaintances.

The confectioner's shop provided the highlight of

the trip. Miss Georgiana bounced like a little girl at the assortment of dainties brought out to honor their arrival. Though Jane and Elizabeth had experienced many exotic dishes, these were among the finest they had ever enjoyed.

Lady Catherine laid in a healthy supply of treats for the boys—to be kept well away from the watchful eyes of their governess, of course. She was so kind, taking such pains to discern what might appeal to the twins and help her to win them over. What a dear, sensitive woman, surely Lady Ellen's kindred spirit.

Darcy sat at the foot of the table and pushed his food around his plate. Both Aunt Catherine and Miss Elizabeth complained of headaches and took their meals above stairs. Without them at dinner, the conversation and the food itself proved very dull indeed. In just two evenings, he had come to anticipate the humor and good natured debate offered by one admiral's daughter.

He avoided Bennet's gaze as much as the admiral avoided his, an unspoken agreement not to mention the morning's debacle, ever. If only Aunt Catherine extended the same understanding.

True, all was not lost. Georgiana bobbed her head courteously and allowed her lips to curve into a smile that was a bit more than merely polite—for her, positively gregarious. Still, she spoke no more than three words consisting of: yes, no, and please. Miss Bennet and Fitzwilliam carried the remaining conversation admirably, though neither provided the sparkle or wit their absent company usually afforded.

Admiral Bennet retired early, allowing Darcy to

excuse himself as well. He retreated to his study. Perhaps in his refuge he might find the answer to his vague dissatisfaction.

Aunt Catherine's journals and ledgers mocked him from the desk. What must she and Miss Elizabeth think of him?

He dropped into his favorite chair with the elegance of a falling feed sack. In all of his school days, only one schoolmaster ever succeeded in making him feel as ignorant and foolish as Aunt Catherine had this morning, and he had incorporated a liberal dose of his cane.

Of course, managing the household required effort and skill, but the sheer breadth of tasks and range of expertise required—no wonder the ladies sported headaches tonight. His surely matched theirs.

In light of his new awareness, two months seemed an optimistic estimate even with the assistance of the most efficient housekeeper. What foolishness to suggest a week sufficient!

Aunt Catherine would receive her apology in the morning, but what of Miss Elizabeth? He slighted her as much as his aunt. She must judge him—

An unseen goad prodded him from his chair, and he paced circles around his desk. Why did her opinion of him matter? He did not need her good opinion.

Aunt Catherine could carry his apology to her and that would suffice.

Miss Elizabeth was too pretty, too intelligent … too suitable … and far too disruptive to his comfort and contentment. She must not be encouraged to raise her thoughts to him.

Nor should he engage any more time entertaining reflections of her.

Elizabeth spent the next two days in careful machinations with Lady Catherine to avoid both her father and Mr. Darcy, whose second hand apology through his aunt did little to allay her general annoyance. Accompanying Lady Catherine on calls to the tenants and long rambles in Pemberley's woods soothed her frayed nerves much more effectively.

She tied her bonnet and slipped on her spencer. Morning had faded into afternoon and Papa and Mr. Darcy should be about their business now. An excellent time to slip out for another traipse through the gardens.

Everything seemed quiet. She crept to the stairs—whose footsteps echoed below? Mr. Darcy was occupied with estate business, the boys with their governesses—

"Miss Elizabeth?" Miss Darcy whispered from just behind her.

Elizabeth jumped. "Forgive me. I was a bit distracted."

"Are you well?"

"Yes, thank you for your concern. I must learn to stop my wool gathering." Elizabeth buttoned her spencer.

"Oh no, you must not stop!" Miss Darcy's eyes grew wide.

The timid Miss Darcy had actually spoken! How had she come to deserve such an honor? "No one has ever told me that before."

Miss Darcy bowed her head and wrung her hands. "I love listening to all the charming anecdotes you tell. You speak kindly, even of those who are ridiculous. Surely such charm requires a great deal of reflection. What better time for reflection than when wool gathering?"

Elizabeth's face flashed hot. She opened her mouth but closed it again when no words came forth.

"Oh! Forgive me, I have embarrassed you! I … I just admired …"

"No, no, do not be concerned. I was only a bit startled. No one else has ever made note—"

"It was most improper of me. I never say the right thing." Her voice hitched.

"Not at all, I am complimented."

Miss Darcy blinked up at her, eyes bright. "Truly?"

Elizabeth touched her hand. "Absolutely."

"Good day, Miss Darcy, Lizzy." Papa strode toward them, settling his hat. "Would you care to accompany me on a turn about the gardens?"

"Forgive me, but no, sir." Miss Darcy curtsied and dashed away.

Poor dear might have gotten her courage up to speak to Elizabeth, but Papa was another thing altogether.

"Lizzy?" He offered his elbow.

Trapped! A refusal now would only bring on scenes more unpleasant than walking with him a quarter of an hour. She slipped her hand in his arm.

They wandered a shady path in the woods. He said nothing, so she answered in kind. Cool breezes darted among the trees, wearing the fragrance of loam and a nosegay of spring flowers. Somewhere in the dense canopy, a bird called to its mate.

"Alston's grounds have paths such as this," Papa murmured, craning his neck toward the birdcalls.

"Much as I admire Pemberley's gardens, I shall enjoy rambling through our own. Perhaps Mr. Darcy or his steward might assist us in finding a competent gardener." She bit her tongue. Why did the wrong things always slip out? Surely he would take the opportunity to—

"Ah, yes, about that." He released her hand and thumbed his lapels. "Darcy offered his help in acquiring a steward for Alston. Given the alacrity with which we wish to accomplish settling in, I suspect it best for me to focus my efforts on the estate and allow you and Mrs. Hill to manage the house."

She stared at him and raised an eyebrow.

He ran a finger along the inside of his cravat and tugged it away from his throat. "Eh ... I imagine this would be agreeable to you?"

Oh, he would very much like to believe that, but it was not sufficient. She cocked her head and drummed her fingers along her arm.

"Aye, Lizzy, just come out with it now."

"With what, sir?"

He squeezed his eyes shut and pinched the bridge of his nose. "A wise captain should trust his crew to know their business and let them be about it. I ... I forgot that for a moment."

Oh, this was difficult for him, but Lady Ellen said it was necessary to make him tolerable to live with. It might not be exactly the confession she wished for. Still, one must accept his apology, plain and simple, without pretty words, for the heartfelt sentiment it expressed.

She returned her hand to his arm. "Mrs. Hill and I shall begin immediately."

He patted her fingers, and they strolled further into the woods.

Thwack! Crack! Whack! Crack!

"What the devil?" He stopped and scanned the trees.

"The boys found their swords! You knew it would not be long." Elizabeth wound her way along a well-worn path to a clearing that must have been the focus of generations of boyish play. In the center, George and Francis faced each other, brandishing well-used wooden swords.

"Papa! Lizzy!" Philip shouted and ran toward them. He hugged his father around the knees. "Miss Wexley gave us permission, sir."

"Of course she did." Papa ruffled Philip's hair.

"Come watch! George and David have never ..." Philips grabbed their hands and dragged them into the clearing. "You can show them!"

"I dread the mischief those four have found." Darcy stalked down the familiar well-worn path.

"You worry far too much, old man!" Fitzwilliam broke into a jog. "Miss Mallory said she gave them leave to play with their friends."

"All four of those boys, unsupervised? What was she thinking?"

"We ran unsupervised all over Pemberley at their ages."

"I know, I know! Consider the scrapes we got into. What might George and David be capable of under the influence of the Bennet twins?"

"I see your point." Fitzwilliam increased his pace. *Thwack! Crack! Whack! Crack!*

"There!" Darcy pointed toward a clearing where he, Fitzwilliam and Wickham had played as boys.

"Right like that! Capital! Capital!! Parry! Yes,

again!" Bennet clapped his hands sharply.

"Don't go easy on him, Lizzy! You can do better than that!" Was that—yes it was— Francis pumped his fists at his sides.

"He is just a beginner. I was easy with you when you first learnt." Miss Elizabeth dodged George's neat thrust.

"Papa!" David bounced on his toes and waved. "Francis and Philip are showing us how to fight with swords!"

"I can see that." Darcy marched to Bennet's side.

"Look what I can do, Papa!" George shouted and swung his sword at Miss Elizabeth.

"Oh!" She spun away and deflected his blow with her sword. "You must remember to announce the start of a bout after you have paused!"

"Sorry, Miss Elizabeth!" George scuffed his toes in the dirt.

"So are you the boys' sparring partner, or their teacher?" Fitzwilliam asked.

"Papa is the teacher." She dipped her head toward her father. "And an excellent one at that."

"But she is very good, Uncle Fitz!" David rushed at them. "I bet she's as good as you!"

Miss Elizabeth's cheeks flushed. How well she looked, eyes bright, color high, gown clinging to her pleasing curves.

"He's right, Lizzy!" Philip appeared at her side. "You are the best sword player in the family."

"Here." David took the sword from George and shoved it at Fitzwilliam. "You try."

Fitzwilliam turned the carved hardwood sword over in his hand. "This is a very fine practice weapon." He winked at her.

How dare he! Darcy winced. No doubt the admiral would take offense—

"Oh yes!" David and Philip bounced in unison.

"With your permission, Admiral?" Fitzwilliam raised the wooden sword in a solemn salute.

Bennet chuckled and dodged backward. "Granted, but do not say you have not been warned. I taught her myself."

"Miss Elizabeth?" Fitzwilliam saluted her with his sword.

"Papa?"

"Go on."

Fitzwilliam and Miss Elizabeth set themselves several paces apart and circled each other in the clearing.

How improper! He should intervene—or at least turn away—but his feet remained fixed in place.

She moved with feline grace and assurance. None on the dance floor could have matched the precision of her movements, the elegance of her style, bewitching him with every step, every clash of wood, every twist and dodge. Stunning, simply stunning.

What would it be like to face such a partner? She met Fitzwilliam's feint and thrust, besting his strength with her agility.

He backed her toward the stand of trees. Her foot snagged on a root, and she fell heavily on her side. Dust and dry leaves swirled up. He slid forward, sword poised to finish the match, but she threw a handful of dirt into his eyes and leapt to her feet.

"Gah!" He staggered back, clawing the debris from his face.

"And touché!" She tapped her sword to the knot of his cravat.

Fitzwilliam wiped his mouth on his sleeve. "That was decidedly ungentlemanly."

"I am not a gentleman." Elizabeth passed the sword to Philip and brushed the dirt from her shoulder and hands.

Bennet approached and placed his hand on the small of her back. "I made sure my ladies were able to protect themselves. You must agree, Colonel, if a woman takes up a sword, it is likely not a gentleman she will be facing."

"You are most correct, Admiral." He handed his sword to an impatient George and bowed. "Well done, Miss Elizabeth. Thank you for the honor of sparring with you."

She curtsied. "If you will excuse me, I should return to the house." Eyes fixed on the ground, she hurried away and straight into Darcy.

"Excuse me, sir!"

The fragrance of honeysuckle followed her. What a marvelous scent! He must stop staring, but how did one tear his eyes from the embodiment of Artemis?

"Pray excuse me." She edged back and dropped a tiny curtsey.

"It was my ... I ... that was the most ..."

"... unladylike display. Forgive me. I forget myself sometimes. We have lived far from civilized society for perhaps too long." She sidled away.

"No, no, not at all. It was ... that is to say, I have never seen—"

She looked aside, eyes bright, and rubbed her shoulders.

What had she understood him to say? "Are you injured, Miss Elizabeth?"

"No, sir. Thank you, I am quite well."

Her entire being contradicted her words.

"George and David are—"

"Excuse me, sir." She dashed down the path.

Oh, that he could chase after her! But his feet rooted to the ground, strength draining with the distance between them.

Elizabeth ran upstairs. No, ladies did not run, but she was not quite a lady. Now, everyone on Pemberley knew it.

Why had she allowed the boys to coerce her into playing swords?

Of all people, why Mr. Darcy to catch her unguarded moment? How he fixed upon her, with eyes so intense— they never left her. He could not even speak to her now. What must he think?

Why ask? No doubt, he regarded her with the same censure that found her everywhere else, marking her as one who did not belong to polite society.

It should not bother her. What consequence for one more to condemn her lack of gentility?

Why did his opinion signify? It should not. It must not. But it did.

Surely, he would always see her, sword in hand, covered in leaves and dirt—nothing but a romping hoyden.

What good to have left London? Disapproval followed wherever she went.

Aunt Catherine swept into Darcy's office, her skirts swooshing like the winds on the cusp of a thunderstorm.

"What can I do for you?" Darcy lowered his book enough to catch a glimpse of her face. Hers was an expression he would just as soon not see.

She thumped her hands on his desk. "What did you say to her?"

"To whom?"

She shot him a milk-curdling glare.

Yes, he knew, but had no desire to discuss it. He lifted his book a little higher. "I said nothing."

"The poor girl was beside herself when she fled to her room." She pulled her fan from her pocket.

"Miss Elizabeth is in no way given to such inappropriate displays." No, she was not going to apply that instrument to him.

Distance, he needed distance. Perhaps the window…who was he fooling? Little good it would do, but he had to try something to deter her.

"What did you find to criticize, Darcy? Was her behavior—"

"Enough!" He whirled.

She stood far too close, her eyes far too penetrating and perceptive. "What happened?"

Escape was impossible.

She edged closer still, tapping her closed fan in her palm. *Shuck. Shuck. Shuck.* He hated that sound.

"Nothing. Fitzwilliam and I found the boys playing at swords with the Admiral and Miss Elizabeth." He stared over her head, anywhere but at her.

Miss Elizabeth had been a sight, sword in hand. How easily she eluded Fitzwilliam's feints. Mesmerizing … He tugged his collar.

"She joined in their games?"

No, he would not acknowledge the question, not even with a twitch.

"She assumed you disapproved—which is not at all difficult, considering the fierce mien you usually wear." The fan slapped his cheek hard enough to sting.

"You go too far, madam."

"I do not go far enough. Your mother would be horrified by your lack of hospitality. My dearest Anne would never have stood for it."

He glowered and sidestepped.

"The poor girl has been through enough. She does not need you adding to her sorrow."

Shuck. Shuck. Shuck.

"What are you talking about?" He ground his teeth and stomped across the room. Away from that wretched fan.

"You are not a simpleton. You can puzzle it out."

"I cannot fathom to what you allude."

"Oy," she chased him down. "What kind of reception do you think a woman like her received from the *ton*?"

"You mean one sponsored by a prince, with a father as decorated and connected as the Admiral, and possessing a handsome fortune?"

She flipped her fan open and fluttered it sharply. "Miss Elizabeth is all those things as well as striking and intelligent, unconventional and outspoken."

"How does that signify?"

"Must I spell it out?"

"I have no time for this. Tell me plainly or leave me."

"The poor dear has been treated infamously by no less than three suitors, men more interested in her fortune and connections than in her." She folded her arms, tucking her fan into her elbow.

"Of what concern is this to me?"

"When she discovered their duplicity, she rejected

them soundly. Naturally, they spread vicious gossip about her to well-connected, jealous women only too happy to take revenge on one so far above themselves in fortune and consequence and character."

Just one of the reasons he avoided London. "And I imagine she told you of this herself."

"Certainly not. The dear girl rarely speaks of herself, or had you not noticed? No, it was her sister—after she inquired what were your intentions toward Miss Elizabeth." She poked him in the chest with her fan.

"My intentions?" He sputtered and edged backwards. If his ears grew any hotter they would surely ignite. "They have been here less than a se'nnight. What intentions—"

"You think you are subtle with those looks you and Fitzwilliam give both those girls."

"Enough, madam."

"They are worthy young ladies. And their fortunes—"

"I am not in need of a woman's fortune to fill my coffers. Pemberley is quite solvent, thank you." He strode to his desk.

"My Anne's dowry—"

"Is set aside for her younger son. I have not touched a pound of it, nor will I."

Her voice softened to something quite tender. "Your management is impeccable."

"Thank you."

"You cannot deny Miss Elizabeth is a brilliant match, though."

"I am in no mood to give consequence to young ladies slighted by other men." He slammed his hands on the desktop.

"Stubborn man! At the very least, as a gentleman you should apologize for discomposing her."

"I do not wish to elevate—"

"Oh do not fear," frost crackled on her voice, "she is certain of your contempt. Your apology will not raise hopes she did not have to begin with." She swished a cloak of indignation around her shoulders and stormed out.

Darcy shut the door behind her, emptiness filling his belly until he sank into his favorite chair. What was more troubling, that others saw his admiration for Miss Elizabeth, or that Miss Elizabeth could not?

He knew her to be upset, but the possibility of hurting her was insupportable. Somehow, he had to rectify the misunderstanding. She must not be somewhere in the world thinking ill of him.

On Sunday, the Bennets joined the Darcy family in their tradition: a relaxed stroll to the village church for service. The crisp morning air encouraged the boys' high spirits. They broke away from their governesses and hovered around Elizabeth, like gulls circling over a ship dock, swooping and chattering, vying for her attention. She grabbed David's and Philip's hands and stooped to listen to their softer voices while George and Francis prattled on, oblivious to their audience.

Mr. Darcy cast sidelong glances her way, but their meaning eluded her. The corners of his eyes crinkled with the lift of his lips. Had he been focused only on the children, she might have called his expression amused. When his gaze passed to her, his eyes grew dark and intense, like Papa's when troubled. Did he desire her away from his sons, too?

"I wish I had a sister like you," David whispered as close to her ear as he could get on his tip toes.

She squeezed David's hand. "I am pleased we will live nearby. I hope to see you often at Alston."

Did Mr. Darcy just smile? What could he mean?

"Tell me of your vicar, Mr. Darcy." Papa stepped between them, sparing her further bewildering glimpses.

"You will find him to your liking."

Indeed they did. Mr. Samuels' gregarious nature and excellent oratory suited them very well. On the trek back to Pemberley, Papa, Mr. Darcy and Col. Fitzwilliam enjoyed a good natured debate over the vicar's text.

Mr. Darcy possessed well-considered opinions and the strength not to concede to Papa's disagreement on those minor points where they differed. Few held their own against Papa's arguments and maintained good humor throughout.

Even fewer men puzzled her so exceedingly.

The morning's conviviality extended into the evening with an invitation for the boys to join the adults at the supper table.

They transformed the meal into a noisy, lively affair, finishing one another's sentences as they described their week's adventures along the streams and in Pemberley's tree house. Their mornings had been spent identifying the best places for fishing in the event Mr. Darcy permitted them to do so.

Francis, of course, had fallen into the stream, requiring George to assist him in getting out. David and Philip kept clear of that particular mischief and reveled in relating the governesses' scolding.

Though she should not, Elizabeth snickered at her

brothers' antics.

Jane did not laugh, but she smiled, a beatific expression few gentlemen could ignore. Certainly Col. Fitzwilliam did not. His eyes remaining fixed on her.

Mr. Darcy, however, seemed unmoved by Jane's charms. No, 'unmoved' was not the right word for it. His eyes lit up when he regarded her, but he did not focus on her the way his cousin did.

Instead, Elizabeth chafed under the weight of his scrutiny.

Her cheeks blazed hot, and she fixed her eyes on her plate. What fault did Mr. Darcy find with her? Her ready opinions on too many topics? Or her willingness to sit on the floor and play soldiers with the boys? Certainly, he still recalled her fencing with them. Regardless, he would not have to search far for a fault sufficient to earn his censure. There were plenty enough for him to find.

She placed another bite of mutton in her mouth and focused on the delicate pattern on the china as she chewed. Perhaps, if she did not lift her face, her cheeks would finally cool.

No, such respite would be too easy. The boys finished their tales and conversation lulled. Mr. Darcy's attention fell to her again. Had no one taught him not to gawk?

She made herself very small in her seat. Perhaps she could conjure an excuse—

Blessed man! Colonel Fitzwilliam filled the silence, regaling them with tales of the tree house's first generation of occupants, including a certain young Mr. Darcy.

Mr. Darcy squirmed and tugged at his cravat during most of the colonel's account.

Elizabeth considered sympathy for him, but no, he deserved to experience as much discomfiture as he had imposed upon her.

Jane joined the conversation, sharing her impressions of Naples, the port where her fondest memories resided. Mr. Darcy ceased his fidgeting.

Colonel Fitzwilliam plied her with questions and enticed her to share further tales. Even Francis and Philip, who had heard them many times, were entranced by her uncanny ability to mimic the accents from those distant shores. George and David sat silent and utterly enthralled, Col. Fitzwilliam with them.

Jane had made another conquest and did not even realize it.

That was the way of things. Jane's admirers extended all over the kingdom though she remained unaware of most of them. Admiral Bennet proved a formidable obstacle to would-be suitors—probably a good thing—but perhaps Colonel Fitzwilliam would be the one to weather Papa's scrutiny successfully.

Chapter 3

DARCY'S EYES BLURRED. He ground his fists into them, but the piles of ledgers and papers, a fortnight's worth, remained stacked on his desk. Prior to the Bennets' arrival, he had been an efficient man. How did well-mannered, gracious guests spin his life arsey-varsey in just three weeks?

Unlike other house parties, which managed to amuse themselves largely without his aid, he found himself constantly in the Bennets' company. Not that they demanded him, no, often enough he worried he intruded upon their merriment. But he was drawn to them, a bee to nectar.

Even dinners lost their staid dignity. Imagine—the man allowed his children to regularly share the table—children! Now, evening meals were often animated affairs, filled with tales of boyish adventures and flights of fancy. Even when the boys were not in attendance, wit, humor and friendly debates flowed as never before. Proper, staid conversation never resumed until they took to the drawing room, and often not even then.

Aunt Catherine fawned over the twins and the Miss Bennets. Georgiana actually spoke in company now. What spell had they woven over her? Who knew his timid little sister was in possession of so much information and so many ready opinions?

Even more bewildering, Fitzwilliam wandered about like a besotted schoolboy mesmerized by Miss Bennet and her enchanting tales of exotic ports of call, many places neither he nor Fitzwilliam had been.

Would the Admiral approve a suitor with so little fortune to offer? She might only be another of Fitzwilliam's fleeting fancies, but with each passing day that seemed less and less likely.

George and David were utterly smitten with Miss Elizabeth. She joined them in the nursery, even sitting on the floor and played soldiers with them. Often, they cajoled her into accompanying them on their adventures where she taught them all manner of knots—a lesson he would surely come to regret.

Far livelier than her sister or Georgiana, Miss Elizabeth proved impossible to ignore.

And ignore her, he should. Aunt Catherine managed his home suitably and those at hand met his need for company. His life was orderly and he was content, very content.

Miss Elizabeth cloaked herself in poise, intelligence and complications. He did not need complications.

Yet, she tantalized him, so different from any woman he had ever known. What exactly had happened between her presentation at court and the recent Season?

A sharp rap sounded at the door.

"Come."

The butler entered and bowed. "Mr. Wickham, sir."

Wickham elbowed past the butler, impeccably groomed as always.

"You received my note."

"When have you known me to ignore an invitation to Pemberley?" Wickham's eyebrows flashed up and he sat near Darcy.

"When have you needed one?" Darcy leaned back and propped one foot on the other. "Why did you not send word when you arrived in Lambton?"

"I did not intend to slight you." Wickham laced his hands and cocked his head.

"You prefer to stay in the rooms above that shabby pub—"

"Living within my means is by no means a reflection of my preferences. No place is more pleasing than Pemberley, but I heard you already entertained company."

"Indeed we do—an Admiral Bennet and his family—that is why I invited you."

"He has daughters?" Wickham braced his elbows on the arms of the chair.

He could not possibly—

Darcy forced a thin-sounding laugh through his knotted gut. "You still retain your sense of humor."

"What have I if I cannot make merry." Wickham's snicker ended in a thin wheeze.

"I promised to keep watch for a situation for you. Such a one presents itself now."

"Tell me more."

"Alston Hall is in need of a steward, an excellent opportunity for the right man."

"Interesting." Wickham rubbed his knuckles along his lips. "You realize Mr. Locke gave me no letter of character when I left his employ."

"I will speak for you. Admiral Bennet will certainly accept my reference. Be warned though. He is an able man and an exacting one. Ran quite the tight ship as far as I can tell."

"How have I offended you that you would send me to the navy?"

"Excuse me?"

"Forgive me. You have always been the best of friends to me. My experience with Locke has left me cynical. He threw me out without so much as the pay he owed me."

"Are you in straits? Do you need money?"

"No, no—"

Darcy opened a desk drawer and handed him a ten pound note. "Here. I am certain your state of affairs will become more secure soon."

Jane had already gone downstairs while Elizabeth remained at her dressing table. Decorum forbade her begging off dinner tonight entirely. She could not be rude to her host.

Mr. Darcy's judgmental stares reminded her of those London offered, though Jane still argued she misunderstood them. At least Colonel Fitzwilliam had been gracious. He was a military man like Papa. Of course he would be different.

Well, nothing to be done but rebuild her mask of respectability and never let it fall again. Thankfully,

Mr. Darcy did not seem the type to gossip, so perhaps this whole incident might fade from local memory. She dabbed away her remaining tears.

A soft rap at the door broke through her reverie.

"Miss Elizabeth?" Miss Darcy poked her head in. "Are you ready to come down for dinner?"

No, she was definitely not ready and might never be. Little matter though. Propriety's demands must be answered. "Soon. I need another pin or two for my hair."

"Let me help." Miss Darcy twisted and pinned the stray locks into place.

"Thank you." She rose and shook out her skirts. Though of the latest style and color, they offered little protection against a thousand insecurities. "Shall we go?"

Why did the length of the staircase always alter opposite to one's desire to arrive at the end?

"Georgiana, Miss Elizabeth." Mr. Darcy bowed as soon as they stepped into the drawing room, his gaze so intense, she nearly stumbled over her feet. He gestured toward an unfamiliar gentleman sitting between Colonel Fitzwilliam and Papa. "May I present Mr. Wickham?"

Mr. Wickham rose and regarded her a few seconds too long. "Pleased to make your acquaintance." The corner of his right eye twitched as he bowed.

She curtsied and tried to ignore the odd prickling along the back of her neck. He had the look and bearing of that arrogant young lordling of the *ton* who—

"Miss Darcy, you are much grown." Mr. Wickham bowed over Georgiana's hand.

"I ... I ... thank you." She snatched it back and

edged toward the settee where Lady Catherine hovered protectively.

"Shall we to go in to dinner now?" Mr. Darcy offered Elizabeth his arm.

Mesmerized, she accepted his offer. How could one man be so utterly unlike another? No arrogance, no presumption, no skin-crawling eyes wandering to her décolletage. He drew her close to his side, sheltered in his warmth, protected by controlled strength. This was no lordling but the powerful, benevolent master of his domain. And he wanted to escort her to the dining room—not Jane, not Lady Catherine, not Georgiana, but her.

Jane leaned on Col. Fitzwilliam's arm. If he looked any more pleased, he risked Papa declaring him spoony. Jane would leave them soon, if not with Col. Fitzwilliam, then with some deserving man.

Elizabeth swallowed the lump in her throat. How fortunate she did not need to marry, and having her fill of the London marriage mart, had sworn off the practice. Papa and her brothers would not be forced to deal with her loss, too.

Tempting smells wafted through the room. Candlelight sparkled off the polished surfaces. Mr. Darcy directed her to take the seat beside him at the foot of the table. He pulled a platter a little closer and carved the joint.

"You keep the finest table I have ever had the pleasure of enjoying." Mr. Wickham tucked his napkin into his collar.

"Considering all the times you have shared it ..." Col. Fitzwilliam sniggered and slid a slice of meat onto Jane's plate. "You ate here more often than at your father's table."

"Given the choice, where would you have dined?"

Papa looked at Mr. Wickham. "You were on easy terms with the family to dine with them so regularly?"

"Mr. Wickham is the son of the late Mr. Darcy's steward." Lady Catherine kept her eyes on her plate as she cut her meat and took a dainty bite.

"I have lived in the shadows of Pemberley all my life."

Mr. Darcy dabbed his chin with a crisp white napkin. He avoided Mr. Wickham's gaze several times and resettled himself in his chair. "Indeed, I am grateful he has."

"I hear a tale to be told." Papa winked at Elizabeth. Few people enjoyed a good story more than he.

Mr. Wickham bowed his head. "You must petition Darcy for the story. It is not mine to tell."

Did Lady Catherine roll her eyes?

"Go on, Darcy, tell them." Col. Fitzwilliam snickered.

Miss Darcy peeked up just long enough to speak. "He saved my brother's life."

"My gracious, what happened?" Jane covered her mouth with her hand.

"It was very long ago, when we were boys." Mr. Darcy pushed a pile of cabbage leaves around his plate. "Not much older than George."

Elizabeth chewed her lower lip. No wonder he searched for his sons so energetically that afternoon. Perhaps concern for them—and not her impropriety—fueled his earlier severe countenance.

Mr. Wickham leaned his elbow on the table and placed his chin in his hand, eyes fixed on Mr. Darcy.

"We were exploring some caves near the ravine at the far side of the estate, prepared as two youngsters might be with a torch and a rope. Wickham stayed at the mouth of the cave, holding the rope I wore around my waist."

"Excellent forethought for so young a man." Elizabeth observed him carefully.

He thanked her with a flicker of his eye. "But not enough. A sudden storm caused a rockslide, trapping me. Wickham suffered a broken arm and a badly sprained ankle. Unable to dig me out, he managed to get back to the house to send rescuers."

"Darcy spent two days in that cave with neither food nor water." Col. Fitzwilliam took a deep draw from his glass. "I never saw Uncle Darcy so undone."

"Hardly surprising as he still wore a black ribbon for my sister." Lady Catherine set her cutlery aside. "He could not have borne another loss."

"How did you make it back with your injuries?" Jane asked.

Mr. Wickham shrugged. "One does what one must in the service of a friend. I found a sturdy stick to act as a crutch and bound the arm to my side with a bit of rope."

"I can only imagine Mr. Darcy's father's gratitude," Elizabeth said.

"He was, indeed, most generous." Mr. Wickham dipped his head. His right eye twitched.

"Uncle Darcy provided his schooling—sent him to Cambridge with Darcy," Col. Fitzwilliam said.

"A fine establishment," Papa mumbled. "I mean to send Francis and Philip when they are of age."

"I believe Francis fancies himself more of a Navy man like you." Elizabeth winked at him. She should not tease him, but he called her impertinent for a reason.

"He may fancy himself whatever he likes. I have other plans for them both." Papa scowled. "What was your course of study, Mr. Wickham?"

"The law, sir." He waved a servant to refill his wine.

"You are a solicitor?" Elizabeth asked. He did not carry himself with the air of a barrister. "Where is your practice?"

"I am not yet so fortunate as to have one." He sagged into his chair. "I hoped to purchase one from my employer, Mr. Locke, whom I clerked for these last two years. Alas, it was not to be."

Silence, thick as an itchy wool blanket, embraced the diners. Jane sipped her wine and kept her eyes down. Knife and fork made nary a clink against the china as Miss Darcy cut her meat. Lady Catherine exchanged a brief look with Papa, whose intent Elizabeth failed to discern.

The suffocating hush lingered until she was certain someone might scream.

"Though you are too polite to ask, I can see you wish to know, so I will tell you." Mr. Wickham settled back in his seat. "His nephew and I both entered his employ in the same month. We began as good friends, but later, he became quite jealous of the favor his uncle showed me. He spoke ill of me, first to Locke's family, then to Mr. Locke himself, culminating in my dismissal."

"How awful." Jane rubbed her knuckles along her chin.

The sympathy Elizabeth should have felt was annoyingly absent. Something remained untold, something naggingly important, something propriety required she not inquire after.

"Not so terrible, for it drove me to Derbyshire to cheer myself with the best company in England." He lifted his glass. "To good friends and good times, may both abound."

The others joined the toast.

"How go the efforts to settle into Alston Hall? That is the name of your estate, is it not?" Mr. Wickham leaned back.

Papa swirled his glass and took a long sip. "The whole process is far too slow."

"Things move much faster when all you need do is give the orders and watch them carried out, eh?" Col. Fitzwilliam elbowed Papa's shoulder.

Papa must think well of the colonel to permit him such liberties.

"It does make me miss the sea at times. Though Lizzy makes excellent progress with the household staff, still, it cannot be soon enough for me."

"One cannot underestimate the advantages of being at home." Mr. Darcy laced his fingers and rested his elbows on the table. "To that very point I have invited Mr. Wickham to join us tonight. Between his experience as a law clerk and what he learned at his father's knee, I am certain you will not find a better candidate for the position of your steward."

"I fear though, Admiral, my lack of references is too great an obstacle to overcome. I quite understand—"

"I saw it enough times in the navy. A man does not always deserve the reputation that follows him. I am willing to take Mr. Darcy at his word and give you a fair go. Tomorrow, we will go out to the estate and you can show me your merits. What say you?"

Mr. Wickham blinked several times. "Thank you. I

only hope to prove myself equal to my friend's confidence in me."

Elizabeth excused herself from the drawing room as early as might be done without inviting uncomfortable questions. Mr. Wickham unbalanced her equanimity and she required safe harbor. She ran the last several steps to her room and pressed her back against the door.

At last! What a … an … an uncomfortable, distressing, annoying—oh! So entirely opposite of Mr. Darcy, how could they be friends?

"Elizabeth?"

Of course Jane would follow. "I am well."

"No, you are not. Let me in."

Elizabeth stepped aside and Jane slipped in.

"You do not like him?" Jane closed the door and led her to sit on the bed.

"How did you guess?"

"Lizzy, you need not be sarcastic with me."

"I am sorry." She laid her head on Jane's shoulder.

"Do you wish to tell me?"

"What is there to tell? He is a disagreeable creature and, if given my fondest wish, I would have nothing to do with him. I cannot believe Mr. Darcy would recommend him to Papa and I dread the thought he may become associated with Alston and our family."

"All this from a single dinner and three quarters of an hour in the drawing room?" She rubbed Elizabeth's back. "Perhaps you are overreacting—just a mite?"

"You used to trust my judgment."

"You did not used to be so prejudiced."

"I am not prejudiced." Elizabeth pulled away and wrapped her arms over her chest.

"You have not said a favorable thing about a gentleman since—"

"Perhaps I have not met one worthy—"

"Or perhaps you have not been fair." Jane retreated to the window. Had they not been on an upper floor, she might have used it to escape their uncomfortable conversation. "I dislike disagreeing with you."

"You do not like to disagree with anyone."

"That is why you should attend to me when I do." Jane's voice bore the barest edge of irritation, the deepest cut she could muster. "I am not insensible to all you suffered whilst we resided in London. I cannot help but wonder though …"

Ah, yes, this conversation once again. "… if it is time for me to lay my caution to rest and start afresh, with a clean slate?"

"You make it sound as if I suggested you put on a motley and take up as a court jester."

Elizabeth rose and stalked to the other side of the room. "Perhaps that would be a fitting occupation for me since—"

"Please stop!" Jane's voice dropped to a hoarse plea.

Elizabeth covered her face with her hands. "Forgive me, I do not mean to be churlish with you."

"And I cannot bear to be harsh with you."

"You could not be harsh with anyone. You are only concerned for my wellbeing, but … oh Jane, it is so hard. I find I do not know, I cannot know, who is trustworthy anymore."

"I am not asking you to trust everyone, merely to

withhold judgment until you have more from which to base your opinion." She relinquished her station at the window and moved to Elizabeth's side.

"How do you make it sound so very reasonable?"

Jane shrugged sweetly, but her eyes scolded like Lady Ellen.

"Very well, I shall give him a chance to prove … himself before I cast aspersions on his character."

"Thank you, now come, sit down, and let me brush your hair." Jane fetched the hairbrush.

Only for Jane would she forestall her better judgment and allow Wickham's actions to speak for themselves.

The clack of wooden swords rang through the grove. The boys laughed and shouted with the freedom of childhood. Elizabeth stood at the far edge and watched from the corner of her eye. Jane sat with them, supervising their play. If only they were installed at Alston and on its grounds, she would join them. But here, she risked Mr. Darcy's dark looks should she be caught. Though they might not be for her, those silent reprimands were to be avoided as much as Papa's.

She craned her neck and peered into the leafy canopy. Pemberley was beautiful and no staff could have made them feel more at home. Mrs. Reynolds found out their favorite foods and they appeared at nearly every meal. Flowers welcomed her on the dressing table every morning. How had they earned such favor?

Only the anxiety of inciting Mr. Darcy's censure made her long for the privacy of their own home. She groaned softly and rubbed her temples. Though she would miss Lady Catherine, Miss Darcy and even Colonel Fitzwilliam, it would be worth it to get away from the constant worry Mr. Darcy induced.

Soon.

She continued along the grove's perimeter. Francis and Philip would regret the loss of their playmates. That could not be helped. No doubt they would host the young Darcys often enough and with them, Lady Catherine and Miss Darcy. Those promised to be pleasant visits indeed. What father brought his children visiting? No, that would not be a problem.

A horse approached and stopped not far behind her. A grunt and shuffling dismount—Papa's trademarks.

She did not turn. "Good afternoon, Papa."

"I hear you enjoyed a productive morning." He lumbered toward her.

His knee must pain him—probably too many hours on horseback.

"The last of the household staff is in place. Mrs. Hill will move into Alston tomorrow and the servants with her. The house should be ready for us in a fortnight." She waited for him to reach her and continued her circuit around the grove. He needed to walk out the stiffness lest he suffer for it tomorrow.

"Capital! I should like to sleep in my own bed again." He clapped his hand to his back.

"Do you not intend to ask Piper to string a hammock in your room?"

"I might at that." He braced his shoulder on a tree. "There's a thought. We could take the room in the attic, the one too small for servants' quarters, and string up several for the boys."

"I would caution you against that if you are still intent on making a gentleman of Francis."

He massaged his knee. "You may have a point."

She allowed him to pull himself upright and set off again.

"I hired Wickham today to be my steward."

She caught her upper lip in her teeth, and quickened her pace.

Papa snorted and hurried to catch her. "Out with it, Lizzy."

"You hired him. What is there for me to say?"

"You do not approve."

"You do not need my approval."

"I should prefer it nonetheless." He grimaced and stumbled.

She jumped to his side, supporting his elbow. "I am sorry, Papa. I cannot lie to you. Something about him … makes me uneasy."

Papa took her arm and they rounded the corner. "Tell me more."

"I … I … do not know precisely; there is something … uncomfortable about him."

"Lizzy," he pressed his eyes and shook his head. His voice shifted into his long-suffering, do-not-force-me-to-be-patient-with-you tone. "You have said the self-same thing about nearly every gentleman you have met since London."

Unfortunately, it was true. Still, it accurately reflected her continued ill-ease. But she had made a promise to Jane, so she would moderate her tone and not sigh. "How did he manage to impress you this morning?"

"His horsemanship leaves much to be desired." He chuckled and paused to rub his leg again. "But he is familiar with the history of the estate and many of the tenants as well. His recommendations were better than I expected."

She grumbled something neither agreement nor dissent.

"If it is any consolation, Piper voiced reservations as well."

Piper, too? That boded ill indeed. She pulled her arms tight about her waist. "And yet you would choose to ignore both of us."

"I am not ignoring either one of you."

"I beg to differ, that is exactly what you are doing." Her foot beat a rapid tattoo on the soft ground.

"I am not."

"How exactly do you see that?"

Mr. Darcy and Colonel Fitzwilliam broke through the trees, engrossed in their own conversation, and crossed their path.

"Good day, Admiral, Miss Elizabeth." Colonel Fitzwilliam bowed.

"Good day to you both." Papa tipped his hat.

"Had you a profitable meeting with Wickham this morning?" Mr. Darcy asked, but his eyes lingered on her.

"I am as impressed as you said I would be and offered him the position."

"Excellent. I am pleased."

"It is good someone is," Papa muttered and frowned at Elizabeth.

"Excuse me." Jaw tensed, she ground her teeth and escaped.

How could he? Why did he punish her for disagreeing with him? He had asked her opinion.

When had it become a mistake to assume he meant what he said? Botheration, she should have kept her promise to Jane and refrained from judgment! At the very least, she could have kept her opinion to herself. She dragged her sleeve across her eyes.

Heavy footfalls pounded after her. She increased her pace. No, no company now, most especially not his.

"Miss Elizabeth, please, wait," Mr. Darcy called.

Her feet betrayed her and ceased their motion. What impossibly stupid thing would he say that she must accept pleasantly?

He stopped beside her. "Thank you."

"As you wish." She resumed her previous brisk pace.

He matched her stride. "I am sorry. I fear my cousin and I intruded on a private conversation."

"There is nothing to be done for it now." Each word tore at her throat.

"You do not favor his choice of Mr. Wickham?"

"Mr. Wickham is your friend, sir. I can hardly answer without risking offense to you. After all your gracious hospitality, it would be most ungrateful of me."

He pulled slightly ahead of her. "Do not be concerned with offending me."

"Excuse me?" Her voice climbed an octave.

"Mr. Wickham is not to your liking. I understand."

She stopped short and gaped at him. Surely she misheard. He would not say such a thing. Would he?

"Have spots suddenly broken out on my face?" His eyebrow rose archly, daring her to examine him further.

She giggled. "No, sir. However it is quite possible

that they will at any moment now."

"When they do, you must tell me, for I am certain they will be a most unnatural color."

Oh, that smile! She had never seen it before. Perhaps that was a good thing. "What color would you consider to be natural under these circumstances?"

"Puce."

She covered her mouth to contain her mirth. Few men encouraged a joke at their own expense—how singular.

He did it again.

Her knees melted just enough to make it ill-advised to walk away.

"Wickham elicits that reaction sometimes." He glanced away just long enough for her to recover.

Much better, she had her bearings again. "Indeed."

"You sound skeptical."

"Not skeptical, but surprised."

No! His lips quirked again. If he continued, she would lose all ability to reason.

"I have known Wickham for so long I see no offense in him. Still, he has the unlucky habit of saying the wrong thing, to the wrong person, at the wrong time. Even to my dear sister."

Her eyes widened. "I noticed he seemed to upset her."

"They have a longstanding awkwardness between them. He only means to tease as an older brother might. But she is of a sensitive disposition." His smile faded and with it some of the afternoon's sunshine.

Now it was gone, she wished its return. Fickle, fickle girl!

"Forgive me, but I see a … a littleness in him that

does nothing to recommend him to me."

He offered her his arm.

Perhaps the longed for expression would reappear if she accepted.

He covered her fingertips with his, so warm and strong.

"Will you tell me what you see in him?" The sharp edge of her voice softened.

"I do not wish to be critical of my father, but I wonder if his excessive kindness to Wickham was in fact a curse. He allowed Wickham to grow up like a brother to me, surrounded by a lifestyle he could not hope to maintain. The best Wickham could aspire to would be a modest home and a gentlemanly occupation."

They left the woods. The afternoon sun tickled her cheek with a warm caress. She squinted until Pemberley's imposing silhouette hid the brightness.

"Through the years, I have detected a subtle bitterness that you, no doubt, noted as well. But who could blame him? His own means would never provide the life he tasted at Pemberley." He shrugged.

They continued on. Gravel crunched underfoot, inviting her to pursue the questions that might push for more than he preferred to reveal.

"You feel responsible for his misfortune?" she asked.

"No, but I do wish to see him in an agreeable situation, for him to finally establish himself."

"Would you hire him as steward for Pemberley?"

"If I thought working for me would not embitter him further, yes, I would." He paused and met her gaze.

His dark eyes glittered with warmth and something

she could not name but it made her insides wobble like calves' foot jelly. Where were the storms and outrages she had steeled herself for?

Words danced just out of her reach. What was this? She was not one to be struck all-a-mort.

"I … I will try to keep what you said in mind. You will forgive me if I suspend judgment until he proves himself to me." Did her voice sound as quivery in his ears as it did in hers?

"That is all I ask, Miss Bennet." He held his hand tight over hers and guided her into the house.

Darcy made his way to his study. The stubborn piles of paper littering his desk refused to budge and mocked him by growing deeper instead. Strolling in Miss Elizabeth's amiable company proved far too pleasant a distraction from the work at hand. Perhaps it was best they would move to their own estate soon.

He sat and reached for the last correspondence from Mr. Locke, his solicitor in London. How could Locke repay all the letters of reference, the introductions, and the referrals that helped establish his practice by dismissing Wickham?

Intolerable!

Despite Wickham's pleas otherwise, he would not sit by passively, but what to do? Was a letter of re-primand and a demand Wickham be reinstated enough, or should he find another solicitor and suggest his friends do the same?

He chewed his knuckle. A letter first, then stronger action if satisfaction did not follow. Where was his pen knife? This missive would require a sharp pen.

Chapter 4

SEVERAL DAYS LATER, Jane and Elizabeth met very early in the morning room to pour over their notes for the pending move. In the subsequent hours, the chamber filled with light and warmth and a plate of Mrs. Reynolds' finest scones and coffee.

"How many times have we done this?" Jane leaned her head on Elizabeth's shoulder.

"Too many." Elizabeth laid her cheek on top of Jane's hair. "It used to be better, though. Lady Ellen had a penchant for making things run smoothly." She tapped her pencil on the nearest list.

Jane yawned indelicately. "I am ready to be done with all this, perhaps even more than Papa. You know I cannot sleep well in the days before we take possession of a new house. Lists and details—"

"And imaginary disasters—"

"Yes, those too, they flood my mind and Morpheus cannot reach me."

Heavy footsteps approached.

"Good day ladies." Colonel Fitzwilliam strode in.

"Good morning, sir." Jane radiated an angelic glow.

Colonel Fitzwilliam was lost, utterly, pleasingly lost. An honorable man, his attentions to Jane even seemed to meet Papa's approval. At the very least, he and Papa shared a mutual respect. His fortune probably did not exceed his sell-out, but Jane had enough to support them comfortably, even to acquire a modest estate. She might safely ignore his lack of affluence in favor of something no one could purchase, character. At last she had a suitor who might do very well for her, indeed.

Elizabeth rose and gestured toward Jane. "My sister has worked far too hard this morning. Would you take her to the drawing room and watch over her while she rests? Without someone to ensure her compliance, I am certain she will not."

Jane's jaw dropped and her face flushed bright.

"Happy to be of assistance, Miss Elizabeth." Col. Fitzwilliam grinned, a delightful expression to be sure, but nothing compared to Mr. Darcy's.

Jane tried to look severe, but failed. No surprise, given the light in her eyes. Though she might not admit it now, she would thank Lizzy for her clever intervention later. An opportunity for time with the colonel should not be wasted. Jane slipped her arm in his and they left.

Now, back to the tasks at hand. Elizabeth sat and pulled Jane's lists closer. She ticked off several points. Those ought to wait until after they were settled. She circled two items to be attended to—

"Miss Elizabeth!" Miss Wexley rushed in, panting,

apron smudged with dirt. "Philip, ma'am. I cannot find him. If it were Francis, I would not trouble you, but Philip—he is not apt to disappear. I searched all the rooms near the nursery, the attics, and the servant's quarters."

"The only time he vanishes is when he is troubled. Do not worry. I will manage him." Elizabeth rubbed her hands together as she left the morning room.

Where to start? Poor Philip, he hated upheaval and despised moving house. Best find him before Papa learned of his disappearance. Despite her best efforts, he still did not understand his quiet son's reaction to disorder and turmoil.

What would soothe Philip's troubled soul right now?

Quiet, the warmth of sunshine and a place the other children would not find him. That meant a room on the east face with windows and books or fine breakable objects. The gallery or the library, the boys were not allowed in the former and avoided the latter. Slow, quiet steps carried her to the gallery.

Were those voices? She closed her eyes and turned her ear toward the doorway. Yes, a deep rumbling whisper and a smoother higher pitched answer.

She inched nearer the door.

Philip stood silhouetted in the window. Beside him, Mr. Darcy crouched on one knee, a hand on Philip's shoulder.

"I understand these times are difficult," Mr. Darcy said *sotto voce*.

"Yes, sir." Philip clasped his hands behind his back, serious beyond his years. "I do not mean to sound ungrateful. Jane and Lizzy, especially, are wonderful—"

"But they are not her."

"No sir, they are not." Philip sniffled.

Elizabeth pressed a hand to her heart. Poor dear, boy.

Mr. Darcy reached into his pocket. "There are bound to be those times when a boy—or a man—will miss his mother more than he wishes to acknowledge to others."

"Yes, sir."

"You must always carry one of these." Mr. Darcy pulled out a handkerchief and tucked it into Philip's hand, "and know where to find a sunny window. I find dust in one's eyes a very sympathetic reason to claim for retreat."

Philip looked at Mr. Darcy, eyes shining. He clutched the handkerchief to his chest. "Thank you, sir."

"Carry on then. You are welcome to stay here until the dust has left your eyes." Mr. Darcy rose and patted Philip's back.

A kindred spirit for Philip! Elizabeth bit her lip and blinked hard. She dabbed her fichu across her eyes.

"Miss Elizabeth!" Mr. Darcy whispered.

She jumped. "I am sorry. I was looking for Philip."

A red stain rose on his cheeks. That tender moment had not been meant for an audience.

"He is a good lad. I gave him leave to remain—"

"Until the dust has left his eyes." The corner of Elizabeth's lips lifted.

"Ah, yes." Mr. Darcy tugged his collar.

"My brother's quiet nature has often been misunderstood. He—and I—will not forget your kindness to him. You may need to prepare yourself for a bit of hero worship, though. He may even wish to discuss books with you."

Mr. Darcy blinked and flashed *that* smile. No, she must not become lightheaded!

"I shall look forward to it. His opinions may well be as fascinating as yours." He offered her his arm and accompanied her downstairs.

Try as he might, maddening distractions tormented the remainder of Darcy's week. Piles of work grew around him. He would master this.

If not disruptions from the boys whose high spirits seemed even higher, a cow-eyed Fitzwilliam followed Miss Bennet offering genteel conversation that hardly fit his typically unpolished manner. He ground his fists into his eyes. Lady Catherine constantly fussed about some aspect of the Bennet's move. Wickham remained perpetually underfoot, seeking confirmation on one point of estate management or another. And yet, the one person he would gladly have seen more of, he encountered least.

Piles of work surrounded him and still she commanded all his thoughts. He dropped his head into his hands and scoured his face.

Anne had never occupied his mind so. But their relationship was congenial and cordial. How much easier that ... if far less compelling.

Gah! He slapped a recalcitrant stack of papers. Best to master it now. He was done with marriage and all fanciful notions of romance and love. Besides, Miss Elizabeth would be out of his house soon enough, her lingering presence no longer to plague him.

He puffed a sharp breath through his cheeks. No, local dinners and parties, even Sunday services would throw them together frequently. Those moments would require them near enough for her to recast her spell.

As if separation alone had the power to break such enchantment. But if distance would not, what would?

He broke the seal on the topmost letter.

The study door swung open and Aunt Catherine fluttered in. Of course! Who better to divert him from his current distraction?

Her interruption was not actually unwelcome, but he dared not let her know that. He threw the letter aside and raked his hair. "What may I do for you?"

She stopped short and peered at him through narrowed eyes. "Are you well, Darcy?"

"I am fine." Little good the lie would do, but making such an admission to her? Insupportable.

"You look an absolute fright." She cocked her head and stepped closer.

He squeezed his temples.

"Your desk is a mess. How unlike you." The little twitch of her brow and cheek—she was mocking him.

He muttered clipped syllables not meant to be heard. "What brings you to my study?"

"Tomorrow will be the Bennets' last day with us." She fumbled in her pocket and pulled out her fan.

"I am well acquainted with the fact or have you forgotten how many times George and David have asked why the Bennets will not continue living at Pemberley?"

"They will miss those Bennet boys." Her eyes crinkled. "Truth be told, I shall as well. They are dear sweet children. I do so love—"

"You did not come to remind me of events in the household." He cradled his head in his hand.

"No, no, I intend to host a party on their behalf."

"A what, madam?"

"A dinner to introduce them to the other families of standing in the area. Otherwise, it may take them months to meet everyone." She snapped her fan open and fluttered it.

How better to break Miss Elizabeth's spell than to invite her back? No, this was the very last thing his shattered equanimity needed. He leaned back and laced his hands in front of his chest. "I do not care to entertain. I never have."

The fan stopped mid-flutter. "But when Anne—"

"I humored Anne's desire to play hostess. Those days are long since passed. We have hosted the Bennets, what, nearly five weeks now. Is that not enough in the way of hospitality toward them?"

She dropped her fan. The tortoise shell sticks clattered on the desktop and her hands planted beside it. Bulging eyes fixed upon him.

The items on his desk became fascinating: the business correspondence, the pen knife to the right, the half-melted stick of red sealing wax half hidden by a folded paper. He did not need to see her to know her piqued expression did not bode well for him.

She did not move—did not even breathe. Her stare singed the top of his head.

Sweat beaded on his upper lip and trickled down the edge of his chin. It fell with a resounding splash on the letter he pretended to read. A low rumble started in his belly and erupted in a snarl.

He lifted his eyes. There was that look. Why did he even try?

"When?"

"A week? Ten days from tomorrow? Which do you prefer?" She straightened and took up her fan. At least she had the grace not to gloat.

"I care not. Simply inform me of the date—"

"You will not make plans to be away. You must be here as host."

He clasped his hands on his desk and glowered. "If I am to be host, then include a guest of my invitation. Wickham."

The fan fluttered faster. "Why do you favor him? I am not sure he is—"

He growled, brow creasing so tightly his head ached.

She snapped the fan closed. "As you wish. He will receive an invitation."

Why had she not argued further? Crafty woman had already anticipated him and intended to capitulate to his demand all along. He had just been managed. Gah!

She tipped her head in victory and left.

Elizabeth woke near dawn the next morning. Shortly thereafter, the elder Bennets and Piper took their leave from Pemberley. The boys and their governess would stay behind for a last full day with their playmates. A modest stroke of brilliance that, giving one less concern for those involved with moving. Though the twins would surely desire to be of help, the effect promised to be nothing short of disaster.

Papa stretched his legs and crossed his ankles. "Mrs. Hill has been on site for long enough now. I cannot imagine that much—"

Piper grunted. He shared a quick glance with Elizabeth and scowled at Papa. Starting the morning with Piper irritated at him did not portend well for the rest of the day. The one upside to that, Piper rarely held his counsel and would freely tell Papa when he was being, in Piper's terms, an arse.

Elizabeth rolled her eyes and thumped the ledger in her lap. "Since you insisted on taking every last stick of furniture that belonged to Mama or to Lady Ellen—"

"And permit my brother's mistress to sully their memories?"

Longbourn estate should have been Papa's, according to his parent's marriage settlements. The legal chicanery by which his brother stole the land eluded her, but the end result was their eviction from the home Papa considered his. Surrounded by reminders of his loss, no wonder he should be so testy this morning.

Piper ducked his chin, closed his eyes and snored.

How she envied him the ability to drop off in an instant and yet stand wide awake the next. Papa claimed it a valuable skill in the Navy. Doubtless, Piper found it even more useful in supervising the twins. Poor Miss Wexley probably would have quit her post by now if not for Piper's generous assistance.

The coach stopped and Piper jerked awake. He handed Jane out and raised an eyebrow at Elizabeth. She shook her head, and Piper shambled off.

She sat beside Papa and twined her arm in his. "You are troubled."

"We have much to do today as you so aptly reminded me." He tugged against her, but only halfheartedly.

"Lady Ellen used to manage all our moves."

Papa muttered something that sounded like '*I am well aware*' and looked away.

"We have never moved her or mama's things before."

"You expect me to permit my conniving, bilge-eating brother to despoil their memories or have the satisfaction of taking even more from me? I think not."

"You miss them."

"Terribly," he whispered through clenched teeth.

"We all do." She rested her head on his shoulder. "Lady Ellen would have rejoiced for the chance to be at Alston, away from your family's influence."

He leaned his head against hers.

Such a pity few ever saw this side of him.

"You must marry again, Papa, soon."

"Have you taken leave of your senses?" He twitched and pulled his arm away.

"Not at all. Some men are happy as bachelors. You are not. I know of only one cure."

"You presume too much—"

"Not at all, Lady Catherine—"

He slapped the seat. "Enough, Lizzy! This is most improper."

"What is improper about expressing my esteem for her? Lady Catherine is all you—"

"I will not have this conversation." He jumped out and limped into the house.

The discussion they did not have told her all she needed to know. She chuckled to herself, gathered her ledger, and followed him in.

The low roar of men's voices rumbled from below

stairs. Wickham had arranged for a team of Alston's tenants to assist their new master. Over their din, Piper's strong voice called out assignments. Papa emerged from the stairway.

Elizabeth dodged. "You look very pleased."

"I am quite satisfied. Mr. Wickham arranged sufficient assistance that we should have all the casegoods unloaded by dinner."

She clutched her temples. "Who is going to supervise these men?"

"What do you mean?"

"Strong backs do not ensure they will assume the proper care with your things. You brought it all this way. Surely you do not want damage now it is arrived?"

"You fuss entirely too much."

She clenched her fist until her nails cut into her palm. At least she managed not to stamp her foot—Papa hated that. "We have not a ship full of sailors trained at your hand, who understand the consequences of displeasing you."

"You believe those chosen by my steward for this task are too incompetent to move a few sticks of furniture?"

"There is a way these things must be accomplished."

He massaged the grey patches near his temples and groaned. "We just need this finished. I desire to be settled into my own home and be done with this distasteful business."

"Why do you not trust me in this? I am quite proficient—"

"And my steward is not?"

"I dare say I have managed the transition of your

household more than he." She took a step nearer, leaned close to his face and whispered, "Your patience is worn threadbare, but the current trial will not last. Your particular and exacting nature, though, remains unchanging. If you progress through this like a runaway horse, expect to spend a month at least discovering one thing after another not done to your satisfaction."

He quivered, frustration pouring off him in waves. "I am not discussing this further, Lizzy."

He would regret his own stubbornness, but nothing in her power would change that. "Lend me Piper to move the strong box into the office. I will ensconce myself in the study and leave you to manage everything else." She stepped around him and pelted down the narrow staircase.

Maddening, frustrating exasperating man! The Navy spoilt him, accustoming him to giving orders with little consideration to how they might be accomplished. He would come to her in a fortnight or two—certainly no less and possibly even a little longer—all humility and confession and apology, satisfyingly repentant for his obstinacy. Until then, the only way to manage was to batten down the hatches, ride out the storm, and clean up the damage afterwards.

Papa needed a wife and the sooner the better.

Elizabeth settled into the study that already sported numerous crates of books, two barrels of bric-a-brac, several trunks of naval paraphernalia and now Papa's strong box. Only tiny trails amidst the detritus permitted her movement through the room.

Best Papa was engaged elsewhere; he had little tolerance for disarray.

Never was there a man so set in his ways. He and Piper placed the desk to match the office in every house they had ever occupied. Soon the rest of the furniture would follow that pattern as well. As long as one were willing to accommodate his peculiarities, Papa was only difficult, not impossible, to please.

A cloud of dust exploded as she dragged a heavy chair across the carpet. Piper would yet need to clean the room. Only he achieved Papa's exacting standards.

Lady Ellen had welcomed Piper's presence even as she laughed at Papa's foibles. She loved him so much. For all Papa's eccentricities, he had married twice for love and treated his wives with the utmost of consideration and respect. Doubtless, that was part of the problem now; he was desperately lonely.

She sat on the floor and rubbed her cheek against the cool leather of Papa's chair. Could Lady Catherine care for him as his previous wives had? Could he love her?

How many times had she caught them together at Pemberley, using the boys as an excuse to stroll out in one another's company? He was a different man in her presence, relaxed—she might even go so far as to say happy. Maybe he was already well on his way to love, but was too distracted to realize it. If so, then she best get their home ship-shape and allow him to focus on other, more important matters.

She clambered to her feet and manhandled the chair into place. The narrow, inlaid table and Trafalgar chairs belonged near the window. The chess board would join them as soon as she liberated it from its packing. Once the table was moved, she would be able to reach the strong box built into the bookcase wall. Thankfully, none of those pieces were as heavy as the stuffed leather chair and she had them in place quickly.

Now for the strongbox. The wainscoting concealed a clever design. The door blended with the other seams in the paneling. The key, wedged in a keyhole hidden in the molding, made the location obvious now, but when removed, it would be difficult to locate.

She twisted the key and the heavy door swung open. Musty air rushed out leaving her coughing and sneezing in its wake. Bother!

Bless Hill for leaving a pile of cleaning rags nearby. She grabbed one and applied it to the inside.

Clink.

What?

She pulled out a key, twin to the one she had just used. Best add it to her chatelaine. How useful, given Papa's propensity to mislay keys. Now to transfer everything.

What a nuisance! The iron clad strong box stood near the door. She wove her way across the room shoving crates and barrels aside to widen the path. If only she had asked Piper to move it closer. Ah well, naught to be done for it now. She dragged the chest close to the wall safe.

She sat back on her heels and opened it. No need to find the inventory, she knew the contents: her mother's and Lady Ellen's jewels, some day to be divided among herself and Jane; folios of papers, including Papa's marriage settlements and will; a leather bound bundle of banknotes—

Unfamiliar footsteps echoed outside the door. She shoved everything into the wall safe and wrenched the key. The safe locked, and the second key disappeared into her pocket.

The door flew open. Mr. Wickham scanned the room, clearly missing her presence amidst the disarray. He shut the door and approached the nearest stack.

Elizabeth's heart pounded loud enough to reveal her location. She slid her hand into her pocket and wrapped her fingers around the reassuring weight of the knife Papa insisted she carry.

Mr. Wickham pushed the top of the uppermost crate aside and rummaged inside.

How dare he?

He replaced the top and turned to Papa's desk.

"Are you searching for something in particular, Mr. Wickham, or do you make it a habit to rifle through your master's things?" She jumped to her feet.

"Oh! Miss Elizabeth, I did not see you." He wore the expression Francis did when caught with a plate of purloined biscuits.

"Obviously." She quickly cleared the distance between them. "What are you doing here? I gave directions not to be disturbed."

"I ... I had not received those instructions, madam."

"I find that difficult to believe."

"I am on an errand for your father."

If his tone became any more placating, she would certainly slap him.

"And the nature of that errand?"

His gaze flitted from one object in the room to

another. "He asked for a set of papers."

"What were the papers he needed?"

"He did not say in particular, only that they were tied with a blue tape."

"No document here fits your description."

He cocked his head and flashed his eyebrows up and down. "Are you certain? If you are wrong, you will have to answer to him."

She rubbed the back of her neck, soothing the tiny hairs standing on end. "I will be happy to. In the meantime, I shall unpack the cat he keeps in his sea chest in case he wishes to use it on either of us."

Wickham's right eye twitched. "You have a very unique sense of humor, madam."

"You think me joking?"

He smiled an annoying, patronizing smirk that cried to be slapped off his face.

"It is time for you to leave, Mr. Wickham."

"Yes, Miss Elizabeth." He bowed and backed out of the room.

She sank onto the strong box and gripped the edges of the box to keep from shaking. That man! He left her skin crawling. Why did Papa not understand?

Piper burst in. "Missy Lizzy!" He knelt beside her and peered at her with his good eye.

How did he move so fast?

"Are you well? I see'd that Wickham fellow scurrying away like someone threatened to relieve him of his jewels."

She covered her mouth to contain a half-hysterical titter to little avail. "I almost did."

"Good on you, lass. He oughtn't been here, most especially not alone with you." Piper's eye narrowed. "What'd he do?"

"He claimed Papa asked for a bundle of papers in blue tape, but I am not sure I believe him."

Piper muttered a string of epithets which would have been the death of most of the *ton's* proper ladies.

"I do not trust him, Piper. All his good looks and smiles—I have no need." She slumped and balanced her forehead on her fists. "Why does Papa favor him so?"

Piper blew out a long, low whistle. "I can't speak for him, ya know, but I 'spect it is the same reason he gived me a chance—"

"But you do not like Mr. Wickham, either."

"Missy, I don't like much of anyone, you know that, and I ain't to be trusting any man where beauty and fortune are in the selfsame lady. The Admiral, he be a better man than me."

"Will you tell Papa what happened? He is so prickly concerning Mr. Wickham."

"Don't worry about nothing. You leave it to me." He flicked his chin toward the door and patted her hand. "They both wilt be having an earful."

Elizabeth fell into her bed, numb with exhaustion. The moon had long since risen high above the trees. Every muscle throbbed, every bone ached, every nerve worn to a threadbare nubbin. The wagons had been unloaded and the largest pieces put in place, thanks to the assistance Mr. Wickham arranged. Though the thought needled her, she was grateful for the extra hands. Still, the amount left to do threatened to overwhelm even her stalwart constitution. Tears hovered, just waiting for the opportunity to overflow.

A soft tap at her door announced the end of her

reflections. If she ignored it, perhaps they would leave her be. The door creaked open and Papa entered.

He sat on the edge of her bed. "Do not trouble yourself to get up."

How would she find strength for another confrontation with him now? She rolled toward him and propped herself on her elbow.

"Piper spoke to me."

She squeezed her eyes shut. The last thing she needed was to fall to weeping. Papa never responded well to tears.

"He told me what happened."

Her spine stiffened and fists clenched. His soft voice did not necessarily mean a quiet temper. Not now, please not now. Her throat cramped around a sob.

"You do not trust Mr. Wickham. Piper shares your concerns."

Those issues were not nearly as material as whether Papa did.

"I did ask Wickham to retrieve some papers for me."

She bit her knuckle.

"But I never told him they were in my study."

What? Her eyes flew open and she sat up.

He took her hand. "You were correct that he had no business in my office. I distinctly told him I had left the lists in Mrs. Hill's office."

"Then why—"

"Perhaps he did not pay sufficient attention to my direction and did not wish to lose face by asking."

She sniffled and dragged her sleeve across her face.

"Go on. Out with it, Lizzy."

"It is nothing."

"Do not prevaricate." He stroked her hand, his fingers gentle despite their callouses.

"He did not at all seem like a man confused." She shuddered. "Papa, he frightened me."

He growled and shifted in the moonbeam. The shadows made his frown deeper, darker and more frightening than it ever could be in the daylight.

"You had your knife?"

"Always."

"Good. I will not have you afraid in your own home. Whilst I cannot protect you from everything, within my walls you will feel safe." He squeezed her fingers. "I am sorry, my dear. The day he frightens you or Jane again will be his last in my employ."

A tear slipped down her cheek. She rubbed it away on her shoulder and laid her head against his chest. Sometimes he found exactly the right things to say.

"You wonder why I hired him?"

She squeaked something affirmative and pressed her face into the soft muslin of his shirt, infused with the scent all his own, the one that made her feel safe.

"He reminds me of Piper, years ago. You know how many are uncomfortable around him. His ways are, let us say, unrefined."

"Positively menacing, at times."

"Indeed, and his distinct visage does nothing to belie the impression. Those unacquainted with him often dismiss him as criminal. He might well have gone that path had your mother not seen something redeemable in him."

"Mama?"

"Yes. She urged me to keep Piper on and I owe my life to that decision. He needed one fair chance to make good. Darcy says the same thing of Wickham."

Just because Mr. Darcy said it of Mr. Wickham did not mean all would be well.

"There are no certainties in people, Lizzy. Some will make right for you and others will fail you. The only thing to do is offer a fair chance for them to show their true colors."

"So you do not trust him either?"

"Not more than he's earned. Certainly not where you and Jane are concerned, I will watch him carefully. Rest easy my dear. I will not allow anything to happen." He kissed her forehead softly and tucked the covers around her shoulders. "Now, sleep. Good night."

He padded away and shut the door.

Elizabeth slept later than usual, not making it to the morning room before Papa and Piper departed to attend their morning obligations. Papa had left her his newspaper and a list of his plans for the day. Dear Papa, though he could be utterly maddening with his inflexible routines, he was also as dependable as the sunrise, not like the dandies and fops she met in London. How good to be well away from such society.

She picked up his list and a scone. Just how many hours did he suppose a day contained? Good thing Piper could keep up with him.

How did Mr. Darcy manage without a man like Piper? She scratched her head. Why was she thinking of him?

Time to focus on the tasks at hand. She found her pencil, flipped Papa's list over and scribbled her own notes. After they brought the boys and their governess to Alston, she and Jane would have to pick up where they left off yesterday. Jane still slept, though. Perhaps she would go alone to fetch them.

Enough dawdling. Eyes on her list, she burst into the corridor. Two steps and she found herself on the floor in a tangle of arms and legs.

"Oh!" She shoved the weight atop her away, elbow ready to drive into the first identifiable target.

"Excuse me, madam." Mr. Wickham scrambled back, sliding along the tile. "Forgive me, are you injured?" He hauled himself onto a knee.

She refused his hand and grabbed hold of the wainscoting. "I am well, sir. Do you normally proceed down the hall at so reckless a pace?"

"No, madam." He stood and offered her a half bow. "Are you in the habit of reading as you walk? If you are, I shall surely take better care to give you a wide berth." His right eye and cheek pulled into the semblance of a smile.

Impertinent. "No, I am not. Pray excuse me." She dusted off her skirt.

Wickham bent and picked something up. "Your chatelaine, I believe." He held up the muddled chains.

"Bother, I will have to untangle these later, thank you." She pushed it into her pocket.

"I just finished a most enlightening conversation with your father." He voice changed ever so slightly, like a violin barely off tune. "He informed me I upset you yesterday. I wish to offer my profound apologies. It was unconsciously done and I pray your discomfort is of short duration. Be assured, I will take greater care in the future to guard your delicate feelings most assiduously." He bowed deeply.

She stammered polite sounds.

"If you will excuse me." He strode away.

She watched his departing form. In all fairness, his apology had been everything she—or her father—might ask for, but it did little to ease her mind or her heart. Why did he manage to discompose her so? Had she become as oversensitive as Jane feared?

Enough! No sense wasting more time on him. She fumbled for her chatelaine and spread the chains in her palm. Bother! Her scissors were missing—and two keys. A quick scan of the floor revealed nothing. They must have skittered under the bookcase which was, of course, too low to the ground to easily reach below. Perhaps Piper could help her later.

❧Chapter 5

A LITTLE OVER A se'nnight later, life at Alston Hall took on the beginnings of normalcy. Papa stopped rearranging the furniture and the twins found their playthings and school books. Items were where they first checked for them. No more dust or musty smells greeted them when they opened doors. In short, the wave of moving frenzy faded into a budding routine.

Some of the weight on Elizabeth's shoulders eased as she and Jane found themselves freed from the concerns of setting up housekeeping. Tonight's dinner party at Pemberley came at the time it should be most appreciated.

Elizabeth stood before her looking glass. Her room, which caught the morning sun, was cool, bathed in late afternoon shadow. How long had it been since she dressed for an evening? She smoothed her burgundy silk skirt a final time.

The flutterings of her stomach—sensations she

had hardly missed—reminded her soon she would face meeting new people, coming under their judgment and scrutiny.

Should she change this for a lighter color? White was so fashionable, though a bit dull.

Georgiana understood her reticence better than anyone else. She insisted the ladies of the area would be most welcoming. More comforting was the intelligence that few unmarried gentlemen resided in the neighborhood. The dandies of the *ton* seemed to think her a prize ship to be hunted for its bounty. Perhaps Derbyshire would not be like London. She worked her tongue against the roof of her mouth to dull the lingering bitterness.

Mr. Darcy never treated her as anything but a lady. He never complimented her father in the hopes of garnering her favor; he never hinted as to the extent of her fortune; he doted on her brothers as much as on his own boys—all things which should have won her regard. Instead, they only magnified the one glaring piece of evidence indicting his judgment as imperfect. Wickham.

She still had not found her keys—

"Are you ready, Lizzy?" Jane called.

"I am." Elizabeth hurried out.

Jane's pale yellow gown suited her so well. Col. Fitzwilliam would surely be quick to tell her so. He was always ready with a compliment, as though, if he did not utter it the moment it entered his mind, the value would somehow be the lesser for it.

"How beautiful! You never wore that gown in London." Jane straightened a bit of trim along Elizabeth's shoulder.

"I am glad you approve." She followed Jane

downstairs.

Philip and Francis pounded after them. At least they were only running and not sliding down the banister. Probably unwilling to risk Papa catching them doing so again.

"Is it time to go 'Lisbet?" Philip grinned up at her, sporting his newly gap-toothed expression.

Elizabeth ruffled his hair. "No, dear. This is not an event for children. Remember? You will be staying home with Francis tonight."

"Not fair!" Francis stomped. "The Darcys are our friends, too. Why should we not be invited?"

"Because," Papa boomed above them. He fastened the final button of his coat and came down to meet them. "Children do not belong at a formal dinner table until they are old enough to display proper manners. Which," he tapped them under their chins, "neither of you is. Need I remind you of what happened the last time you joined us at dinner?"

While amusing, their quarrel over the best methods for frog catching devolved to throwing potatoes. Papa's only choice had been to reacquaint them of the meaning of 'kissing the gunner's daughter' and banish them from the dining room.

"No, Papa." Philip bowed his head.

Poor Philip felt Papa's reprimands so. Francis, though, barely noted them. He looked to Jane, presumably for sympathy, but he would find none from her.

"Even Mr. Wickham is attending and he works for you. How can it be a fancy affair if he is invited?" Francis pouted.

Elizabeth stiffened. Wickham at dinner?

"The other guests are none of your concern." Papa

tugged his sleeve. "Piper will take charge of you for the evening. He has work for you to do."

"Awww, no, please." Francis stomped and pumped his fists at his sides. "We studied all day with Miss Wexley. You are going to a party. Can't we have some fun tonight?"

"Enough out of you." Papa turned Francis by the shoulder and swatted him. "Go sit in the foyer and wait for Piper."

The twins trudged downstairs and dropped into the hall chairs.

"I saw the coach approaching just before we came down," Jane said.

The door flung open, revealing Piper with George and David at his sides.

"Oh, Papa!" Philip squealed and rushed to his friends.

Piper winked as well as his scars allowed. A menacing look even when he was pleased, it became truly fearsome when he was not. "I'll just be taking 'em outside 'till you have left. No sense letting 'em spoil your finery. We'll string up the hammocks in the attic for the night."

"You will take your berth with them?" Papa descended several more steps.

"Indeed sir, poor Miss Wexley ain't prepared for hammocks." Piper swung two fingers like a hammock in a storm and clutched his stomach, tongue lolling, then led the boys outside.

Elizabeth chuckled and followed Papa downstairs. "Perhaps, I should stay home—"

"Piper has managed far worse than the likes of those little breeches without your help. Let them be." Papa's eyes narrowed, and he read her like the morning paper. "You are trying to avoid Mr. Wickham."

"I have no wish to spend an evening in his company." Elizabeth sighed.

"Then do not. Plenty of other guests will be available to entertain you."

Jane laid her hand on Elizabeth's shoulder. "You truly have nothing to worry about."

"You give him entirely too much notice. Has he troubled you since I spoke with him?"

"No, sir."

"Let the matter drop. Do not waste this opportunity to become acquainted with our neighbors, and do not insult Lady Catherine's hospitality." He pushed the door open and led them to the coach.

She settled into her seat, the cool leather, soft as butter, its smell comfortingly familiar and safe. Papa was right. Wickham avoided her and, save his apology, had scarcely spoken a dozen, proper, and necessary words to her. The pleasure of Pemberley's hospitality should not be forsaken for her unnecessary sensitivity. Instead of Wickham, she would dwell—or at least attempt to dwell—upon the great advantages of an evening spent in amiable company.

Bennet rubbed his knee. The pain no longer kept him awake at night, now that the rigors of moving had eased. Regular doses of Lizzy's willow bark tea helped as well, though he dare not tell her lest she force more of the vile liquid on him. Dear girl, so much like her mother and stepmother. She ran his home, and him, with a gentle efficiency and peace that saw him through the darkest storm of his life.

What would he do without her?

The first refreshing breezes of evening worked to clear away the heat of the day as the coach stopped at Pemberley's front stairs. He pushed the carriage door open and handed his daughters out. When had they become young women whose beauty stole his breath as surely as a northern gale? They would leave for homes of their own soon making Alston a lonely place indeed.

Lady Catherine awaited them at the top landing. How odd and warmly flattering, the lady of the house, not the butler, came to greet them. He straightened his cravat.

"Good evening," Lady Catherine kissed Jane's and Lizzy's cheeks. "How much we have missed you in just these few days!"

"Us, or our brothers' way of entertaining George and David?" Lizzy's brows lifted and she cocked her head. Her eyes twinkled.

How easy she was with Lady Catherine. Bennet swallowed hard. It was almost like seeing the girls with Ellen.

Lady Catherine laughed.

Funny, he had not noticed the sweetness of the sound until now.

"Silly girl! Though the boys miss their mates, you can be certain Georgiana and I have been at loose ends for female company since you left us. She is quite put out with only me to advise her embroidery."

Bennet paused at the base of the stairs. A familiar ache opened somewhere near his heart. *You must remarry, Papa … Lady Catherine …*

He shifted from one foot to the other and kneaded his thigh, just above the throbbing scar. Dratted knee!

Ellen had nursed him so patiently through that injury. She had teased him then: *how lost would you be without a wife to tend your needs.* Was that what Lizzy saw?

Blast and botheration, they were right; he missed the companionship of a woman and not just of the baser sort men bought. He longed for a partner, a friend, an equal to share his burdens, his interests, and to share hers.

Could a man find affection thrice in one lifetime? It seemed too much to ask, but a marriage of convenience would not suit. To be alone in the company of one's wife? Ghastly thought!

Lady Catherine was handsome enough to tempt him, though she did not match Fanny's stunning beauty or Ellen's quiet grace. He enjoyed his conversations with her, her mind every bit as quick as Lizzy's. Equally important, she doted on her grandsons and their friends as few women of her station would. She also befriended his daughters. So perhaps … perhaps.

He tugged his sleeves and climbed the stairs. With any luck, she did not notice his reliance on the banister.

Lady Catherine ushered the girls inside but lingered on the landing.

Waiting for him?

"Good evening, Admiral."

How had he missed the loveliness of her eyes, a peculiar shade of grey that changed with the color she wore? Tonight, they matched the blue of her gown. He peeked through the door. "Are we the first to turn up?"

"The others should not arrive for a quarter hour at

least." Her fan flickered. "I thought you might be more comfortable if you were settled in to greet them, rather than sweeping into a room already filled with strangers, so I suggested an earlier time to Jane. Is that to your liking?"

"You are most considerate. The girls, Lizzy in particular, will appreciate your forethought. Thank you." He offered her his arm. "Shall we?"

She tucked her hand into his elbow, where it felt right and natural, and they sauntered into the house.

Darcy trotted down the stairs, yanking at his cuffs. The plan to have the Bennets arrive early was brilliant—not that he would tell Aunt Catherine so. She was apt to become insufferable when told she was right.

Heaven forbid she knew the true reason behind his reticence for this party. He dreaded sharing the Bennets' company—Miss Elizabeth's company—with their neighbors. Her attentions should belong to him alone. Not that Vance or Henry were likely to garner her notice.

Vance read little and cared even less for thoughtful conversation. Though he possessed a talent for entertaining, a discerning Miss Elizabeth required more than mere entertainment. And Henry, a decent enough fellow, but quite incapable of talking about anything save himself. She despised those who only spoke of themselves.

He straightened his cravat. Why should he be concerned how Miss Elizabeth found his neighbors? She may like any of them she found appealing. She could like the whole lot if she wished! His life had nothing to repine and every reason for contentment.

Content is not happy. Why did Aunt Catherine's words continue to haunt him? Bah!

He paused at the landing. Miss Elizabeth chatted with Aunt Catherine. Stunning, simply and completely stunning. How was one to breathe in the presence of such perfection? She belonged here, in his home, mistress of Pemberley.

What was he thinking? Displace Aunt Catherine?

Below him, Aunt Catherine beamed at Admiral Bennet. Her eyes sparkled—a woman well pleased with a gentleman's attention. The Admiral best not trifle—gah! How had he gone from son to father-protector in a single thought? These Bennets addled his mind!

He shook his head and descended the remaining steps. Somehow, he would master this!

"At last, you join us!" Aunt Catherine normally produced her fan after such a statement, but her hands were engaged with Admiral Bennet's arm. "Have you encountered Fitzwilliam somewhere upstairs as well?"

"I am here."

Darcy jumped and looked over his shoulder. How satisfying it would be to remove Fitzwilliam's insolent smirk.

"Good evening." Fitzwilliam bowed.

Miss Bennet and Miss Elizabeth curtsied, clearly struggling not to laugh.

"It is a pleasure to see you tonight." Darcy might have tried not to smile, but the effort would have been a waste. How could he remain taciturn in the presence of such beauty?

"We appreciate your invitation," Admiral Bennet

said. "My daughters are ready for some diversion."

"It is our privilege to offer it." Aunt Catherine glanced from Fitzwilliam to Miss Bennet. "Shall we proceed inside?"

Darcy approached Miss Elizabeth. "Would you care for a turn about the garden before the rest of the guests arrive?"

"What a capital idea! Miss Bennet?" Fitzwilliam offered his arm.

"Shall we, madam?" Admiral Bennet cocked his head at Aunt Catherine.

"You are quite inspired, my boy." Aunt Catherine led the group into the garden.

The young people dispersed to opposite sides of the rose garden, still in view of their chaperones, but distant enough for somewhat private conversations.

"They are excellent men." Lady Catherine's voice was soft and wistful. She must count them more as sons than nephews. "I owe them a great deal. Are you not curious as to why I would be living at Pemberley?"

"It is not a gentlemanly question to ask. You need not explain." Bennet adjusted the length of his gait to accommodate hers.

She studied her feet and perhaps his as well. "See how they look at each other, Darcy and Elizabeth. I am not sure they understand it yet, but I do. You should recognize what kind of man shares those moments with your daughter."

"My Lizzy has little intention of marrying."

"So she told me. It is no wonder, given the men of the *ton*. Darcy is different. Eventually, they will come to their senses. When that happens, they do not need a protective old goat of a father interfering with their happiness."

He stopped mid-stride and stared at her.

She shook her head and shoulders enough to ruffle her taffeta—a disgruntled hen about to peck for her place in the yard. Did she think it made her appear formidable?

No, not that. Too much contagious good humor glittered in her eyes.

"So you wish to tell me, and I do not object to hear it."

"I must beg your patience as the story goes back some time." She gestured toward a bench and they sat. "My father, the Earl of Matlock, arranged my marriage with a younger son of a wealthy gentleman, just after my sixteenth birthday. Both Sir Lewis and I had been very sheltered. He delighted in his new freedoms. As soon as I fell with child, he left for an extended visit to London, only returning after Anne's birth."

Tension radiated from her like heat crackling from a fire. Bennet slid his hand close to hers, their gloved fingertips touching.

"Forgive my indelicacy, but on his homecoming I … I noted … evidence of the French disease on his person. I locked the door against him, knowing too well what—well, enough said. Needless to say my actions displeased him. He left for London and there he remained for much of our marriage. I need not describe the following years for you. No doubt, you have seen men ravaged by the disease. The pox took his mind and, in his last five years, he became alternately melancholic and violent. Darcy happened upon Anne and me after one of his worst episodes."

He laid his hand on hers. "Even in the grip of disease, that is unconscionable."

She sniffled and bit her upper lip. "Fitzwilliam, then but a captain, removed Sir Lewis from the estate and took him back to London. Darcy brought us to Pemberley, a month from his twentieth birthday."

Protective even then, a most admirable trait.

"Darcy had lost his father only months before, yet he still insisted upon taking us in. Thus, he married Anne." She pulled a handkerchief out of her pocket and dabbed her eyes. "They enjoyed an amiable match, until she died with David's birth."

"I am sorry you lost her."

She blinked rapidly. "At Sir Lewis' passing, I discovered that he had impoverished Rosings, leaving us almost nothing to live on. Had Anne not been mistress of Pemberley, we would have been reduced to genteel poverty."

"I had no idea."

"Darcy insists my grandsons need me and will not hear of me living elsewhere—not even Pemberley's dower house. He is a man after your own heart, sir." She dodged his gaze.

He took her chin and guided her to look at him. Too familiar a gesture, but they were too old to be bothered by the notion of compromises.

Oh, she was lovely in the glow of the sunset. Vulnerable and strong, she had known adversity and still prevailed in the midst of the storm, the very kind of companionship he longed for. He marshaled all his strength not to kiss her.

The setting sun bathed Miss Elizabeth in a warm glow. Though he tried to deny it, her absence from Pemberley distracted him even more than her presence. How foolish to have tried to convince himself of the great advantages of distance from her.

How did one court a woman like Miss Elizabeth? One immune to flattery and small talk, who had traveled more broadly than he, with understanding quick and sure, rapier wit and a keen ability to see through to a man's core. No wonder the *ton* demonstrated little tolerance for her. She did not belong in London; she belonged here, at his side. If only he could convince her.

What was that? In the corner of the garden, Bennet and Aunt Catherine sat far closer than propriety allowed. "What is he thinking?"

Miss Elizabeth caught his arm. "Wait."

Bennet leaned in and brushed his lips against her forehead. She tipped her head up and he kissed her.

"How dare he exercise such familiarity?" Darcy ground his teeth, heat rising along his jaw.

"Stop it," Miss Elizabeth whispered. "Can you not see? He is comforting her. She just shared … something with him and is distressed."

"It is not proper."

"Hang the talk of propriety. She is a widow; he a widower—both with well grown children. Give them some leave to know how to conduct themselves." She squeezed his arm hard. "That is my father you speak of. Do you accuse him—"

"No." He released the breath that had lingered too long in his lungs.

"Papa will not trifle with her."

"Of course, you are correct." He placed a hand

over Miss Elizabeth's, her peace translating to him. "I am sorry. What I—"

"Envisioning a parent courting takes some adjustment. I remember when he courted Lady Ellen." Her lips twitched. "It is not easy to come to terms with the notion of our parents engaging in something so … youthful."

"Has she told you?"

"She shared some of her story with me."

"Then you know she has nothing."

"I expect that is what she just explained to Papa. You see his response. Wealth will not buy what he needs. He does not admit it … he is lonely. I think Lady Catherine might be as well."

He bit back the argument dancing on the tip of his tongue. "I never considered that."

"Leave them to know what they are about. If they choose each other, please do not—"

"I doubt she would allow me to hamper her intentions. But I assure you, I will not interfere in the manner they decide to be happy." As if he—or anyone else—could hope to stand in the way of a determined Lady Catherine de Bourgh.

"Thank you." She lifted a shimmering gaze to him.

Oh, that he might have the Admiral's boldness to kiss her as her full, crimson lips begged. What a delightful notion. He leaned closer.

"Our guests approach."

He jumped and whirled toward the voice. When had Fitzwilliam and Miss Bennet come upon them? Confound him! Fitzwilliam enjoyed this little game of his far too much.

"Perhaps we should go inside and give them a few moments more," Jane murmured.

Darcy caught Fitzwilliam's eyes, eyebrows rising.

"I noticed." Fitzwilliam slapped Darcy's shoulder. "She is not your daughter or your sister. Relax. I can think of no one better suited for her. She deserves an amiable man."

"I am glad you agree." Elizabeth's countenance lifted in a smile Darcy would rather have reserved for him alone.

Darcy dipped his head. She rewarded him with her eyes and the world was right again. He adjusted her hand in the crook of his arm. Greeting his guests with Miss Elizabeth at his side would be quite satisfactory.

Elizabeth steeled herself for the foyer. Papa could not have missed the looks Mr. Darcy cast his way, but he would not fail to make the best of the opportunity afforded him with Lady Catherine. Unfortunately, their stolen moments put her in the position of meeting guests without their hostess. She must conquer this reticence, but her last Season remained so clear in her mind.

Mr. Darcy's shoulder brushed hers. He stood close, unwilling to relinquish her arm. His protectiveness should have been bothersome, even presumptuous, not oddly comforting. Best not examine further lest she lose the trifling measure of consolation it offered.

Mr. Wickham burst through the door first. Naturally! Who else was more fitting to open the party?

"Good evening, Darcy, Miss Elizabeth." Wickham bowed. "So kind of you to invite me."

His leer clung to her bosom like a leech. Horrid

rakeshame!

Mr. Darcy cleared his throat. Shoulders pulled back, he grew several inches taller to tower over Mr. Wickham.

Pleasing solicitude indeed.

Wickham edged away, but his lecherous grin did not fade until Papa and Lady Catherine entered. On a stern look from Papa, he removed himself from the foyer. That performance might just cost him his job. Happy thought indeed.

She and Mr. Darcy scooted aside to make room for them. A family arrived and with them a transformation of Lady Catherine into consummate hostess.

"May I present Sir Allen, Mrs. Vance, Master Vance and Miss Vance?" She gestured toward the new arrivals.

Sir Allen reminded her of the print shop caricatures of armored knights of yore, everything pointy and shiny and slightly askew. His wife's matronly figure made up for his gauntness. Ginger haired and fresh-faced in a fashion plate sort of way, Miss Vance appeared just as Georgiana described her—a sweet, if somewhat unimaginative girl.

Master Vance bowed over her hand. "Charmed to meet you, madam."

A softer image of his father, he might have been handsome save for the vacant look in his eyes.

"Likewise, I am sure." She curtsied.

Mr. Darcy stood rigid—a cough or sneeze would surely shatter him. His lips stretched in an expression vaguely like a smile, a thin and tense mien, worn as one wore a hat or cravat, to show and impress. Why should he need to wear it now?

The Vance's passed by.

Would his churlish bearing remain? Perhaps it was time to claim a headache and escape. She chanced a glimpse at him.

He searched her with eyes so animated, she nearly gasped.

The useless fops of the *ton* saw pounds when they considered her, reducing her to a finite number, calculable in horses, carriages and houses. Mr. Darcy saw something else, but what?

His air suggested it something very, very pleasing.

Another couple swept in.

"May I present Mr. Henry and his sister, Miss Henry?" Lady Catherine glowed, whether from her comfort in her role or the man standing beside her, Elizabeth could not discern.

They exchanged bows and curtsies.

If Mr. Henry added one more frill to his cravat, she might have dismissed him as a dandy. Instead, he came off as mildly vain and self-absorbed. Given the time it would take to tie such a monstrosity, what else might be accomplished in a day? Beside him, Miss Henry was a daisy left several hours too long in a dry vase; commonly pretty, but wilted along the edges.

Mr. Samuels, the vicar, and his wife followed; both white-haired and jolly, and very much to her liking. Three Albertsons trailed them. Mister, Missus and Master John, whose wide eyes and stammered greeting bore testimony to his recent entrance to polite company.

Mr. Darcy seemed to find his good humor as he chatted with the young man who shared his passion for fine horses and hunting. Perhaps now she would not have to endure the grumpy master of Pemberley all evening.

"Shall we adjourn to the dining room?" Lady Catherine said, her hand still in Papa's arm.

Elizabeth winked at Papa. His brows pulled together in an imitation of a scowl. He twitched his eyebrows at her hand in Mr. Darcy's arm and cocked his head. Her cheeks tingled.

Papa offered a little wink of his own and escorted Lady Catherine away. She should know better than to tease him so. No one escaped such an encounter unscathed.

"Miss Elizabeth?" Mr. Darcy's sonorous voice near her ear was more caress than address.

A spark raced down her spine. She fought to keep the surprise—and dare she admit—delight off her face. It would not do to be so open, certainly not in company.

"Shall we?"

She could only nod, her voice too untrustworthy to use.

The dining table overflowed with a multitude of dishes. Their fragrances perfumed the air. Elizabeth's mouth watered as she identified many Bennet favorites among them. Though polished and formal, the room glittered with the warmth of candle light and the promise of good conversation. Lady Catherine and Mrs. Reynolds had outdone themselves.

Mr. Darcy took his place at the foot of the table, insisting Elizabeth and Jane sit on either side of him. Lady Catherine occupied the head with Papa.

"Were your brothers much surprised?" Colonel

Fitzwilliam asked, eyes sparkling and full of Jane.

Jane glowed with confident happiness—something she often did in the Colonel's presence. "They were most pleased, though I feel sorry for Piper tonight."

"Is it true your brothers are identical twins?" Master Albertson sawed at a juicy slab of meat.

He had not yet grown into his appetite. Soon her brothers would display the same ravenous tendencies. But his manners! Elizabeth laced her fingers in her lap. She must not take the knife from his hand and cut his food properly. "Yes, they are, much to the dismay of their governess."

"Are they the same age as Master George?"

How did Master Albertson manage to form words around the chunk of mutton in his mouth? Tomorrow, she would begin addressing her brothers' table manners. "A bit younger, I believe."

"What a trying age." Miss Vance sipped her wine and cast furtive glances at Mr. Darcy.

"I suppose, though I find them enjoyable." She fought to blunt the sharp note in her voice. What audacity, to criticize her bothers without even knowing them.

Mr. Darcy harrumphed. She caught his gaze and his eye twitched in the barest of winks.

So, Miss Vance had little sympathy for children. Mr. Darcy tolerated her, but nothing more. Elizabeth's hackles smoothed.

Mr. Wickham leaned over his plate and covered his mouth with his hand. He caught Miss Vance's eyes. "I have been told Miss Elizabeth finds them most amusing and is their master at teaching them sword play. She quite despises all other pastimes in comparison. "

Master Albertson looked up from his plate, his cheeks puffed with potatoes and peas. His eyes bulged to match his cheeks. Even he felt the affront.

Bile burned the back of Elizabeth's tongue. While Papa might tease, it was an intimacy not offered beyond the family circle.

Colonel Fitzwilliam's and Mr. Darcy's matching stormy expressions did not bode well for Mr. Wickham.

"She is a wonderful sister and her brothers and my nephews adore her," Miss Darcy said, her voice strained to breaking.

How much courage had she mustered for that remark?

"Miss Vance," Colonel Fitzwilliam said, a touch louder than required. "I understand you and your brother are recently returned from Bath. How did you find it?"

Dear man, Colonel Fitzwilliam. She must thank him later. For now, she focused on her plate. Cut, chew, swallow the tasteless, dry bit. Sip the flavorless wine and try to ignore it all.

In truth, how could Mr. Wickham's banter compare to the brutal gossips of London when it more resembled the familiar teasing of old friends. The roiling of her insides and the trembling in her hand—she must maintain herself under better regulation. This was not London and she would master this. She drew a slow, deep breath and exhaled even more slowly.

Her favorite pie made the second course pass quickly. Near the end of the slice, her sense of taste returned and she appreciated the piquant fruit and savory, flaky crust.

Sooner than she expected, Lady Catherine rose and gathered the women to the drawing room. Elizabeth lingered behind.

Miss Vance chatted with Miss Henry. Their words muted with distance but their expressions made their topic clear. Who did they find more offensive, though, Wickham or herself? Only the rigors of the drawing room would reveal that, but perhaps it could wait for a few moments.

A cheery fire lit the room, where tea, coffee and biscuits waited. She hesitated until the others seated themselves, and sat as far away as might still be deemed polite. Perhaps easing into company would be best.

Lady Catherine insured the ladies conversed comfortably and joined Elizabeth on the settee. "Are you well, my dear?"

"I am fine."

"No, you are not." She patted Elizabeth's wrist. "I heard Mr. Wickham's dreadful remark."

"It is nothing."

"You will yet learn not to lie to me." Lady Catherine clucked her tongue. "His remarks were spiteful and rude and inappropriate. No one here faults you. He damaged his own reputation, not yours."

Elizabeth dared not meet Lady Catherine's eyes.

"He is an inconsequential, jealous and vindictive man who resents that you see through his façade of civility. Worse, he begrudges his station in life and counts your father's generosity as a slight against his ridiculous notions of entitlement."

Had she ever told Papa so?

"The boldness of him knows no bounds. He once

offered for Georgiana."

"Surely not!"

"As much as you and your sister have encouraged her to converse with you, I thought she would have told you."

"We never spoke of him at all."

"Perhaps that is not so surprising, given how the whole incident affected her. He made an offer to her, the advantage wholly on his side, which she refused. To make matters worse, he claimed the whole thing but a jest. Afterwards, he continued to tease her, not unlike what he did to you tonight. She took it quite to heart, hence her shyness now. I despaired she would ever speak three words together in company until you came to us."

"Why does Mr. Darcy—"

Lady Catherine pulled out her fan and fluttered it close to her face. "You know how Mr. Wickham saved Darcy's life. There were other, less dramatic incidents when my nephew found himself at odds with one or another of his peers and Wickham soothed the offended parties and negotiated understandings. I confess to long wondering if Mr. Wickham did not manage to manufacture those incidents to curry favor with Darcy and his father. But that may just be my suspicious nature." She snapped her fan closed. "I suppose when you are convinced you owe a man your life and many favors beyond, you can be persuaded to overlook a great deal."

"Papa and Piper are similarly indebted to one another, but Piper is nothing like Mr. Wickham."

"No, he is not, nor would your father tolerate it. I dare say he will be quite displeased with Mr. Wickham tonight."

"He heard?"

"I fear Mr. Wickham will soon be seeking other employment. Your father does not suffer insult to his daughters." Lady Catherine clasped Elizabeth's hands. "Please, do not judge my nephew by his generosity. He would rather fail by giving too much than too little." She rose and joined the gaily chattering ladies.

Elizabeth fidgeted on the settee, too agitated to sit. Surrendering to the ill-ease, she pushed to her feet and slipped out of the drawing room. She gulped in the hallway's cool air, a balm to her ragged throat. A few moments more and her composure would surely resurface.

Scraping, heavy steps heralded the men's departure from the dining room. No! She was not ready to face any of them. Not yet. A servant's door promised refuge.

Darkness and the smells of dust and stone greeted her. The door tapped shut a moment before those footfalls entered the corridor. Several passed by.

"So what think you of Miss Elizabeth?" Wickham asked, *sotto voce*.

"I found her most pleasing and very pretty indeed."

Master Albertson was a dear boy.

"And you?"

"She is pretty enough I suppose, but the *ton* quite dismissed her. I am not disposed to give consequence to young ladies rejected by other men. She is certainly not handsome enough to tempt me."

"I will not listen to this!" Mater Albertson stomped away.

She pressed her ear to the door. Silence. It served

her right for hiding in the servants' corridor, just one more impropriety to add to her list of transgressions. She rubbed her eyes with her palms, ducked out and directly into Mr. Darcy's waistcoat.

"Oh excuse me. I …" Her voice betrayed her. Had she only a moment to prepare, she could have covered her distress passably well. His dark eyes bored into her soul and discerned far more than she wished.

Darcy caught Miss Elizabeth's arm as she stumbled into him. Confound it all, she heard! Nothing else explained the distress her eyes. "Please forgive me. I should never have invited him."

She stared up at him, mouth open as if to speak, and licked lips that begged to be kissed. Her dainty hands tightened around his upper arms. Oh, for the Admiral's boldness! He would sweep her into his embrace and insist she never leave.

Propriety demanded he free her from this compromising situation. Preserving her honor was more important than indulging his passion.

For now.

He steadied her on her feet and forced his hands to release her. Propriety made a cruel mistress.

"You need not apologize for him. It is nothing." She smoothed her bodice, her voice only a whisper, a wraith of what it should have been.

"His words were both ungentlemanly and untrue." He studied her. "Worse still, he has hurt you."

She turned away. Were her hands trembling?

"May I escort you to the drawing room?"

A little color faded from her face. "Please, I need

some fresh air."

"I often find myself in need of such a respite. Allow me to show you one of my favorite places." He ushered her through nearby French doors to a quiet balcony. "Should you require anything, do not hesitate to ask. I will have a footman wait just inside the hall to attend you."

He bowed and called the servant to his new station. As much as he wished to stay and comfort her, urgent business demanded him. He tugged his coat and strode to the drawing room.

At his entry, the conversation paused but soon resumed its former hum. Wickham approached the table where Vance and Henry played cards. They dealt him in, though Vance rolled his eyes and Henry wrinkled his nose. Had Wickham always been such unwelcome company?

Wickham talked through the entire hand. Instead of dealing again, Henry dropped the deck on the table and left, Vance on his heels. They marched to Darcy.

"You will forgive my boldness." Henry twitched his shoulders and puffed his chest, a young bantam preparing to take on the established rooster. "I know your fondness for Wickham—"

"He has gone too far this time—completely outside the bounds of taste and manners. Just as one might expect of a person of his … quality." Vance folded his arms and tried to stare down his nose at Darcy but, a hand span shorter, the effect was lost.

"It is a good thing Miss Elizabeth was not in the room to hear his nattering." Henry jerked his chin toward the admiral.

"You realize, if her father gets wind of it, you may well host a duel on your front lawn," Vance said.

"Really, why did you even invite him?"

Darcy lifted an open hand and grunted. He set his jaw and marched straight to Wickham. Poor young Albertson, who stood talking with him, pulled at his cravat and scuffed his feet, eyes darting about, probably looking for escape.

"Excuse me, I need to speak to Wickham," Darcy said.

Albertson ducked away with a whisper of thanks.

Wickham propped his shoulder along the wall and tapped his toes against the hardwood floor. "Why the serious expression? This is a happy occasion. Can you not enjoy your own party, or did Lady Catherine force it upon you? Never fear, I shall cheer you and you will soon make merry with the rest of us." He winked and his attention wandered to Miss Bennet and the young ladies gathered around her.

An unsavory transformation took place. Wickham's countenance became a dog's, slavering over delicacies not meant for it.

How could he have been so blind? "I need to speak to you privately. Come." He jerked his head toward the door and stormed into the hall.

Wickham's footsteps rang on the marble, just off tempo from his own, fighting for preeminence in the narrow space.

Elizabeth gulped in the milky smooth night air, relishing the way it trickled into her lungs, easing the rawness. What was Wickham's flea bite compared to the *ton*? Enough hiding. She would face Mr. Darcy's guests for better or worse.

Too few steps took her to the drawing room. She

paused at the drawing room door and listened. How odd, neither Mr. Darcy's nor Mr. Wickham's voice came from within. Where were they?

She smoothed the front of her skirts and forced herself into the populated room.

Lady Catherine appeared at her elbow. "I am so glad you have returned, my dear. Your papa was growing concerned."

"Yes, I was," Papa whispered in her ear.

She looked over her shoulder. He stood close, his chest nearly against her back, a wall of warm strength that would not fail her. Dear, dear Papa.

His large callused hand found hers and gripped it hard. "This is not London, Lizzy. Come see. No one is listening to that fool's blather."

Oh dear! Tomorrow, Wickham would face a tongue lashing that would make him wish for the cat. Hopefully, Papa did not expect her to bear witness to the event. Not that Wickham did not deserve it, of course, but an angry admiral made for a fearsome sight.

She scanned the room.

"Darcy stepped out with Wickham." Papa shared a knowing glance with Lady Catherine.

"Do not trouble yourself with that now. Mrs. Samuels and Mrs. Henry would much like the opportunity to sit with you a few minutes." Lady Catherine took her arm and led her in.

Instead of the distain for which she had steeled herself, Elizabeth met open warmth and welcome, a group ready to embrace her in conversation and companionship. She pressed into Lady Catherine's steady shoulder.

Mr. Wickham, it seemed, was tolerated in their

midst for Darcy's sake, but his behavior this night went too far. Miss Vance declared her hope Mr. Darcy would ask him to leave. She could abide the company of tradesmen, but socializing with servants? Abhorrent!

Darcy shut the door. "You know why I called you away."

"You do not even invite me to sit? Oh, you are in a foul mood." Wickham brushed his lapels. He dropped into a chair near the fireplace and propped his feet on a stool

Darcy stomped toward him. "I did not invite you here tonight to insult my guest and the daughter of your employer."

Wickham flicked his hand. "Pish, posh. Where is your sense of humor?"

"Her father will have something to say about this and I for one would not relish that conversation."

"Then he is without humor as well. Anyone who heard will attest it was all in jest."

"You best leave now."

"You are throwing me out?"

"I am asking you to leave."

"I never thought the day would come that you forgot what you owe me." Wickham tossed his head, affected as a stage actor delivering well-rehearsed lines. "They told me you were like the rest, that I was a fool to save you as I did. You have changed, Darcy, and not for the better."

"It is time for you to go." He opened the door and signaled the footman. "Show Mr. Wickham out."

"Yes, sir."

Wickham sauntered past Darcy, the servant trailing a step behind.

Darcy sagged against the door's cool wood. How many times had Fitzwilliam tried to convince him to do this? What made the difference tonight?

Elizabeth.

He would have excused Wickham's cavalier treatment of any other, even Georgiana. Foolish, foolish, foolish!

No, more self-recriminations now. He had guests to attend and apologies to make.

Lilting strains from the pianoforte filled the hallway—Georgiana's playing? Who convinced her to play before company? How was such a change wrought? Of course! Miss Elizabeth stood with her, turning the pages.

Did the presence of her friend bolster her courage or did Wickham's absence? His guts twisted all the way to his heart.

Soft, light notes trailed off to gentle applause.

"Will you play another?" Bennet asked.

Aunt Catherine squeezed his arm and beamed. Who knew the brusque old seaman could sound so fatherly and encouraging?

Georgiana peeked up, face glowing. Miss Elizabeth whispered something in her ear.

What had Georgiana expected—critique? No, most likely she anticipated an ill-mannered tease. Dash it all.

This was how his sister should be treated. Never again would he tolerate any less.

Georgiana rose. "Perhaps after my friends have

played, too. Miss Elizabeth?"

Miss Elizabeth's eyes widened and she inched back, her face frozen in the same expression Georgiana usually wore when asked to play. No wonder they took to each other so readily.

Miss Bennet and Bennet hastened to her side and conferred a moment.

Bennet tipped his head toward the bookcases. Aunt Catherine slipped away and brought back a leather case.

Quick hands revealed a carved pipe, and Bennet blew a sweet note that Elizabeth matched on the pianoforte. Miss Bennet laid her hand on her sister's shoulder as Bennet began a haunting melody. Miss Elizabeth came in a few lines later, weaving a tight harmony so intriguing Darcy nearly missed Miss Bennet's voice soaring above the instruments in—was that Italian or Latin?

Italian. Darcy peeked through half-lidded eyes but saw only Miss Elizabeth, lost in her music, supporting her father and sister, urging their best performance whilst she remained quietly—and contentedly—out of the spotlight. Her focus, the wrenching intensity of her visage gripped him with a palpable force. He lost himself in the music and the longing.

He jumped at a thunderclap of applause. When had they stopped playing? "Please, another."

Miss Elizabeth pulled back from the pianoforte and peered at him.

He pressed his hands together and cocked his head.

"Girls?" Bennet asked. "Something lively per-haps?"

"Yes, Papa." Miss Bennet leaned down to whisper

in her sister's ear.

Miss Elizabeth's fingers danced through the opening lines of a sea shanty. Bennet alternated playing and singing, a rich baritone that harmonized with his daughters' light melodious voices.

Whilst Georgiana played more skillfully, Miss Elizabeth infused a life into the music not unlike the air she brought to Pemberley. The halls had been so empty since the Bennets departed for Alston.

Rousing applause ended the song, but Bennet insisted Miss Vance take their place and play for them.

Poor girl, she hardly compared with those who had gone before her. She tried to decline, but Miss Bennet and Miss Elizabeth plied her with sufficient encouragement and Miss Bennet promised to turn pages for her, so she finally capitulated.

His feet carried him toward Miss Elizabeth, but what to say to her? He could not stand dumb and gawk at her, though he would have liked nothing better.

"So, Darcy, what did you think of our trio?" Aunt Catherine asked, eyes shining.

"Extraordinary."

Miss Elizabeth clasped her hands before her. "I am pleased you enjoyed it."

How could he do otherwise? "You should prepare yourselves. The favor of your performance will be highly requested after tonight."

"Such is the hazard of being new in the neighborhood." Bennet adjusted his cravat and dusted his lapels.

"Do not think so meanly of us." Aunt Catherine's fan appeared and fluttered gently. "It was a most worthy performance." She flicked her fan at Miss Vance, who fudged and slurred her way through not-so-difficult passages. "Not all are so well favored."

"She merely needs opportunities to practice her display in order to become truly proficient. The poor girl is painfully self-conscious." Bennet raised an eyebrow at Miss Elizabeth.

She ducked from his gaze.

"I believe we keep additional music in the armoire. Do help me look for something appropriate for Miss Vance." Lady Catherine pointed with her fan.

"As you wish, madam." Bennet gestured for her to precede him.

They slipped away.

Darcy edged closer to Miss Elizabeth. "The pieces you played tonight were entirely new to me. I enjoyed them very much."

"Those are among Papa's favorites." She tipped her face up toward him.

How easily he lost awareness of everything around him when she turned her attentions to him. Did she understand this power she wielded over him?

He licked his lips. "Please allow me to apologize."

"Excuse me?"

He offered her his arm. She took it and followed him to an open bay window.

"You overheard what Mr. Wickham said in the hall. I am without words to apologize for him."

"He is responsible for his deeds, not you."

"I made a mistake in inviting him. He does not belong in this company. I ... I asked him to leave and will not include him in future gatherings."

Her eyes widened. "I do not know what to say. Your friendship with him—"

"Has run its course. I wish to consider new friend-ships." He took her hand and raised it to his lips.

Chapter 6

THE NEXT MORNING, Darcy sat in his office, savoring coffee and memories of the previous evening.

What joy was his! Miss Elizabeth returned his regard, and yet she would not shrink from voicing her opinion. So much fire! What assurance and strength! Anne, so broken by her father's disdain and the desperation of their situation, had been far too grateful to ever question him. Though they had rarely argued, such easy circumstances left him craving something more, to be challenged to be greater than he was, to think differently, and to see through other's eyes. Oh, for such an inspiration! Miss Elizabeth would offer that in spades.

He picked up the pound cake he had scavenged from the kitchen. How thoughtful of Mrs. Reynolds to insure it was available to him.

Rap. Rap. Rap.

Whose knock was that? What a beastly hour to

bother a man. "Come."

Wickham shouldered the door open and sauntered in.

Of course—who else would intrude so early? Darcy dropped his cake and brushed his hands over his plate.

"May I trouble you for a few moments? We left on a most unpleasant note yesterday." He slipped into the leather chair across from the desk.

Could he wish to see anyone less this morning? Darcy forced his scowl into something moderately pleasant.

"Have you not forgiven me, yet? Most unbecoming of you." Wickham laced his hands behind his head. "That Bennet woman has discomfited you."

Darcy wound his hand around his still warm coffee cup. The delicate china quivered in his grasp. Mrs. Reynolds would be displeased if he crushed it and coffee spilt over his desk.

"You have always been so ... so ... temperate where women are concerned." Wickham's lip curled back in an expression Darcy had once read as amusement. "It is high time you took interest in a woman. Considering Anne's disposition ... it makes one wonder—"

Darcy slapped the desktop.

"My, you are testy this morning. You cannot tolerate a wee bit of jest."

"If you came merely to torment me, you know the way out."

"That is no way to treat a friend who came only to do you a favor."

Darcy rubbed his tongue against the roof of his

mouth. Perhaps a bit of coffee might wash away the cotton-wool. "Tell me, or leave. I am in no temper to play games."

"I wish to warn you about Miss Elizabeth Bennet."

The unmitigated gall! Darcy dropped his cup onto its saucer, sloshing coffee on the desk.

"Forgive me for being the bearer of such information, but I would be no friend to you were I to keep it to myself."

"Stop now."

"You must listen … though I speak about your favorite. I cannot allow you—"

"Allow me? You cannot allow me? When did you become master over me?" Darcy planted his hands on his desk and half-rose in his seat.

"Calm down, old friend, all I ask is that you listen. You were told of Miss Elizabeth's cruel treatment by the *ton* and, like a true gentleman, you believed the tale. I contacted several of my friends to learn more detail and discovered she earned their censure with her wanton ways. Good society had little choice but to cut her. She brought it upon herself."

"You stoop to new lows. I will hear no more." Darcy charged around the desk, barely restraining the urge to grab Wickham by his cravat.

Wickham dodged behind the chair. "I … I would not believe it myself if I had not witnessed her despicable behavior firsthand."

Darcy stopped short.

"One morning whilst I worked, she threw herself at me. She begged me to—no, I cannot share such things. Suffice to say, I was like Joseph in Potiphar's house. What could I do? I pushed her away and fled."

"On what grounds should I accept that flight of fancy?"

Wickham shoved a small pair of scissors and a key, both clearly broken from a woman's chatelaine, into Darcy's hand. "The chains caught in the buttons of my coat when I shoved her off me."

The objects matched Miss Bennet's.

"You doubt me?"

"Why would she throw herself on you?"

Wickham stood straighter and pulled his shoulders back, though he kept the leather wingback between them. "I am not good enough for her, too poor, too low, to be of interest to a woman of quality, particularly with a prize like you for the winning?"

"How dare you speak of a gentlewoman—"

"So you rather I left you to pursue her, believing all her smiles and coy looks were reserved for you alone, whilst she was inviting me to her bed?"

Darcy's fists quivered for a target. "Out! Get out!"

Blank eyes stared at him as though he were a complete stranger.

"Now go, or I will assist you out."

Wickham slammed the door behind him.

His hands shook, denied their desire to be clamped around Wickham's throat. He ran the dainty, broken chains through his fingers. So fragile, so wrong that they dangled limply in his grasp when they should be actively serving their purpose with their mistress.

What had Wickham done to acquire them? If he laid a hand—but no, surely Miss Elizabeth would not keep secret an assault on her person. Bennet—or Piper—would have killed Wickham as soon as look at him if that had been the case.

Then how? Miss Elizabeth certainly had not thrown herself at him.

He picked up his cake and crushed it. Crumbs fell through his fingers.

This would not do. He had to see her and the Admiral, though heaven alone knew how he might explain himself.

Midmorning sun streamed through the study window. Shadows played along the carpet and climbed up Bennet's chair. Piper stood just behind him, appearing for all the world as though he paid no attention. Only fools assumed Piper inattentive.

"I expected you much earlier." Bennet waved sharply. "Do not linger like a fool in the doorway. Come in."

Wickham sauntered in and sat close to the imposing oak desk. "I had to attend Darcy before I came."

Under the table, Bennet's left hand tightened until cramps shot through his arm. "And how did he compel you? Is he your master?"

"No, he is not. He is my friend—you are my *Master*." The word lingered on Wickham's tongue, a curse not a title.

Piper's scarred eyelid tightened. Blue veins in his neck stood out, throbbing.

"I am here now. What may I do for you?" Wickham dipped his head, his smile so false it begged removal.

"Explain yourself."

"Pardon me? I have not the pleasure of understanding you."

Fingers laced, Bennet leaned forward. "Perhaps you are not accustomed to dealing with a man of my ilk. Your prevarications do not fool me, nor do I find them amusing. Your friend may tolerate them. I do not."

Wickham's right eye twitched. "I shall keep that in mind."

"Explain yourself." Bennet's face shaped into an expression known to wither young seaman and seasoned officers alike.

"What am I to explain?"

"Last night! And if you pretend not to comprehend me, Piper will throw you out on your bloody arse." Bennet thumped the heel of his hand on the desk.

Wickham jumped.

Good, he was not entirely senseless. Not entirely.

"You cannot possibly hold a few idle words against me."

"Indeed? How come you to that conclusion? A man's words are the ultimate judge of his character. Judged by every idle word … out of the overflow of the heart … and all that." Bennet tapped a worn Bible on the corner of his desk.

"You sound like a Sunday morning fingerpost."

"I have not noticed you warming a pew Sunday mornings to be able to tell what a vicar sounds like."

"I heard all the sermons read as a boy. Why endure them again?"

Piper sprang across the desk and grabbed Wickham by the collar. "What place had you to be talking about Missy Lizzy that way?"

Wickham barely blinked.

No upright man remained so calm in the face of

Piper's fury.

"I certainly meant no offense by any of it."

Piper tightened his grip until Wickham's cheeks flushed. He slapped at Piper's fist.

Bennet rose and leaned into Wickham. "Under what circumstances do you believe your words might not cause offense to a lady—or her father?"

Piper shook him until his teeth rattled and dropped him, a boneless ragdoll, to the chair.

"I … I …" He rubbed his throat. "In actuality, it is all in how you look at things. If one wishes to find offense, one will find it wherever one looks. I had not taken you for the variety of man whose thin skin would lead him to—"

"Cease the useless prattle!" Bennet rounded the desk and stood very close to Wickham. Close enough to smell the growing ill-ease in the rude, self-important little coxcomb. "You have fooled Darcy into thinking you his friend for far too long. Does he know how you mock him to those below his station?"

"That is no business of yours!"

"Perhaps not. Though I am now sufficiently convinced of your character. Good day, Mr. Wickham. You are dismissed. Remove yourself from my cottage immediately."

"You have not paid—"

"Your salary? What of your rent? Not to mention the meals you have taken here, the supplies Hill noted you removing from my pantries …" He pulled a slip of paper from his pocket. "Ah yes, candles, a bucket of coal—no that is two buckets, soap, beer, bread … shall I go on? All told, at this point you owe me for your upkeep."

Wickham scuttled back. "That is absurd."

"You did not take these things? Piper will agree when he goes to the cottage to check?"

"Ah … no …"

"You believed them your due? Part of your salary, I suppose?"

"No …"

"I know, you considered it a gift." Bennet folded his arms and drummed his fingers along his shoulder. "I imagine you are accustomed to supplying yourself from Pemberley's larder and just assumed the privilege would be extended here as well."

"Yes, that is—"

"Rot! Moreover, I doubt Darcy recognized what you were about either. You are a thief." Bennet cracked his knuckles.

"How dare you!"

"If you are not out of that cottage and off my property by sundown today, I will bring the magistrate the remains of the prig who imposed himself on my family. Do I make myself clear?" Bennet reached for where his sword should have hung.

Wickham scrambled away. "Abundantly."

"Show him out."

"Aye, sir." Piper grabbed Wickham's upper arms, dragged him from the office, and shut the door behind him.

Bennet sank into his chair and slapped his forehead. Lizzy would be pleased—and relieved. She had her mother's sense about people. At least she was gracious in her victories. Meager consolation that it was.

Elizabeth fastened her day dress. They still had not found a ladies' maid—ah well, that was the least significant servants' position to fill. In time, the staff would be complete. In the meantime, she would enjoy the quiet of her own thoughts in the morning.

Whatever Piper had done with the boys the night before rendered them so exhausted they slept well past their usual waking hour. Perhaps he should contemplate a career as a governess. She giggled, imaging the look that thought might earn her—one that would frighten most grown men. The dear man.

She sat at her dressing table and unraveled her braid. Feelings from last night sprang free with her hair. The silver-handled hairbrush slipped from her fingers and clacked against the marble tabletop. Eyes shut, she threw her head back. How to make sense of it all?

Wickham behaved exactly as she expected he would, like the fops and dandies of the *ton*.

But everyone else displayed their displeasure with Wickham most openly, as openly as their approbation of her. Derbyshire was definitely not London.

And Mr. Darcy—her breath hitched. He removed Mr. Wickham on her account. The mirror revealed a pink stain spreading across her cheeks. The attention he had given her—even Jane commented on it.

How they giggled over that last night! It seemed he really liked her, the way Papa liked Lady Catherine.

Was such a thing possible? She had shut the idea away for so long, but now it stood staring at her: a man she could like and respect well enough to marry.

Did he have any desire to become *spliced*—as Papa would say—again? He already had his heir.

Her child—oh, had she actually thought that? If

she bore him a son, he would never be Darcy's heir. A sad reality she could not change. She tucked a final pin in her hair. Surely though, with his assets and her dowry, there would be some kind of legacy for her children. But still—

She pushed herself up. Enough reflection. If she hurried, she might yet take her morning walk before attending to the household.

Sunrise was well past. Hints of sticky warmth flew on the gentle breeze. Thin clouds shielded the sun but would not last the heat of the day.

The kitchen gardens called to her—the perfect place for a morning ramble. What was that? No—piglets loose in the garden!

At least she wore sturdy boots and an old dress this morning. She shouted for the gardener's boys and dashed after the nearest piglet. There was a knack to catching the creatures—one she had not quite mastered.

The diversion soon lost all novelty, and her temper grew short. Apparently, creatures existed less mindful than her brothers.

By the time the piglets were returned to their pens, her good humor had gone the way of her gown, soaked in mud and sweat, and sporting not a few tears. Bless it all, she would have her walk this morning—she earned it. She straightened her bonnet and retied its ribbons. A final instruction to the gardener, and off she went.

The joys of country life—still, better than being in London. Perhaps now she would find some quiet.

"Miss Elizabeth!"

No—no, not him! Not now, not in her current dishabille.

"Miss Elizabeth?" Mr. Wickham sniggered and tipped his hat. "You look quite remarkable this morning."

"It is no concern of yours, sir." She tried to dodge around him.

He sidled over and blocked her way. "How unlike you to be so ... casually attired. Quite improperly exposed as well." His gaze slid down along the neckline of her gown to her bosom where tears revealed her chemise.

She pulled her shawl over her décolletage. Horrible, vile creature, standing far, far too close.

His right eye twitched; his cheek jumped in time. The same corner of his mouth drifted up.

Piper would have slapped that thought out of his mind. If only she could do it herself. "You best leave Alston lest Papa find you here. Whatever threat he offered, I assure you, he meant its entirety."

Wickham's lip curled. "Your opinion weighs heavily with him."

"I am honored he seeks my opinion." She stepped backwards and slid her hand into her pocket. Trembling fingers wrapped around the cold, solid weight of her knife and flicked open the blade. It quivered with every beat of her pulse.

"You advised him—"

"That is no concern of yours." The trees to his left closed any escape, but the path opened to his right. She felt the way behind her. A beastly large tree blocked that route.

He narrowed the distance between them. "You should reconsider your recommendations to him—immediately."

"I think not." She slipped her hand behind her

back.

"You will regret the consequences if you do not. Look at you, common as a barber's chair, a little bit of brimstone come to the neighborhood." He spat at her feet.

Had this been the first time she heard herself described thus, she might have broken, but the *ton* formed in her the mettle for men of Wickham's ilk.

"I visited Darcy this morning to give him proof of your cockish ways—a piece of your chatelaine broke off when you threw yourself at me begging for me to blow off the groundsills with you. Gentleman that I am, I ran off, leaving you untouched."

"You are a bad liar."

"He thanked me most profusely for the intelligence and intends to keep his distance lest you entrap him in marriage."

Surely he would not, he could not, believe—

Wickham towered over her, fetid breath stinging her eyes. "Petition your father to restore my position or I will poison the entire neighborhood against you."

"No one here cares a jot what you say. They all rejected you last night."

"Then I suppose you will have to marry me." He grabbed the front of her dress and wrenched the weakened fabric.

The muslin cried out and shredded. She whipped her knife around. The blade bit into his hand and held fast.

He howled and released her.

She pelted down the path, barely seeing where she went. A string of epithets fit for a sailor followed her. Branches snapped at her face and tore her bonnet back. She stumbled and pitched forward, catching herself on a long a tree trunk. Panting hard, she looked up and screamed.

"Dear God, Elizabeth!" Darcy sprang from his horse and ran the last few steps to her, Fitzwilliam on his heels.

He slapped back the underbrush determined to keep him from her.

Mud and was that—yes it was ... blood splattered her torn gown. Damn it all! "Are you injured?"

She blinked several times. Did she not recognize him?

"Mr. Darcy? Colonel?" Her voice was more plea for help than greeting.

"What happened?" Fitzwilliam asked over Darcy's shoulder.

Her gown gaped open, revealing the lace of her chemise. Darcy draped his coat over her shoulders and pulled it tight around her. "You are bleeding."

She lifted her hands before her face as though seeing them for the first time. "No—it is not mine—it is Wickham's."

Ten heartbeats passed.

"Where?"

She pointed.

"Get her back to the house. I will deal with him." Fitzwilliam dashed for his horse and trotted away.

"I did not—he grabbed me—used my knife." She clutched Darcy's coat to her.

Every muscle in his body tensed to protect her. "I will see him run out of the county."

She peered at him, eyes wide and vulnerable, so very vulnerable. "You did not believe him—what he told you this morning?"

"No, heavens no!"

Bennet might have his hide, but dash it all! He wrapped his arms around her and pulled her tight to him. She nestled into his shoulder and shuddered. This was exactly where she belonged.

He stroked her back, willing his hand gentle all the while his belly roiled. What had Wickham done?

"Papa dismissed him earlier," she whispered. "He petitioned me to change Papa's mind."

'Petitioned' was a most politic choice of words. An unlikely possibility under the best of circumstances.

"You struggled with him?"

She peeked up at him. A valiant little light glimmered in her eyes. "No, not very much. Most of the damage can be attributed to piglets loose in the garden." She giggled into his lapels. "I … I detest piglets right now."

"Truly? But the blood?"

"Papa insists Jane and I carry a proper knife. Wickham grabbed for me and I struck his hand … Piper will be cross that I did not aim for something more vital." She tittered again, a hollow shadow of the normally rich, joyful sound. "Papa commissioned that knife for me. He will be most vexed I have lost it."

"I doubt that will be his first concern." He tucked her head under his chin. "I could never forgive myself had he harmed you." Surely she heard the thunder in his chest.

"The worst harm is to my gown. Thankfully, I never particularly liked this one."

"None of that changes the fact he threatened you."

"He intended to force Papa to make us marry."

"Fool." A growl rumbled through his ribs. "I expect Piper might kill him first, unless your father precedes him."

"Piper is every bit as protective as Papa and without so many scruples. He cultivates a host of unsavory connections. Papa says it is worthwhile to have a rogue or two on your side in a squall."

Lucky Bennet to enjoy such resources. "I cannot object. His motives are most pleasing."

"Why did you trust Mr. Wickham when the signs of his duplicity were so clear?" She huddled closer.

Dearest, loveliest Elizabeth, who else would not let him go unchallenged, even in a moment like this, hold him accountable so faithfully, especially when held so close to his heart? Perhaps, if he held her long enough, he might be able to hear her thoughts. Would that they could stay here until then.

"Clear to you, who are a sterling judge of character and unencumbered by the past experiences that muddied my discernment."

"Do you know how he came into possession of my chatelaine's pieces?"

Surely she did not—

He craned his neck and peered into her face. Dear God, she did! "I know you did not throw yourself upon him as he claimed. I could never believe such a thing." He produced the chains from his pocket and dropped them into her hand. How difficult to part with even those little bits of her.

"Mr. Wickham ran into me in the hallway and we took a spectacular fall. I found these and two keys went missing. I never considered him capable of the sleight of hand to steal them so easily."

"What of the key still gone?"

"Perhaps Wickham has it."

"You need a locksmith then. Should I recommend one to your father?"

"I expect so."

"Will he even admit me to speak with him?"

"Papa is not one to hold a grudge. Besides, you were here to rescue me. That will please him."

"But does it please you?" He laced his fingers in hers, an intimacy too intense to bear without a kiss.

How would Bennet see it?

How did he?

He had barely kissed Anne. Theirs was more a friendship based on duty—ardor played little role. Their relations were pleasant enough—for him. Did Anne feel the same? She never said. Passion, all that the Bard wrote of, was foreign to him.

But now, he held the embodiment of everything he desired—beauty, wit, charm, affection and worth. How could he not but try to possess it? He lifted her hand, so warm in his, to his lips and kissed it.

"I …" her voice hitched and quivered with her fingers. "I am very pleased." A flicker of kindred passion glimmered below her lashes.

Lightening shot through his spine. He tipped her face up to his. Summoning every fragment of self-control, he gently caressed her lips with his. Was this her first kiss?

It may as well have been his.

So sweet, an intoxicating nectar, he could never drink enough.

Her breath tickled: short, shallow flutterings, tentative and shy. She was on unfamiliar ground as much as he.

Too soon, he pulled back to nestle her head under his chin. "Need I apologize?"

"No."

He heard her dear, wry, little smile.

"May I speak to your father?"

"What option have we? There is no hiding anything from Papa." She turned in his arms to face at him. "His fondness for Lady Catherine will be to your material advantage." The sparkle in her eyes demanded another kiss.

He obliged.

Bennet grumbled and raked his hair for the hundredth time. Taking on a man with a bothersome past always presented risks. Sometimes it worked in one's favor and other times—

He tipped his chair back looking for answers on the ceiling. Lady Catherine warned him just as Lizzy had, but he had been too bloody stubborn to take heed of either. Ellen would scold him now if she could see. And she would be right.

With Wickham gone, he must begin again—and this time, listen to his advisors. Alston was a sound estate. If they made it through harvest to next spring, it would be a legacy to pass to his heir. He rubbed the back of his neck.

"Papa! Papa!" Francis caught himself in the doorway of the study, panting.

Philip slid into him, knocking them both pell-mell across the carpet into a heap like a pile of puppies.

Philip propped up on his elbows. "Mr. Darcy is bringing Lizzy to the house on his horse!"

"They are riding together!" Francis climbed out

from under his brother. "That is not proper, is it father?"

"Will Lizzy be in trouble?"

"What's this? Stuff and nonsense—" Bennet pushed to his feet.

"It is true." George poked his head in. "We saw them."

David's head bobbed energetically. "She is wearing my Papa's coat but it is not cold."

Francis ran to the window and pointed. "Her hair is all rumpled and her bonnet is missing."

Icy knots tied his guts like furled sails. Two wives had already been torn from him. Not again—surely not again. He sprinted across the room, leapt over the boys and into the hall where Piper met him.

Darcy's horse stopped at the bottom of the front steps. Lizzy perched awkwardly in front of him, in a posture anything but proper.

"Lizzy!" Bennet reached for her.

"I am well, Papa." She slid into his arms, clutching Darcy's coat tightly around her.

He steadied her shoulders, his heart crashing against his ribs in storming waves. "No, you are not. Who did this?"

She sniffed and wiped her face with the edge of her tattered fichu. "Mostly the piglets—"

The four boys tumbled from the front door, elbowing one another and shouting.

"Piglets?" Francis squealed. He fought to get past Piper's arms.

"Yes, they got loose this morning." She craned her neck to look at them. "You four should go and check and make sure they are still secured. Then you might help the gardener repair the damage."

"May we, Papa?" George asked with far greater solemnity than his bouncing suggested.

Darcy slid off his horse and waved them on. "Go ahead, all of you."

Lizzy shivered in Bennet's arms. He placed his hands over hers and gently pulled the great coat back. "The piglets did not do this."

He would kill the man who did.

"Wickham." She closed her eyes and her chin quivered just enough to break his heart.

He snugged Darcy's coat around her and pulled her to him. Piper's eyes narrowed and his jaw tightened. Wickham had crossed the wrong family.

"Perhaps it would be best to go inside." Darcy gestured for the front door.

Hill met them and bustled Lizzy upstairs.

Bennet stood at the base of the stairs, staring after her. He counted his breaths, each one slow and deep. He had not been a captain who favored the lash, but he might just make an exception now.

Piper tapped his shoulder and jerked his chin toward the study. Bennet stalked off with Darcy close behind.

"I saw him off the estate. Followed him halfway to Lambton just to be sure." Piper gripped the back of the wingback chair, his arms cording.

Bennet growled and slammed his desk. "I had an interview with him this morning. He said he visited you before he came to me."

"I thought he might apologize for last night," Darcy raked his hair, "but he did not. Instead, he sought to poison me against your family. I threw him out and warned him never to return."

"Desperate men," Piper muttered and glanced out

the window.

"Did you see him?"

"No, I came upon her after she escaped him. He intended to compromise her and force a marriage."

"It would serve him right if I let him marry her. She'd cut off his bollocks before he got to use 'em." Bennet closed his eyes and savored the image.

"I believe she nearly did. She is certainly not defenseless."

"She shoulda slit the bloody bastard's throat." Piper paced across the room. "I will finish the task for her, I will."

"If the wound she dealt him festers, it would be greater punishment to allow him to suffer with it," Darcy muttered. "It is a rare woman who can keep her head under such a circumstance."

"No woman in my care is defenseless, even if she is alone. Lady Catherine will be no different."

Darcy turned aside and sniggered.

"You find humor in that?"

"Forgive me. Not at all. I merely pictured Aunt Catherine with a knife."

"Certainly not." Bennet drummed his fingers together. "In the orient, there are those who use a fan as a weapon."

"You cannot be serious."

"I rarely joke."

"She is vicious enough with the one she currently possesses. I will not have such a thing in my house." Darcy rubbed his chest.

"No matter, she will not be living with you when I give it to her."

"Elizabeth insisted your intentions toward her were honorable, though you have taken improper liberties with her."

"You would call me improper? Given the position I just found you in with my daughter, I should be asking you of your intentions."

"I intend to convince you to permit me to court her."

Their eyes locked. Darcy did not back down.

"Your marriage was not as felicitous as my own. I require better for my daughter."

"I married Anne out of duty, not love. I was faithful to her in marriage and in friendship, but we were too dissimilar and she far too grateful to me for more. But your daughter—"

"It is to your credit that you do not desire her because you are in need of capital." Bennet stomped across the room. "But the only reason I do not cast you out is you finally showed the good sense to throw Wickham aside."

Darcy leaned his forehead on his palms. "My father encouraged me to dismiss him. I wish he might have lived to see it happen."

At least he admitted to his own errors, certainly a point in his favor, particularly if he considered a life with Lizzy. "Loyalty and faithfulness are admirable traits when they are rightly placed. I am not currently convinced of the soundness of your judgment. Prove to me you are worthy to entrust her safety to and I will accept you as a son."

"May I begin by recommending a locksmith? Wickham gave me one of Miss Elizabeth's keys and her scissors—"

"The blackguard stole them, he did." Piper pounded his fist into his palm.

"She said another key is still missing."

"I have taken precautions, but give me your locksmith's name and direction, nonetheless."

A knock sounded at the door.

"Come."

Fitzwilliam strode in and handed Bennet an object in a bloody handkerchief.

Piper leaned over his shoulder. "It be hers."

"I followed his trail as far as I could, but lost him. He did not lose enough blood to slow him down much. No doubt she surprised the hell out of him." Fitzwilliam dropped into a chair.

"She shoulda gone for the vitals. I taught her better. She and me are gonna have some words."

No doubt the words would be largely from Piper's side alone, short, terse and loud. How did Miss Elizabeth withstand Piper's ire?

"Perhaps it may be best this way. If she mortally wounded him, the investigation might be … troublesome." Bennet rubbed his temple. "It is enough she escaped."

"I am impressed with her clarity of mind." Fitzwilliam braced his elbows on his knees. "Forgive me, I must ask—"

"Yes, for all her disposition is milder, Jane is as adept and as well armed as her sister. She would have done the self-same thing, though she might have apologized before she ran off."

Piper snorted.

Fitzwilliam guffawed. "Whilst it pleases me to know it, what I was going to ask is, what moved you to such an unconventional course? Did your wives approve?"

"I suppose I was selfish, keeping my family as close as I did. Port cities are often less than genteel. I insisted my wives and daughters were protected in every possible way, including the ability to defend themselves."

"They learned faster than most sailors I taught. Right clever gals, all o' them." Piper rocked slightly on the desk.

"Miss Elizabeth is quite proficient with a wooden sword." Fitzwilliam winked at Darcy.

Now was not the time.

"She be deadly with a real blade." Piper pulled out his handkerchief and polished the dirt off Elizabeth's knife.

"No doubt." Darcy rubbed his knuckles along his lips.

"The greatest irony is none of them ever had need of it until we came back to London." Bennet threw his hands up.

"What happened whilst you were in town?" Darcy asked.

Piper pitched forward and shot him a glare more powerful than a musket ball. Muttered swallowed invectives rumbled from his corner of the room.

So this was a more sensitive subject than even Aunt Catherine expected.

"He has the right to ask." Bennet waved him down.

Fitzwilliam whirled on Darcy. "I cannot believe you actually—"

"Spoke to me first?" Bennet rapped his desk. "Do not think I have missed—"

"Not at all, sir." Fitzwilliam grinned and saluted. "You miss nothing under your command."

"Keep that in mind. As to your question … it is appropriate you understand—both of you—before your connections to my daughters deepen."

It might be better if he did not learn the name of the man who hurt his Elizabeth. Revenge was too tempting. Darcy settled back, his throat too tight to swallow.

"You are well acquainted with London society. My daughters, with their fortunes and connections, are quite eligible matches, particularly for second sons and peers in mean circumstances." Bennet laced his fingers together so tightly his knuckles went white and stared directly at Fitzwilliam. "Jane experienced her share of spirited suitors, but they were not so … energetic in their pursuit as Lizzy's."

Fitzwilliam chuffed what could only have been a sigh of relief. Lucky man.

"Elizabeth's lively disposition attracted much attention from a number of well-born young men, lacking in capital, but not ambition. With her keen sense of people, she quickly penetrated their facades and cast them aside."

"Of course," Darcy murmured, "she has little tolerance for their ilk."

"Indeed, not." Bennet leaned back in his chair, its joints creaking under the force. "On two separate occasions, a suitor attempted to compromise her into marriage—as if I would condone such a union. She escaped the first without bloodshed, but the second will carry a pronounced scar across his right cheek as a reminder. Nearly put out his eye."

"The hell-born babe yapped it were Missy Lizzy who came at 'im, unprovoked. She shoulda slit his throat."

"Perhaps." Bennet clenched his jaw. "The magistrates pronounced her innocent, having acted only in her own defense. Needless to say, a wave of cruel talk followed—"

A facial scar should be obvious enough. Darcy stroked his chin. That family and their associates would never—

"Miss Jane woulda done no different, neither. For all her pretty looks, she ain't one to stand any imposing on her."

Bennet closed his eyes and bobbed his head. "Both of them were sullied by the gossip. Anyone who associates with them will be tainted by the talk as well."

"My family avoids London for good reason. I will not feed my sister to those hell hounds and harpies."

Fitzwilliam crossed his legs and looped his hands over his knee. "You do not follow the accounts of my family, I suppose. My elder brother creates enough scandal for us all. We can weather whatever else might come."

Bennet tapped his lips. "That would be Viscount Hightower?"

Better to forget that intemperate relation existed whenever possible. Fitzwilliam covered his face with his hand.

"You may also add Sir Lewis to our list of unfortunate connections."

"Most men would be trying to convince me of the strength of their connections and how those would overcome my daughter's shortcoming, not airing their dirty laundry."

Darcy opened his mouth to speak, but shut it again. No sense losing the ground he had just gained.

"Then I have your consent—" Fitzwilliam leaned forward.

"No."

Piper's lips shaped into a hard line no sane man would cross.

"Excuse—"

"Stow it, Colonel."

"See here, sir!"

"I have not denied you, either."

"Then what?"

"My daughter is fond enough of you and the company you keep does you credit." Bennet gestured toward Darcy. "But you have as much to prove to me as your cousin."

"Prove to you?"

"Yes. How will you provide for her and her children?"

Fitzwilliam's jaw dropped.

"I am too well aware of the plight of a younger son." Bennet rubbed his palms together. "You live with Darcy and your aunt. Is this by amiable choice or the object of necessity?"

Fitzwilliam squirmed.

Few discomfited Fitzwilliam. What a pleasure to observe a master leave his self-assured cousin twitching.

"My daughter may have a fortune—which I credit you with having never inquired after, but I could hardly consider handing it over to one who might squander it."

"I would very much like to take offense and indulge in a bit of high dudgeon. But I cannot." Fitzwilliam writhed against the leather upholstery. "What do you require?"

"Proof you are trustworthy. How can I entrust a man not responsible with his money with a treasure like my daughter?" Bennet tapped his steepled fingers together.

"What do you require of me?"

"Find evidence to prove it to yourself—in all likelihood that will be sufficient for me."

"Yes, sir." Fitzwilliam's jaw set.

Darcy knew his look. There would be no living with him until he solved the puzzle and conquered this foe.

"Now, regarding Wickham—"

"I will send men to spread word we are searching for him and offer a reward for locating him. His friends do not tend to be the loyal sort," Darcy said.

"The girls shouldn't be going out without me or a footman with them," Piper said. "A guard should be set up, all watches, as well—two men in the halls."

"Is that necessary?" Darcy asked.

Bennet slapped the desk. "The bastard attacked my daughter. He has been stealing from my larder and most likely yours as well. Now he is cut off from it all. What do you think he will do?"

Darcy dragged his hand down his face. "You are correct. I am far too much in the habit of making excuses for Wickham."

"It is time you see that." Bennet snapped. "I expect you to implement the same measures at Pemberley. Your sister and Lady Catherine need no less protection than Jane and Elizabeth."

"Probably more," Piper muttered.

"If you do not, have no doubt, I will bring them here and ensure they are properly protected."

"You overstep yourself, Admiral. They are my family and my responsibility."

"Prove it." Bennet's eyes added—*and yourself.*

Darcy stole a quick look at Fitzwilliam. "I will station footmen as you suggest and the ladies will not go out unaccompanied."

Fitzwilliam's brows climbed high. He must be enjoying the spectacle: Darcy capitulating to another's will. But dash it all! Elizabeth was worth it.

Chapter 7

AFTER THREE DAYS' SEARCH produced no signs of Wickham, Piper reluctantly agreed to call off the efforts. Still, he had confided to Darcy that several of his friends promised continued vigilance since Wickham owed them debts, too. Despite the presence of watchful footmen in Pemberley's corridors, life slowly regained normalcy.

"He may actually have left," Fitzwilliam muttered over his teacup.

Lady Catherine harrumphed as she arranged her taffeta with one hand and fluttered her fan with the other, the embodiment of a broody hen. "I, for one, shall not be sorry to see the end of him at Pemberley. Admiral Bennet's suppositions proved correct—Wickham helped himself to my pantry, something not even your sons have done."

"How astonishing to hear you agreeing with Bennet." Fitzwilliam set his tea down.

She slapped his leg with her closed fan.

"Madam!"

"You best temper your teasing before Bennet acquires the gift he mentioned." Darcy smirked behind his newspaper.

Lady Catherine whirled on Darcy. "Excuse me?"

"She will not be here to use it upon us and he will play hoist with his own petard." Fitzwilliam's merry eyes contradicted his sober officer's mask.

"Our dear aunt will not dare attempt to manage him as she does us." Darcy winked.

"Whatever are you blathering on about?" She smacked her fan into her palm.

Shuck—shuck—shuck

"Nothing at all, Aunt." Fitzwilliam grinned.

"Do stop teasing." Georgiana rearranged the biscuits on the nearest platter.

That look, that tone, so reminiscent of Elizabeth's. He set his newspaper aside and hunkered down beside her. She turned her face away.

"You are afraid." Darcy laid his hand on hers.

She blinked and offered a weak smile. "No, no, I am—"

"Trying to comfort me. But I should feel the full force of my error. Do not shrink from that, dearling. Forgive me for remaining loyal to him for far too long."

"It is difficult to regard loyalty a fault. You are the most dutiful man I know."

"Just not the wisest. I am committed to change, though." He squeezed her fingers. "I was wrong to have brushed aside your feelings and made light of his offer for you. Will you please forgive me?"

"With such a pretty apology, how could I not?"

Her smile was genuine this time. "You are the best of brothers."

"Someday, I hope to deserve your high regard." He hauled himself to his feet. "Aunt, do you know how much Wickham took from the larders?"

She struck her palm with her fan. "I instructed Mrs. Reynolds to keep a list whenever she observed the stocks did not add up correctly. Her records should provide you what you require. What are you going to do?"

"I am not certain yet. He must be punished, though I cannot reconcile myself to seeing a man who was once my friend hang."

Fitzwilliam leaned back and balanced one foot atop the other. "Some kind of friend, belittling you behind your—"

Darcy raked his hair. "Yes, I am aware of that, and yes, I forgave him."

"Another thing I fail to understand. What would give you to ignore his egregious treatment of you?"

"Consider how difficult he found school—the poorest student who relied on the charity of another. In spite of that, he did me a service you do not now, and may never, comprehend."

"Enlighten me." Fitzwilliam pitched forward on his elbows.

"I would like to understand, too," Georgiana whispered.

Darcy braced his forehead against his palms. "Scholarship came easily for me, but school proved far less so. Noise and crowds and unfamiliar people are my bane, even to this day. Whereas others are able to talk of nothing for hours, I cannot. I had no idea how to join in and was vilified for it. You know my

dislike of games. For that, they judged me prideful.
Surrounded by my peers, I felt so very alone."

"Darce, I had no idea."

"Should I have advertised such a thing? How
better to make my humiliation complete?" He trudged
to the fireplace and braced his hands on the mantle.
"I petitioned father to send Wickham to permit me
someone familiar nearby. His presence eased the way
for me, allowing me to study his example and begin to
learn those ordinary skills most acquire without effort.
He realized I observed him, and it amused him.
Whilst he spoke ill of me at times, he did not revealed
the true nature of my discomfort. I will always be
grateful he kept my secret."

"I never realized your gratitude came from such a
source," Aunt Catherine whispered.

"It does not mitigate my error in ignoring his
misdeeds, though. I will change that."

Lady Catherine cocked her head. "So Admiral
Bennet—"

"Will have the proof he needs—or I will take his
daughter to Gretna Green."

Fitzwilliam barked a hoarse laugh. "Be serious!
Piper would kill you, assuming the Admiral does not
do it first."

"Miss Elizabeth's consent is the only one I need."

"You would go against her father?" Georgiana
gasped and clutched her heart.

"If I must, but I will try to give him what he asks
for first."

"Georgiana is right. You are the best of men."
Lady Catherine set her fan aside and bustled to his
side.

"No, Aunt, I am not, but I am trying." He craned

his neck to look at Fitzwilliam. "How are you getting on with those papers for Bennet?"

"Progressing well, now I have gotten over the astonishment." Fitzwilliam laced his fingers and stretched his arms. His knuckles popped.

"Astonishment? Over what?" Georgiana asked.

Fitzwilliam joined Darcy at the fireplace. "Some years ago, when I joined you here at Pemberley, I requested your brother's help to manage my meager funds. I confess, I have not followed the reports closely, as I did not like being reminded of my own penury. However, between Darcy and his solicitor, the results are beyond all my expectations. I can no longer claim poverty."

Mrs. Reynolds appeared in the doorway. "Sir, the post." She extended a silver tray with a fat, sealed letter.

"Thank you." Darcy took the missive. Its sharp corners cut into his palm. Bad news, no doubt. "Excuse me."

Darcy stalked to his study and threw the letter on his desk. *Clack!* The sealing wax hit the wood. The decanter of port caught his eye and called to him.

No, the drink might allow him to ignore what was unpleasant.

He pinched the bridge of his nose and dropped into his chair. It creaked and complained as he reached for the missive. A bit of the seal, cracked by the desk, fell away and bounced along and off the desktop.

Mr. Locke's crisp, neat script greeted him. No doubt he managed to offend the solicitor with the officiousness of his last letter. Now, he would need to recant nearly every word.

He scrubbed his face with his hands. Best do this thing quickly.

Mr. Darcy, I am pleased my prior work met your exacting standards. I regret you now desire to end our association.

You have always been a fair man. I pray you might permit me to present my case and perhaps reconsider.

I understand Mr. Wickham is your particular friend and, as such, you promoted him to me. The sad facts of the matter are that his performance was, from the first day, wholly and entirely disappointing.

I enclose, for your examination, documentation of his work habits. He arrived late and left early nearly every day. Though I docked his pay, his practices did not alter. These complaints alone were not enough to warrant his dismissal. Your favor earned him an extra measure of patience.

Darcy dropped the letter. Only a few weeks ago, he would have consigned it to the fire without reading another word. He bounced his fist on his desk and relished the sting.

… Items 'borrowed' from the pantry … rent not paid … gambling debts … creditors coming to the law office, disrupting … books and accounts not balancing … young ladies … Locke's daughter …

Darcy's hands trembled. Locke only hinted at the extent of Wickham's transgressions, but he had to know more and recompense what he could.

Darcy slept poorly and woke early. Before anyone else stirred, he visited the kitchen for something to break his fast whilst he worked. Only a few issues to deal with and he would be free to go.

The door flung open. Fitzwilliam burst in and planted his hands on the desk. "Do not argue. I am going with you."

"Excuse me?"

"Mrs. Reynolds told me of your plans—rather, I forced her to tell me. Your staff is either fanatically loyal or scared to death of you. It is difficult to discern which."

"Bennet's staff is scared, mine is loyal and you are not accompanying me." Darcy tucked his ledger into a drawer. "It is my doing, and I should bear the undoing of it."

"Precisely why I'm coming with you. You are too apt to shoulder responsibilities that are not your own."

"I recommended him to Locke."

"Balderdash! If Locke hired him because of you, it was to curry favor for his own benefit. If he suffered, it was from choosing to lay aside his own good judgment. Your sense of duty is far too developed."

"I do not recall you complaining when you benefited from my overdeveloped sense of duty." Darcy pushed back from his desk.

"Indeed, and I am not proud of it. I took advantage of you and am most heartily ashamed of myself for it."

What had Fitzwilliam just said?

"Do not look so surprised I came to be sensible of my error."

"I never asked—"

"That is the problem. You never do. You determine your duty and do it, setting aside all your own needs and wants. You try to take care of everyone, and it is excessive. At some point, you must let us fend for ourselves. Allow me to stand on my own and not rely on you so much."

"You never asked for—"

"I never needed to." Fitzwilliam threw his hands in the air. "You anticipated everything. Where Father ignored me and gave me little, you have given too abundantly. Let me be my own man. Let me make mistakes. Let me suffer for them. I will be all the better for it."

Darcy pressed his arm over his ribs. They had been boys the last time Fitzwilliam punched him. That blow hurt far less.

Fitzwilliam sat on the edge of the nearest chair. "If you intend to take Miss Elizabeth as your wife, you need to mend your ways. She is not a woman who will tolerate so much caretaking."

"What do you consider Admiral Bennet?"

"He is a commander, not a caretaker. There is a difference. Trust me."

"You suggest I am not suitable for her?"

"Rein in your generous nature just a bit, and you will be entirely suitable." Fitzwilliam leaned close. "Do you really mean to take her to Gretna Green?"

Darcy chewed his knuckle. "We have not spoken of it, yet."

"I thought not. She will say yes."

"How nice you are so certain."

"Yes, I am, but Bennet is right. You need reform as much as I. Habits are difficult to change. You require someone to hold you accountable."

"I will not excuse Wickham this time nor smooth his way. For once, he will feel the weight of every one of his mistakes." Darcy forced a lackluster chuckle. "But knowing I must answer to you will not hurt, I suppose."

"I can be packed in an hour."

"No. Wickham remains unaccounted for. Do you wish to leave Lady Catherine and Georgiana unprotected in our absence? Piper still accompanies the Miss Bennets whenever they journey away from the house. Alston's footmen still patrol its halls. It hardly behooves us to do less."

"Your footmen—"

"Will never be as vigilant as you or I." Darcy pushed up. "Stay and protect my family—our family—whilst I travel. I will heed your warnings, but I cannot allow you to accompany me."

"I do not like the notion."

"I do not need you to like it. I need you to do it. Did you not say I asked too little of you in the past. See, I am changing my ways."

"This is not what I intended." Fitzwilliam grumbled and rolled his eyes. "I will stay."

"Thank you." Darcy picked up his bag. "I will return as quickly as possible."

Fitzwilliam clapped his shoulder on the way out.

Darcy settled into his coach and directed his driver to Alston.

He worried his knuckles against his teeth. The sun barely peeked over the horizon—far too early to pay a call. Still, Bennet did not sleep much past dawn, nor did Elizabeth.

Oh this was foolishness, appearing at their door at such a ridiculous hour! What would he even say? He should give this up and be on his way to London.

The carriage jolted over a familiar rut in the road, the one marking the narrow drive leading to Alston manor.

Too late. Bennet, atop his proud bay, approached.

How would he explain himself? He slid open the side glass.

Bennet brought his horse close and touched his hat.

Darcy rapped on the roof. The coach stopped and he jumped out. The admiral dismounted and gestured for Darcy to join him.

"You are up and about early this morning." The admiral's face was drawn up in maritime knots.

Clearly, he did not welcome company, so why did he invite it?

"I suppose I am, but the journey to London is a long one and I prefer to make an early start."

"London? To see your solicitor?"

"Yes. Wickham recently worked for him—"

"You will have him draw up settlement papers as well."

"That is on my agenda." Darcy gritted his teeth and braced for the storm.

Bennet's steps grew firmer, more purposeful. He snarled and glowered: a mask that would frighten his seamen—and most other men—into submission. "You are determined upon my Lizzy."

Sunrise was a bit early for a confrontation, but best have done with it. "Absolutely."

"Have you forgotten, you have neither my permission nor my approval."

At least he did not mince words. Was there a mast nearby for him to tie himself to weather the coming gale?

"Perhaps you have forgotten, she is of age. Your approval is a luxury, not necessity."

"You would go ahead against me?"

How many could say they had seen a genuine look of shock on the admiral's face? At some time in the future, Darcy might appreciate being one of the few. For now, it seemed a dangerous clique in which to claim membership. Nonetheless, Bennet would understand while he might command Alston, he did not command Pemberley or Darcy.

"No, sir. Not if presented with any other alternative."

Bennet sent a rock skittering into the tall grass.

Surviving the first onslaught was a good sign. "I wish to see her before I depart."

"This is an uncivilized hour to pay a call to a lady."

"Would you not deem me ungentlemanly for leaving her without explanation or word?"

Bennet growled something unintelligible.

What a joy he must have been on shipboard morning watches.

"Will you permit me to call on her or not?"

Bennet pushed on several more steps and muttered syllables that sounded like '*A man who would go to Gretna Green will go behind my back anyway.*'

"I asked you a question, sir. Am I to expect the courtesy of an answer or not? Admiral Bennet!" Darcy stopped. Tall grasses tickled at his elbows. "If you have issue with me, you will speak outright and look me in the eye whilst you do it."

The grasses parted and Bennet whirled. He stomped to Darcy and stopped far too close for comfort. "Very well, I hold you responsible for Wickham, for all he has done."

"What? Responsible for—"

He stabbed Darcy in the chest with his fingertips. "Your judgment is suspect at best, and if you think I am going to permit an unworthy soul to carry off my Lizzy, you are sorely mistaken."

Now he came to the truth of it—Elizabeth. But perhaps a frontal assault on Bennet's reasoning was not the best approach. "Whilst I am as appalled as you at Wickham's behavior, I am not responsible for his actions."

"You should have thrown him out on his arse when he offered for your sister."

Darcy gritted his teeth. "You are correct. I erred, believing his excuses."

"Little good admitting it now."

"What more shall I do? I cast him off for his insults to your daughter and did not for a moment have faith in his calumny against her. I am on my way to see my solicitor to learn the truth of his behavior in London. Shall I murder him in cold blood as well?"

The faced each other, watching for the first move. Had they swords, they would have been drawn by now.

Aunt Catherine had warned him to expect this reaction. He would not easily release his favorite. *Do not let his bark intimidate you,* she said, *he would test what you are made from. Remember, you seek to take his favorite from him. He will not let her go easily. Do not worry. He will, in time, see things as he should.*

Why had he believed her?

"Papa? Mr. Darcy?"

Elizabeth approached from the house. The rising sun glowed in a halo behind her, his angel of deliverance.

"I told you not to walk alone—"

"I am in no way alone, Papa, given that I am talking with you." The sweet little smile he loved so well quirked the edges of her mouth.

Only she could get away with such a response.

Bennet harrumphed and slid the sword he did not have back into its scabbard.

"What brings you to Alston so early, Mr. Darcy?" She curtsied and looped her arm in her father's.

"I am for London this morning and came to take my leave." He tipped his hat.

"How kind of you. Papa enjoys company on his morning jaunts."

Did she not realize she played with fire? Bennet was apt to explode into vitriol at any moment, yet she poured kerosene near the spark. She winked at her father.

He grumbled something unintelligible.

"I had hoped to obtain his permission to call upon you as well, madam."

Bennet's face tightened. Was he trying to contain a fresh tirade?

And yet, Elizabeth did not falter, turning to him with a beatific smile.

"I am going to the morning room. Stay to the gardens within view of those windows." He stormed away.

Darcy offered her his arm. The gardens looked especially lovely—lovely and delightfully admiral-free—this morning.

"Papa is in high dudgeon for so early in the day." She blinked up at him, eyes twinkling.

Must she be so tempting and with her father certainly watching from the windows? A man could only tolerate so much!

"It would be foolish to expect anything else. He is displeased with me in general and my unmannerly, early arrival served to inflame his ire further. Finding yet another fault to credit to me was not the balm his spirit required this morning."

She snickered. "His temper does sometimes get the better of him."

"He is angry over Wickham—and whilst I cannot entirely blame him—"

"He is scarcely being reasonable either."

"That thought had occurred."

"It crosses the mind of any who deal with Papa long enough." Irresistible impertinence danced on her lips.

"So then his indignation is a passing thing?"

The light faded from her countenance. "Not at all. Do not take his ire lightly. It is very real."

Most fathers would have been pleased at his interest in their daughter. But not Bennet—no one interested in Elizabeth would please him.

He placed his hand over hers on his arm. The penetrating warmth of her fingers soothed his ragged nerves.

He stopped and glanced at the house. A cloud passed overhead, allowing them to see into the morning room. Piper had just entered with the boys. Bennet would be distracted for at least a few moments.

He stepped in front of Elizabeth and grasped her hands. "How do you feel about his attitude toward me?"

"It troubles me exceedingly."

"You are aware we do not require his consent."

"Consent for what?" She turned her shoulder.

"Do not hide from me." He took her chin and guided her to look at him.

The questions in her eyes sliced through his composure. Why did she doubt him? Why—of course she would. When had he ever properly expressed himself?

"My dear Elizabeth, you must allow me to tell you how ardently I admire and love you. Almost from the first moment I met you, my heart, my mind have been so distracted, I scarce could consider anything else. If only you knew how many times I played your sword battle with Fitzwilliam over in my mind, wishing it was with me instead."

"No, do not tease me so. If you cannot be honest with me, I—"

"I do not understand."

"What of all your severe looks? I detected no signs of regard in your countenance then."

Ouch!

"Foolishness that, attempting to convince myself of my contentment in life—all the while you were showing me my emptiness."

Her lips rounded into a delightful little 'o' and the creases around her eyes eased.

He bent to touch a kiss to her forehead, but his self-control proved insufficient and he brushed his lips to hers. Better judgment demanded he should stop, but a brief taste inflamed him more. He pulled her to him, desperate for her warmth in his arms, her breath on his skin, her heartbeat against his. She was the completion of his every barrenness, the fulfillment of his every desire.

Without a doubt, he would not find love, this kind of love, more than once in his life. He dare not let her slip through his fingers. His chest constricted. Aching for air, he pulled back and met her gaze.

Her eyes shimmered and a tear glittered on her cheek.

A tear.

Why tears?

He willed his hand not to tremble as he lifted the tear to his lips.

"Forgive—"

She laid a finger over his mouth and shook her head. "Do not apologize."

His heart resumed its rhythm. Did she feel his arms quake with the force?

"I ... I cannot object to your attentions. I know it terribly improper—"

He stopped her words with kisses. She melted into him, lips soft and warm below his. Hunger, consuming hunger gripped him. He could not bring himself to stop until forced to pulled back mere inches to gasp for breath.

"No dearest, I will not permit you to even think that. Those accusations in London were untrue. You are indeed all that is good and proper and I find it most desirable the lady I would court desires me as much as I her. Never, never apologize for that."

She bit her lip and sniffled.

"Why the tears, my love?" He brushed another away, each drop rending a little tear in his heart.

"Papa is difficult and maddening and stubborn, but please, do not make me choose between the two of you."

He looked over his shoulder. Piper blocked the window. Bless that man! "How do I satisfy him?"

She looked into the sky as though the answer might be found amongst the clouds. "I have never seen him so unreasonable. I do not recognize him at all right now."

"Do not expect me to give you up, not for anyone's opinions."

"Even his? He does not frighten you?"

"Not nearly as much as the prospect of life without you." He cupped her cheek and stroked her brow with his thumb. "When I return, I will try to negotiate a peace again. If he does not relent, mark my words, dearest, loveliest, Elizabeth, I will carry you off to Gretna Green in the middle of the night and bring you back my wife."

"No! You—we—could not."

"I suppose you are correct." He brushed away another tear and placed a kiss on the top of her head. "But I do intend to acquire a special license so the vicar might marry us some afternoon in the family chapel and come with us to explain the fact to your father."

Her eyes widened and she gaped.

"Surely he would not harm a man of the church."

She trailed her fingers along the edge of his jaw. "You are not joking, are you?"

"Not at all." She had agreed to be his wife and she would be. He searched his memories for that moment, for the exact words, the precious look in her eyes ... "Dear Lord, I am a fool!"

She stiffened and tried to pull back, but he held her fast.

"I was so certain I had, but I only did so in my overactive imagination."

"What are you talking about?"

"The biggest, most colossally stupid oversight of my life. I never actually asked you—I—forgive me. I have been utterly blinded by my love for you. So much so, I completely overlooked—" He dropped to his knee and touched his forehead to the back of her hand. "Elizabeth, I love you more than I ever imagined possible. Would you consent to be my wife?"

"Oh!" She covered her face with her hands.

He jumped to his feet and pulled her into his shoulder. She was crying—sobbing. Heavens above, what had he done?

Piper no longer stood in the window. No doubt the Admiral would be storming out soon. Hang it all!

"Elizabeth?"

"I am sorry—I am being missish and silly—"

"You are neither. Please forgive this overbearing fool for not to having asked you properly until now."

"I never dreamed anyone would—"

"Then you are not displeased with me?"

Her eyes shimmered. "Not at all."

Thank Providence! "Am I to understand that as a yes?"

"Yes."

His hands and feet tingled. So this was the sensation of supreme happiness. "Then I shall find a way to win your father before we marry or reconcile with him after. In either case, you, Elizabeth Bennet, will be my wife. Soon."

"You are a very confident man, Mr. Darcy."

"With you in my arms, I could hardly be anything else." Her full red lips demanded a kiss, and she must be denied nothing.

He pulled her into him, immodestly, indecently, so close no secrets remained between them. One hand seized her shoulders and the other her waist, finger-tips ranging a hair's breadth further than they should.

She tipped her head up and received his lips on hers, meeting his desire with one of her own that tore through him like lightening. Was it possible for a woman to be as ardent as a man?

Obviously, this one treasure was. How could he ever let her go?

Their tongues met and his knees threatened to buckle. He clutched her more tightly, only for her dainty fingers to bite into his waist and back. Her hand slid, just a fraction, just enough to fan his passion dangerously hot.

If only—no, he must not permit those delightful, dangerous thoughts. "Elizabeth, I must … I cannot … you are too perfect … if I do not release you now, I …"

She stretched on tip toe and whispered. "I know." Feather-like lips brushed his ear and suckled his earlobe for the barest of seconds.

He threw his head back and groaned. "Woman, do not tempt me so. I am but a man—one your father would not hesitate to murder where I stand if he had any inkling of what my thoughts were right now. I promised to do everything in my power to broker peace with him, but I unless I separate myself from you immediately, I … I cannot …" He kissed her again.

She kissed him back, just once, then stepped away. "You are right." Her cheeks glowed and a fine sheen of perspiration dotted her upper lip. "Perhaps that would be best for both of us."

He grabbed her hands. "I will watch you to the house."

She licked her lips. "How long will you be gone?"

"Not one moment more than necessary. A week,

ten days at the most."

"Not so very long."

"Too long to be without you, but worth it to be free to marry as soon as you are willing. Very soon, I hope."

"Very soon" She lifted her chin and smiled bravely.

He kissed her hands and forced his fingers to release her. Each step she took toward the house, away from him, carried the force of a physical blow. How could he endure even a se'nnight apart from her?

Halfway to the house, Elizabeth slowed. An encounter such as she just had must be savored, especially since chaos would erupt as soon as she entered Papa's domain. Her skin thrilled with the feel of Darcy's hands. Surely her lips were swollen, hair disheveled and complexion heightened. If Papa had not observed everything from the windows, a single glance and he would read it all in her eyes.

He would not be pleased.

So be it.

Papa might be accustomed to having his way, but as Lady Ellen and now Lady Catherine said, a little disappointment once in a while would not kill him and might even be good for him.

She paused a few steps from the door. Oh the storm that awaited her! Papa's anger was a fearsome thing, one she avoided at all costs. No chance of avoiding his wrath today. But what was Papa's wrath to Mr. Darcy's love?

Perhaps it was best for her to remove herself from

his command and leave him to his new lady. She would only be in the way when Lady Catherine took over as mistress, benevolent and gentle though she may be.

Piper opened the door for her. "That weren't—"

"Perhaps not."

"He see'd you."

"I do not care. I love him and he made me an offer of marriage—not for my fortune nor my connections, but he wants me for myself alone. I will marry him. Do not think I am some hoyden—"

"I know you ain't, Missy." He patted her shoulder. The dark eye buried in his craggy face twinkled. If only he could make Papa understand—

"Elizabeth Frances Bennet!"

She cringed. His command deck voice threatened to shatter her fragile composure. Boy-sized footsteps pounded up the stairs. No doubt their governess would have little trouble keeping the twins to the nursery this morning.

"My study, now!"

Had Mr. Darcy not already been for London, she would be out the door running for Pemberley. Why had he left her alone to face Papa?

No, that was not fair. Had he any idea of what awaited, he would not have left.

In light of Papa's tone, Gretna Green might be a good notion.

"Missy, it don't do to keep him a-waiting."

Piper escorted her to the study. If only Hill and the footmen did not look so sympathetic. Perhaps Papa had already railed at them? Had that abated his wrath or only encouraged it? Her knees turned rubbery, and each step grew heavier than the last. How could she love Papa so much, but in moments like this, fear him in equal measure? At sea, he found it to his material advantage, but at home?

Papa stood at his desk, back to her, hands clasped behind him so tightly his knuckles went white. His posture spoke everything that needed said. She could leave now and consider herself duly scolded. Why stay any further? Piper gave her a little push.

She gulped and minced in. The door clicked shut. Papa did not stir. The knot in her belly only grew as she approached the desk and stood at attention.

His chest heaved with deep, ragged breaths the same way it had when she marked that uncouth young lord's face with her knife. Did he compare Darcy to that vulgar mushroom, whose bollocks she would have happily dangled from his watch fob? He best not or—

Papa turned, wearing his dour admiral's mask, the one that cowed enemies into surrender, and fixed his steely gaze on her.

She lifted her chin, blood thrumming in her ears. With boldness only Mr. Darcy roused in her, she met his flashing blue eyes. Few dared challenge him when he was in high dudgeon.

"I am shocked, truly and deeply appalled."

Of all things he might say to her right now, it would be that. If she clenched her jaws tightly enough, perhaps she might avoid uttering those plentiful words that would not help her cause.

He stalked around the desk and pulled up short beside her. His hot breath burned against her face and ear. "I never dreamed I would witness one of my daughters in such a compromising position. After what you endured in London, why permit such liberties, much less be a willing participant? Perhaps I misjudged—"

Her eyes narrowed and her jaw hardened. She could play his game, if he so desired. "The same behavior is not troublesome when exhibited by you and Lady Catherine?"

He slapped the desktop. A loose pencil and stick of sealing wax jumped. "There is no comparison."

"Why not? I find the two quite similar. In fact—"

"How dare you!"

"You do not deem your behavior improper? How intriguing." She tossed her head. "I found your liberties quite—"

"You encroach upon my privacy?"

"—enlightening." She allowed the corners of her lips to drift upwards just a mite. Had he not forced her to this, she might feel guilty. "Though your interactions with Lady Ellen were even more … educational."

His cheeks flamed, and he sputtered.

"Did you forget how unguarded you and she were? Have you any idea how scandalized you left poor Jane? Lady Ellen told Jane and me to consider you both an example of marital felicity when you kissed and embraced in the corners of the library, and that we should hope to be so fortunate as to find an affectionate man."

The veins in his temples stood out, purple and throbbing. "My comportment is not in question!"

"No? Did you not wish to examine the boundaries of appropriate behavior for *unmarried* individuals? Or is it possible you have forgotten you are just as unmarried as I?"

"Elizabeth!"

"Enlighten me as to the ways our conduct differs from yours and Lady Catherine's in Pemberley's library the other day?"

"How dare you!"

"Or is passion acceptable for you but not for a younger man and woman?"

"Lady Catherine is not a maiden—"

"She was married six weeks before her husband abandoned her for other diversions and she locked her door to him since—close to thirty years ago? That barely qualifies her as an experienced woman."

He slapped the desk. "You will cease such indelicate—"

"All these years, surrounded by naval men, in foreign ports of call, have left me with little delicacy. No wonder you are so disappointed in me. I am shockingly indelicate."

"How can you say that?"

"Many reasons. To start with, I can swear as vociferously as you and understand the meaning of every word I am saying. What delicate lady can do that? Shall I go on?"

Papa's jaw worked like a trout languishing on deck. His eyes bulged, intensifying the similarity.

"At least Mr. Darcy reserves his cavorting to his betrothed."

"His what?"

"You have not even asked Lady Catherine to marry you and yet you take, and she permits, such liberties with her person."

"Betrothed?"

"Is it not far more disturbing for two unengaged persons to be romping about than two who are—"

"I have not consented to a courtship, much less an

offer of marriage."

"Do not forget I am of age and do not need your permission."

"You would go against me?"

"Will you remain so utterly unreasonable?"

Papa paced across the room, hands locked behind his back. "He is not worthy of you!"

"Because he made an error, or because he would take me from your house?"

He growled deep in his throat.

"Do you think you can keep me here forever? That Lady Catherine can be my mother as Lady Ellen was? She is my friend, but I am no child."

He winced.

Had she exposed the truth of the matter? Could this be less about Mr. Darcy than about—

"Not another word regarding Lady Catherine."

"As you wish." She flashed a tight smile and spun on her heel.

He grabbed her upper arm and forced her back. "I am in no way finished with this conversation."

"Nonetheless, I am."

The air between them crackled. "You will not speak to me in this manner."

"How then shall I address you when you are acting like a fool?"

He took her chin in his hand and held it hard. "I require respect in my home."

"You expect respect when you offer none?"

"What are you blathering about?"

"Mr. Darcy has shown you honor and respect, yet you offer none in return."

"I have been civil."

"Your behavior this morning was nothing short of

rude and intolerable."

"My behavior? My behavior? Shall we consider the licentiousness I just witnessed from both of you? Right in front of my windows no less. How interesting you seem easy making light of that display."

"Would you not rather know what is happening? We were both aware of your observation. If you prefer, we can easily make certain our assignations are far less obvious than your own."

"He all but compromised you, in my own garden!"

"And I encouraged him wholeheartedly."

"Do you not take the danger seriously? Your reputation hangs in the balance."

"If I am compromised—" She leaned in until they were nearly nose to nose. "—make us marry."

"I am ashamed of you."

The words struck like a slap in the face.

She recoiled and grabbed the desk for balance.

"Ashamed!"

So he relished the pain he inflicted. How could he?

"You declared yourself so concerned about your reputation in London. What am I to think? I swear, Elizabeth, moments like this I have a mind to—"

"To what? Flog me like a sailor?"

"I have seen men flogged for less lip that you have given me this morning."

She strode to the sea chest and seized a dirty canvas bag. Her fingers fumbled with the complex knots. The worn cat fell to the floor. Muttering an unladylike invective, she snatched it up and hurled it at his chest.

"You only mean to hurt me anyway! Why not do it properly?"

At last, he was without words.

"Go ahead and do it. You may as well finish what you have begun. Make sure and do it right and proper to boot." She quivered before him, but he would not see her flinch, no matter what he did.

The soft creak of reluctant hinges heralded Piper's shuffling steps.

He laid a hand on Elizabeth's shoulder. "Go on, Missy. Ya be done here for now."

She hesitated, but he shook his head. He turned her and gave her a slight push.

The door shut quietly behind her.

"I have not dismissed her!"

"What the bloody hell be ya doing?" Piper ripped the cat from Bennet's hands and flung it into the corner.

"You saw her this morning as well as I."

"Aye, I did."

"And you defend her?"

"He's a widower of five years and he keeps no mistress."

"You cannot be sure."

"Ya think I would let him near Missy Lizzy if he kept another woman in the wings?"

"Why did you not tell me?"

"Did you ask with your eyes full of Lady Cathy?"

Bennet grumbled. "He will compromise her if they continue on their course."

"Let them marry."

"Let her marry a man I do not trust?"

"You're being a damn fool. He be more trustworthy and honorable than any other man you bloody well know."

"How have I come by this intelligence?"

Piper shook his head and spat into the fireplace. "Selfish bastard. You want to keep hold of her so bad, you're driving her away."

"Never."

"Daft too, now."

"Piper!"

"She sees you wantin' to hurt her—has she ever said that? In all the years—you scolded her, lost your temper, even made her cry—did she ever say you was only trying to hurt her?"

Bennet snarled. Not Piper too—he was supposed to be an ally.

"Has she ever balked at your correcting—no—not Missy Lizzy. She never done nothing but try to please you—more than any other living soul! The moment she finds a man you should be proud to call son, you start acting like—"

"Enough!"

"You keep this course, she'll marry Darcy, and have nothing to do with you again. Lady Cathy won't have you for it neither. If you be wanting either of your ladies at your side, you best start rethinking your tack." Piper stomped out and slammed the door.

Bennet flopped into a nearby chair and dropped his face into his hands. What had he done? Lizzy held his heart and soul, was the one who understood and supported him when no one else did. She tolerated him in his worst moments and helped him connect with his sons and even Jane. In the dark days after Ellen died, she bore the depths of his grief. Would she really abandon him? No, it just was not possible.

He slipped out of the study and stole upstairs to Lizzy's room.

The door sat barely ajar. He peeked in.

Soft morning light silhouetted her in the window. She stood straight, shoulders back, chin up, as he always taught her. That was his girl. Sometime along the way, though, she had become a striking, elegant woman.

When had that happened?

A slight shift allowed him to make out the line of her face. She had her mother's eyes, but his jaw. Her chin quivered in the light and … what … wait—those were tears on her cheeks.

Of course, their heated conversation would have upset her. Perhaps tears should be expected. But Lizzy almost never cried.

She blinked and swiped the back of her hands over her eyes. Soft steps took her to the closet where she knelt on the floor and dragged something large and heavy toward her.

Her trunk?

The lid banged hollowly against the wall. She lifted a pile of fabric and stood, letting the liquid silk trickle down to the carpet. Creamy gathers, embroidered in a complicated pattern, puddled near her feet.

Good Lord! Was it—yes, Fanny's wedding dress. That sentimental, soft hearted—she had saved it, passed it to Lizzy before she died.

He never knew. Of what else was he unaware?

Lizzy smoothed it over her waist and twirled, shadows of the little girl she had once been.

"Oh Mama," she whispered, voice ending in a squeak. "I love him—" Her chin dropped to her chest, and she gulped in a shuddering breath. She flung the dress on the bed and collapsed into a sobbing heap on the floor.

Bennet staggered away. He made it to his chamber and shut the door behind him, falling against the wall. His chest fused into a searing knot while his belly turned to ice.

Bloody hell, Piper was right.

Chapter 8

THE TRIP TO LONDON usually offered a welcome respite for reflection, particularly if he made the journey alone. But today, Darcy's meditations brought no comfort.

He must make things right for Locke, for Miss Elizabeth, for everyone. How was such a thing to be accomplished?

According to Fitzwilliam, the best course of action was to take no action at all.

But to sit by and do nothing? If he did not fix things, ensure everyone was taken care of … what would happen? The thought reverberated, rattling through the carriage, louder and louder, taunting, threatening.

What would happen?

Caretaking was as natural as breathing. Could those he loved manage if he shirked his most sacred duty?

Could he?

Where would he be—who would he be, if he did not ensure … everything?

He fell back against the squabs. What had he ever been able to control? His best efforts did not save Anne's life. Fitzwilliam still was not a man of independent means—but he argued his own lack of initiative contributed materially to his situation.

Darcy had encouraged him for years to take more action, but Fitzwilliam never did. What made the difference now?

Bennet, of course–overbearing, meddlesome, controlling—he scoured his face with his palms.

Was his judgment so faulty? Was he untrustworthy?

No, Bennet had overstepped himself on that account. Pemberley prospered under Darcy's management. Rosings Park … when he first took over, it appeared David would inherit only debts and a decaying manor house, but now he expected the estate to be solvent years before David received it.

Darcy exhaled heavily. His judgment was good, but not perfect. He had done too much … too much for Wickham, for Fitzwilliam—and it would stop.

What to do with himself if not managing those concerns?

Love Elizabeth.

Of course. He slumped against the sidewall, tension flowing away in waves.

This was what Bennet had been asking! Would Elizabeth be his first priority? Darcy closed his eyes and sighed.

Absolutely.

The next morning, Darcy called at Locke's office.

"Mr. Darcy?" Locke jumped up from his desk and trundled to the doorway.

Locke's cravat sat askew and his waistcoat buttons mismatched their button holes. Glasses perched precariously on the end of his nose, ever ready to fall, but miraculously holding in place. His right index finger bore a permanent ink stain framing the chewed fingernail. How did so brilliant a solicitor appear for so very much like the most incompetent apprentice clerk?

Locke's documents were meticulously detailed and free of the common loopholes and dodgy language which plagued other solicitors' work. He had proven himself trustworthy through long years of association. It would be a dreadful shame to lose the relationship now.

"I was not expecting you, sir." Locke rubbed his hands along his breeches. "I received no letter, sir."

"I sent none. I had, though, hoped to discuss your letter." Darcy pulled it from his pocket and flicked it with a finger.

"Ah yes, I must beg your indulgence, sir. I fear I wrote it in a fit of pique and I have regretted it from the moment I posted it." Locke ran a finger along the inside of his collar.

Darcy lifted his hand.

Locke's mouth continued to move a few seconds after his last words stopped.

"Is there some place we might sit privately?" Darcy glanced over Locke's shoulder.

"Of course." Locke waved Darcy to follow as he shambled past a pocket door, down a narrow hall that canted decidedly to the left, and through a crooked door streaked with cracking red paint.

Locke muttered and shifted a pile of papers from the large wingback chair to a lopsided table nearby. He stumbled over a doorstop left in his path. Darcy caught his elbow and steadied him. Locke kicked the stop to the baseboard and trudged to the desk, shifted another pile to the floor and he dropped into his seat.

His uncanny memory made better sense—how else could he manage to find anything in the suffocating heaps of paper, books and ephemera? Doubtless, others asked the same questions. Without the Darcys' and Matlocks' support, Locke's business would have failed.

Locke coughed into his hand. "You wished to speak with me?"

Darcy tried to lay the letter on the desk but found no space. He smoothed it over his lap. "I came to discuss the matter of Mr. Wickham."

"I thought as much." Locke swiveled his chair and leaned down to a pile of ledgers on the floor. From the center of the pile, he removed two. He scooted his chair about, rifled through a stack of paper and selected half a dozen sheets. The rotation completed with a stop at his strong box for several envelopes, and he returned his attention to the desk.

Darcy drew a breath, but Locke lifted a hand and twitched his head.

With shocking precision, he stacked ledgers on the left, staggered papers along the center and lined the envelopes on the right. Fingertips touched each document, closing his eyes briefly with each one. He nodded and lowered his hand. "Proceed."

"Regarding Mr. Wickham, your letter," Darcy

lifted the sheet, "details a number of transgressions, some trivial and others rather serious."

He tapped the nearest ledger. "It was entirely inappropriate for me to bring those concerns—"

"Stop!" Darcy would have slapped the desk had there been space enough.

Locke jumped.

"I did not come to demand an apology."

Locke jerked upright and removed his glasses. He tipped his head to peer at Darcy as though the change of perspective would reveal another man in his office. "Indeed, sir? How unexpected." He polished his spectacles against his sleeve and balanced them on the tip of his nose.

"Now we have established that, perhaps we may continue."

"Am I to understand you are withdrawing your support from Mr. Wickham?"

"You are correct."

Locke lifted his hand and swiveled his chair. Several moments of shuffling and muttering produced more journals, paper and envelopes.

Such a damning collection of evidence against Wickham. "How much harm—"

"This looks rather serious, no? I am a meticulous man—"

"I count on that fact. Now, regarding Wickham?"

"As to that, I do take precautions with all my employees to mitigate the damage they might—"

"Stop." Any more dithering and what little patience he had left would evaporate. Darcy planted his elbows on the chair arms and resettled himself. "Since my own hasty letter, I have made a number of discoveries regarding Mr. Wickham. I hope to gather information to inform my next actions, not to rescind my patronage."

Locke exhaled sharply and sagged into his seat. He pulled a handkerchief from his waistcoat pocket and mopped his sweaty brow. "Your support and that of your good father before you has meant a great deal to me and I would—"

"The matter of Mr. Wickham? How much damage?"

Locke opened the first ledger. "Before I begin, I assure you, despite Mr. Wickham's best efforts otherwise, I experienced few actual losses due to his … ah … questionable practices."

Darcy closed his eyes and let his head fall back.

"It may not appear so; however, I am acutely aware of everything and everyone connected to my business. Better, cleverer men than Mr. Wickham have tried to take advantage of me with no success."

"But your letter—"

"As I said, it was written in a moment of vexation. I noted his attempts rather than his successes. All this before you is documentation of his activities, not evidence of the damages."

"I am much relieved."

"Appearances may suggest I need a keeper, but be assured, I do not." Locke's lopsided mouth curled around a chuckle. "I would like Mr. Wickham to get what is coming to him. No doubt, I am not the first he has tried to cheat."

Alston's larder, Pemberley's pantries, gaming debts in Lambton… "You are correct."

Locke unfolded a set of papers and snapped out the creases.

Two hours later, Darcy tucked a quire of foolscap,

lined with Locke's precise handwriting, into his portfolio. The evidence against Wickham was clear, objective and overwhelming. The theft from Locke's pantry alone was enough to see him hang.

Bile coated his tongue—would he ever lose the taste?

How drastically he had underestimated Locke's ability to take care of his own business? Perhaps Locke was not the only one he misjudged. There was no 'perhaps','—definitely. Another habit he would end today.

"We have done enough for one afternoon. I shall return in the morning to discuss several papers I need you to draw up." Darcy stood.

"Thank you, sir. I will await your call."

Darcy tipped his head and let himself out.

Nine days after Darcy's departure, Elizabeth and Jane craved fresh company and escape from the confines of Alston. Lovely man that he was, Piper allowed them to accompany him into town on errands and even offered to pick up Miss Darcy along the way—assuming of course, 'Colonel Fitz' would agree. A smile from Jane and a promise from Piper were all he required to grant permission for them to enjoy Lambton.

Bright sun and air soft with a gentle breeze welcomed them into town. A break in the heat promised rain, but not soon enough to ruin their afternoon.

Piper accompanied them to the butcher, grocer and chandler, though he waited outside the door most of the time. No doubt he used those stolen moments to communicate with contacts he would not wish the young ladies exposed to.

Best not tell Georgiana about that. Poor girl could barely speak to him. Every time he even looked at her, she blanched and shrank away.

After visits to the linen draper and milliner, they claimed fatigue and pleaded for a stop at their favorite confectioners. Piper grumbled but acceded. After all, the confectioner's shop with dainty furnishings and refined, expensive delicacies did not exactly attract ruffians.

"I promise. We will not leave until you come for us." Elizabeth peeped over Piper's shoulder as Jane and Georgiana sat down at an exquisite little table near the window.

"No." Piper stomped to them. "Ya mustn't sit here." He grabbed the back of Georgiana's chair.

She sprang to her feet. "Why ever not?"

"We might be seen from the street sitting there. We must not flaunt the fact we are without our guardian." Elizabeth patted his scarred cheek.

"Do not give me any of your lip, Missy." Piper poked her shoulder. "Or have ya forgotten how ya baptized your knife in 'im?"

Elizabeth shuddered and reached for her pocket. "I shall never forget." Beastly unfair of him to offer such a reminder when she was only enjoying a little levity.

"Then do as I tell ye and sit 'ere." He pointed at a table in the corner, partially hidden by a tower of shelves. "The owner likes your blunt well enough. He'll make sure ye are served well." Piper stomped to the preferred table, pulled out a chair and set it down with greater force than necessary. "You mayn't see the passersby from here, but they don't need fine ladies like ye gawking at 'em no how."

Jane and Georgiana sashayed arm in arm and sat where Piper instructed. He scowled at Elizabeth and she slipped into the remaining seat.

"Thank ye." He signaled the serving girl, whispered something in her ear and tucked a coin in her hand. She curtsied and hurried off.

"We shall be fine." Elizabeth smoothed the tablecloth. "Besides, you are certainly tired of lace and linen and ribbons. You have earned a rest from female frippery."

He folded his arms and glowered. "Ya wish to be talking of your young men outsides my hearing so's all your chatter willn't go back to the Admiral."

Jane blushed and looked away. Georgiana bit her lip and trembled.

Elizabeth mustered her sweetest voice. "It took you long enough to notice."

Piper growled, but it became a good-natured roar. "Then by St. George hisself, just say so. Be straight with me, Missy. Ye know that."

"Yes, sir."

"And don't be calling me sir, now. Else sure as I stand here, I'll box your ears."

"Yes, Piper." She blinked meekly. "We will wait for you to come for us."

"See ye do." He grumbled and shambled out.

Other patrons craned their necks to watch his departure. The door clattered shut, and they whispered among themselves.

Jane and Elizabeth dissolved into peals of laughter. Tears ran down their faces. Georgiana pulled a neatly embroidered handkerchief from her reticule and gave it to Jane.

"Thank you." Jane dabbed her eyes, still snickering.

Elizabeth gulped back the remaining giggles. "Piper still frightens you." She patted the back of her hand to her cheeks.

"He frightens anyone of good sense." Georgiana glanced toward the doorway.

"Piper is a dear soul," Jane said.

"You say that as if it were obvious. I doubt his own mother calls him dear."

"Actually, she does. We met her once." Elizabeth sniggered. "You must understand, he maintains his frightening mien because it serves his purpose. Be not mistaken though, you will find no one more loyal."

Jane folded the handkerchief. "Serving under Papa earned him substantial prize money, enough that he has no need to remain in service. He continues on with us by choice."

"Piper is as family to us, an eccentric uncle we cherish."

"George and David adore him. Richard respects and trusts him, but still …" Georgiana's shoulders twitched.

The serving girl appeared with a tray of lemonade and dainties. "Your man said to bring you a bit o' everything an' see you had all you cared for." She placed the blue and white china carefully in front of them, curtsied and retreated.

"How kind of him to spare us the agony of choosing among so many wonderful treats." Georgiana's hand hovered over the plate bobbing between a tiny tart and a square of marzipan.

"Here, take them both." Jane dropped them on

Georgiana's saucer.

"Oh no, I could not." She pushed her plate toward Jane.

"You can and you must," Jane pushed it back, "for neither I nor Lizzy prefer those."

"What would you like Lizzy? The chocolate cream must be calling out to you … Lizzy?"

Elizabeth pressed her finger to her lips. She angled herself to spy around the shelves and out the window.

"What is it?" Jane leaned forward and craned her neck.

The bell on the door tinkled and heavy, shuffling footsteps followed. Elizabeth ducked behind the shelves.

A man approached the front counter. His dirty coat and stooped back resembled every other villager in Lambton. He carried a bandaged hand in a sling around his neck, hat pulled low over his eyes.

Blast it all! His words were too muffled to hear. If she could just make them out, she might be entirely certain. "We must leave. That is Wickham."

Jane gasped.

"No, surely you are mistaken." Georgiana's hands hung in the air, ready to push back the ugly possibility.

The man at the counter angled slightly toward them. His right eye twitched.

"Did you see that?"

Georgiana squeaked.

The serving girl hurried past.

Elizabeth grabbed her arm. "Is there a back door?"

"Yes, mum, but only us who work here use it."

"Take us now and you may keep the remains of the coin our man gave you." Elizabeth tried not to look at Wickham.

"Yes, mum." She beckoned them to follow and led them behind another shelf and into a narrow, dark corridor, past a drafty stairway to a storeroom where the backdoor was cracked open. Sunlight streamed in.

"Speak of this to no one." Elizabeth seized the girl's hand. "Our man will be most displeased if he learns you have betrayed us. Whilst I would never order him to harm anyone, he is apt to do as he wilt when his back is up."

"Yes … yes, mum." The girl dropped in a shaky curtsey.

Elizabeth took Jane and Georgiana's hands and sprinted outside.

"Where are we going?" Georgiana cast about.

Long shadows danced along the cobble stones and chased an orange cat from her hiding place. Barrels and boxes were heaped near several doors. The cat pounced on something small and squeaky behind one of the piles. Heavy smells of hard work and life hung between the buildings.

"Out of this alley. Too many dark corners and too few people." Elizabeth started toward the main intersection.

"Piper mentioned he intended to call upon the vintner, the shoe maker and the blacksmith," Jane said.

They emerged from the alleyway. Elizabeth scanned the street. "He is friends with the blacksmith. He would go there last to visit a mite and give us time to enjoy ourselves."

"Where is the blacksmith?" Georgiana bit her lip.

"This way." Jane pointed.

They rushed into the large intersection. Breathless,

they slowed to a brisk trot. It would not do to attract too much attention. Three more intersections and a quarter mile of street passed, and the familiar clang of the smithy's workshop greeted them. Several steps from the shop, Elizabeth peeked over her shoulder. No one, at least no one she could see, followed.

"What the devil be ya doing here?"

Elizabeth jumped.

Piper squeezed her shoulder hard. "I told ye ta stay put. Ye promised me—I don't like it when a promise—"

"We saw Wickham." Elizabeth grabbed his coarse hand.

His posture and expression shifted from uncle to soldier. "Are ya sure?"

"Who else would have his arm in a sling and a twitchy eye? I am certain."

He muttered a string of epithets. Georgiana blushed from her shoulders, her eyes nearly popping from their sockets. No doubt Col. Fitzwilliam curbed his language around her.

With a final snarl, Piper led them inside. The smithy, a burly man, with tufts of rugged red hair escaping the leather strap holding back the rest of his mane, stopped his work. His face and arms were smeared with soot and sweat, his smile barely less menacing than Piper's.

They would be safe here.

Piper clapped her shoulder, "Ye done good, Missy. I should have knowed you wouldn't dare disobey a direct order lest it were for a nigh on good reason."

Georgiana's astonishment would have been laughable under difference circumstances.

He clapped her shoulder, too, though more gently.

"It be well, Missy Darcy. Quit trembling, now. I ain't unreasonable, just a mite fearsome." He winked and turned to the smith. "I needs see if I can find him. Your wife be strong enough for a morning call?"

"She were churched this week, and the babe be strong and healthy. Company'd be welcome to her." The smith stroked his scraggly chin. "I'll be going with, just to remind him, friendly-like, of the debt he owes me. The apprentices can watch the house and shop well enough in my stead."

Two broad shouldered, barrel-chested young men, brothers no doubt, stepped forward shoulder to shoulder, hands balled into fists that could shape iron. Apparently Wickham owed them something too.

"Always pleased for a good man to cover my back."

"I'll tell the wife." The smithy ambled toward the cottage behind the shop.

"His apprentices are kin to his wife. You'll be safe here. Stay until I come for you. Mrs. Smith is a sweet girl. I know ye better than to think yourselves too high for the likes of such a simple home. Come."

He led them along a rose-lined path to a neat, if quaint, cottage. The smithy showed them to a tidy, cozy front room and introduced his wife. The windows sparkled and crisp striped drapes fluttered in the breeze that wafted the roses' perfume inside.

"Don't leave the house," Piper whispered in Elizabeth's ear. "It may be a while. Don't go nowhere." He ducked out the door with the smithy.

Thankfully, Jane stepped up and carried the conversation. Dear sweet Jane. She always knew what to say and how to say it. Soon they were cooing over the baby and chattering like old friends. Doubtless, more visits like this would follow.

Even so, the visit's pleasantness did not over-shadow the specter of Wickham's threat. Elizabeth shuddered. Papa would be most displeased.

One of the smith's apprentices brought Bennet Piper's message: Come to Pemberley—Wickham.

When he left the Navy, he expected to leave such calls to battle behind as well, but now all those dearest to him were in jeopardy as real as any he had faced at sea.

He pushed his horse to its limits all the way to Pemberley, arriving before Piper and the ladies. Lady Catherine received him in the drawing room where he paced the path along the fireplace, huffing and grumbling as he went. Damn fool, Piper, not to be there when he arrived.

"You will wear a track in the carpet if you do not stop." Lady Catherine stepped directly in front of him and wagged her finger. With her tight lips and head cocked, she was not quite laughing at him, but far too amused—impertinent, just like Elizabeth.

He stopped short and towered over her, nostrils flaring.

She thumped his chest with two fingers. "Do stop your show. I have no need of it nor am I impressed by it."

"You will—"

"I will what?" She rose on tip toes and glowered back at him as few dared. "Let us establish one thing clearly, from the start."

"And what would that be?"

"We are not at sea. This is not the Navy, and you

will not stand in the center of my parlor barking orders at me." She tapped his waistcoat with each point.

"Excuse me, madam? Do you suggest—"

"Do not order me about like some seaman."

"I was not—"

"Yes, you were." She planted her hands on her hips. "I will have you acknowledge that I am a capable first mate. I expect to be considered as nothing less."

Only Ellen had dared speak to him with such fire. Heat rose in his belly.

She pulled up a little straighter. "Remember, I kept Rosings running, alone, the years of my husband's madness."

He dropped his chin to his chest. "Yes, Cathy."

"Much better. Now tell me." She nestled into him, her warmth a soothing balm as she fit into the hollow space near his heart.

He kissed the top of her head, savoring the fragrance of her hair. Lizzy was right. Ellen had warned him of the same things. His loneliness ran far deeper than he would ever admit. Cathy's presence brought it into sharp relief.

How soon could they arrange a wedding? He held her more tightly but relished her closeness a little too much. Best keep himself under good regulation.

"Forgive me, I must move. I am not one to be still with so much on my mind." He stepped back.

"Of course." She edged out of his path, a wry little smile on her lips.

"I cannot abide that blackguard still in the county. None of you are safe until he is gone."

"You would order him hung from a yardarm?"

"Indeed. At the very least he deserves to be lashed about the Fleet." He growled and spun on his heel. "You think he has earned less?"

"No."

"How could Darcy allow this to continue all this time—to harbor that snake in his home, never considering what damage might be done? He is responsible—"

Lady Catherine whipped her fan out and slapped her palm. "Enough!"

"You do not need to defend him—"

"Yes, I do." She stomped three steps toward him. "I understand you are angry and I do not fault you for that. But place the blame rightly. Darcy acted out of duty—the strongest lesson his father taught him. Nearly every act of his life has been motivated by his sense of responsibility, not his preferences or comfort. Toward Wickham, toward Anne and me, toward his cousin ..."

Bennet's brow rose. "Fitzwilliam?"

"Ah, yes, you never asked, and neither of the boys is so forthcoming."

Sarcasm did not suit her.

"My nephew the viscount indulges in many of the same pastimes Sir Lewis enjoyed. Fitzwilliam voiced his displeasure, and it led to a rather spectacular row. My dear brother, the earl—who by the way knew full well of Sir Lewis's indulgences and did nothing— threw Fitzwilliam out and cut off his allowance. Darcy refused to stand by and watch Fitzwilliam disowned for condemning the viscount's lifestyle."

"I had no idea."

"He purchased Fitzwilliam's commissions and made sure he advanced and lived comfortably, opened his home when Fitzwilliam retired and even mediated a restoration in the relationship between the earl and him. Everything Fitzwilliam has, he owes to Darcy. Everything I have, I owe to Darcy. Everything Wickham has, he owes to Darcy."

"Darcy owes that cur a duty?"

She threw her hands in the air. "How could he possibly owe any duty to a man who recently displeased you? You blind, arrogant, self-important sham of a commander."

He leaned in toward her. "Woman, you go too far."

She stopped him with her fan.

"How dare—"

"Easily. I will defend my boys, even from the likes of you. Do not forget, Wickham did save Darcy's life. I would not be here, nor would my grandsons have been born, had Wickham not acted to rescue Darcy. I am grateful. Did you question Piper's motive the first time he saved your life, or did you consider yourself lucky? Did you not believe you owed Piper something for his service?"

Bennet grumbled and wrapped his arms around his waist.

"What is more, all those years Darcy was away at school, you have no idea how he suffered."

"Suffered? The schools he attended are nothing compared to the life a seaman endures."

"You are insufferable!" She fluttered her fan faster than usual. "Have you not noticed the bond between Philip and Darcy? As Lizzy is just like you, Philip is like Darcy: a quiet intelligent boy who is not at ease in a crowd. Whatever Wickham's motives, he helped Darcy through the crush of school days, introducing him, including him, teaching him how to make friends and be acceptable to others. The same service Francis and Lizzy perform for Philip."

"Now you find fault with my son? And you dare compare my daughter and son to *him*?"

"Do you deny Philip is uneasy in company? The poor lad took nearly a week before he spoke to me and only then because I discovered his favorite sweets. Now, he is easy enough with me. In fact, I am honored he seeks me out to tell me his secrets, but I had to work diligently for the honor. He needs the help Lizzy and Francis offer to overcome his natural reticence."

"It is not the same."

"How so?"

Bennet snarled and turned away.

She slapped his shoulder with her fan. "You are a piece of work, laying the blame on my nephew, whilst not accepting any of your own."

"My own? What exactly do you hold me accountable for?"

"If Darcy is at fault for Wickham's actions, then you are equally liable for your daughter's unfortunate experiences in London."

"You cannot—"

"Indeed I can." She balanced on tiptoe and glared lightening into his eyes. "You failed to protect Lizzy from improper suitors as much as Darcy failed to control Wickham. In fact, this dreadful affair with Wickham is on your head more than his."

"Mine?"

She flipped her fan open and waved it before her flushed face. "You chose to hire Wickham despite your best advisors' warnings. Remember, neither

Lizzy nor Piper were entirely comfortable with him. Granted, you thought Lizzy's judgment compromised because of London, but to ignore Piper?"

"I gave Wickham a chance as I did Piper and other men through the years."

"Is he the first to have failed you?"

"No."

"So you knew it a possibility, and still you took him on?" She slapped his other shoulder with her fan. "Take responsibility for your choice. Do not blame others."

"You have gone too far, woman."

"I will not stand for it any longer."

"You will not stand?"

"No sir. I love my nephews too well to connect myself with a man who would mistreat them and look down upon their kind and generous natures."

His cheeks tingled and stomach knotted. "What are you saying?"

Her voice chilled, like the icy wind that presaged a gale. "You are a better man than you are acting right now. I married a man who did not live up to his best, and I will not do so again."

"How dare you liken me to Sir Lewis?"

"I will not tolerate a man who does not offer me his best."

"You will not have me?"

"Not if you continue on so stupidly."

He blinked hard, trying to clear the haze in his mind. She did not mean—

"You cannot imagine a woman—a woman in my circumstances—refusing all you offer with Alston and your connections? Or that your behavior could be so poor as to overcome the inducements?" Frost formed on her words.

Bennet stalked to the window and flattened his forehead against the cool glass. Her accusations lay like a sodden cloak, heavy and chilling across his shoulders. He gripped the window sill, breath fogging the panes.

Her reflection skated along the glass, ethereal and revealing. She watched him, but the determined glint in her eyes did not fade. No doubt, she would abandon him if pushed to choose. Just as Piper warned.

Ellen and Fanny were good wives but not quiet, soft spoken ones, his strongest supporters and harshest critics. Though they may not have always been right, their opinions were always valuable. He had learned to listen to them and weigh their words carefully. Cathy sounded so much like them.

She faced the fireplace, back rigid, offering no quarter.

The woman he already considered his companion and partner stood ready to walk away from him. Loneliness buffeted his ribs with the force of a hurricane.

He slipped behind her and wound his arms around her waist. She stiffened a bit at his touch.

No, he could not lose her now! The top of her head nestled under his chin and he rocked her to him. "Oh, Cathy."

She leaned back into his chest and wrapped her arms over his. "I know you do not like to be out of control. Do not allow that to get the best of you. You are better than this. Do not punish Darcy and Lizzy for your choices or for Wickham's."

He held her tightly.

"The thought of letting her go tears at your very soul. She is the child who is your spit and image. It is especially painful to permit that one to leave you."

So this was what it was like to be stripped bare and exposed to view. This woman uncovered the nakedness of his soul and did not flinch nor judge but merely named the mysterious specter haunting in the shadows.

She turned in his arms and tugged his head down to press her cheek to his. "You do not understand yourself, but I do."

"You are right, my dear. I am a stubborn old—"

"Stubborn, but not a fool. Sir Lewis was a fool, and I will not suffer one again."

He pulled back and held her, their noses almost touching. "Thank you for your confidence in me."

Feathery fingertips stroked his jaw.

Oh, that touch ignited far more than she realized. She was playing with fire—and the dear minx knew it! He swallowed a wholehearted laugh—though, from her expression, his eyes betrayed him.

"I have every confidence in you. Now, show my boys the same. Fitzwilliam will prove himself to you easily enough. You have done him a favor by pushing him to a bit of self-reflection. But release Darcy from your unfounded resentment. He will respect you all the more for it. There is no better match or protector for Lizzy."

"I know." His words barely escaped the tightness in his throat.

"And you will have me to keep you company in her absence." She winked.

He drew her in sharply, so close her velvet breath caressed his face. Her lips parted in silent invitation, one he could not resist. She held nothing back. Heat flowed through him, liquid and fiery. Her passion matched his as their tongues twined.

"Cathy," he growled in her ear and nibbled the side of her neck. "Marry me, soon."

She stroked his back, leaning into his kiss. Her hands drifted to his waist, teasing, but not breaking his self-control. "You took long enough to ask. I thought my nephew would have to call you out for compromising me."

"I have not yet begun—"

The front door creaked open and Piper's distinct footsteps echoed in the foyer.

Bennet growled.

She patted his cheek. "This is probably best, all told. We should be a good example for our children."

He grumbled, offered her his arm, and escorted her out.

The final day's journey back to Pemberley started late and did not improve. What should have been a few short hours burgeoned into an arduous day that included a thrown horseshoe and a broken carriage wheel.

What other calamities awaited? Surely highwaymen would be bearing down on them soon. Gah! Darcy shook his arms, the air in the coach so thick and heavy he might drown within. All hopes of meeting with Bennet today lay dashed with the remains of the wheel by the side of the road.

Now it would be at least another day until he could see her. He banged his head against the soft squabs. If one more thing went wrong, he would abandon the carriage and walk the rest of the way.

By the time he approached Pemberley's border, every aching, travel-weary limb vibrated with thrumming energy. As the coach passed Pemberley's final gates, he rapped on the roof and the coachman stopped. He bounded out and sucked in fresh air tinged with a cold edge, refreshing as food to a starving man.

He left a trail of stiff tension and anxiety in the uncut grass and found vestiges of his good humor along the way. Light poured through the front windows, inviting, welcoming him. Home, finally.

George and David tumbled through the door and nearly knocked him to the ground.

"Papa! Papa!"

He embraced them. How could anyone not long for the warmth of their children, squirming and wriggling to get closer? Unseemly? Bah—this was the stuff that made life's trials bearable.

"I missed you too." He kissed the top of each tousled head and relished the scents of boyhood and dirt.

Their governess dashed out. "I am sorry, sir—"

"Do not worry. I am happy to see them." He stood, a boy hanging off each hand. "Now, you must go back with Miss Mallory."

"But Papa! We have barely seen you!" David tugged his hand.

"You may join us for tea in the drawing room tonight."

"Thank you, Papa!" George clapped.

"Come, boys." Miss Mallory ushered them into the house. She paused and cast another look of apology over her shoulder.

Fitzwilliam met him a hair's breadth before Mrs. Reynolds. "Why did you not send word?"

"I am glad to see you too, and my travels were ghastly. I appreciate your overwhelming concern." Darcy turned to Mrs. Reynolds. "Has dinner been served?"

"Yes sir, we just finished."

"Send a tray to my study. I shall be there presently."

She curtsied and hurried away. No doubt she would add his favorite biscuits and tea to the tray as well. Oh, it was good to be home.

Fitzwilliam took his portfolio and led the way to the study.

Darcy shut the door behind him. "You wish to talk?"

"Surprisingly perceptive of you." Fitzwilliam placed the case beside the desk.

"I am weary with the trials of traveling all day and my patience is sorely tried."

"Perhaps you should go back then, for you will only find more to try you here."

Darcy sank into a chair near the fire and rubbed his eyes. "Have you no welcome news?"

"And reduce your burdens? Why ever would I do that?"

"Perhaps because you live under my roof and eat the food from my table, quite heartily I might add. And stop sitting on the arm of the chair. The boys have already picked up on that bad habit of yours. Their governess does not need you aiding and abetting their ill manners."

"It sounds as if you are anxious to be rid of me. To that end, I have been considering properties—"

"Surely this is not what you need to discuss right now." Darcy squeezed his temples.

"No, it is not." Fitzwilliam slid onto the chair and sat up very straight. "Is this more to your liking?"

Had his journey not been trying enough? How could he deserve this as well?

"How was Locke?"

"He is still my solicitor. The settlement papers are drawn—though Bennet is likely to find plenty of minutia to pick apart."

"Do not be too certain. Aunt Catherine had some strident words with him."

"Blast and bother! Do not tell me she has interfered in my—"

"Interfered is one way to describe it."

Darcy slapped the arms of his chair. "Meddling woman has stepped beyond—"

"Do not dare say that to her face or she will hunt you down and haunt you for the rest of your days."

"She is haunting my days right now."

"A fine banging thing that you have worked up a good lather over something! You have allowed us all far too much latitude in the name of duty."

Darcy covered his eyes and clutched his temples. "What did she do? It is not as if I had much favor with Bennet to start."

"So I heard. That was a prime performance just before you left."

"Dear God, are the servants talking?"

"They would, if not for Piper. Fear not, dear cousin. You have that man's approbation. He will not have an ill word spoken about you by anyone. Threatened to cut tongues out I suppose." Fitzwilliam wagged his brows. "It was him who told me."

If Darcy's face grew any hotter, it would surely burst into flame.

"Relax, old man, it is good to know a core of—"

"Enough!"

"No need to be sensitive! I, for one, am pleased to discover you are as much a man—"

"I said enough!" Darcy sprang to his feet. "I am appalled my lack of self-control may have caused Elizabeth further grief with her overbearing father!"

"Fear not, you do not lack champions. You can be certain Piper had a pretty word to say to him."

Darcy snorted and raked his hair.

"As did Aunt Catherine. It was something to see—or rather hear about—her tongue unleashed upon someone other than us! Such a proud old hen finally pecked the rooster himself."

Darcy braced his elbows on the mantle. The 'rooster' could not have appreciated that. "How is this supposed to help me? Surely he will be more set against me now."

"She told Bennet she would not have him if he interfered with you and Miss Elizabeth."

"I do not need her to bribe him—"

"Do not fool yourself—she is not so selfless. She dotes upon her grandsons and will not jeopardize her ties to them for anyone. Do not forget she harbors a certain fondness for you as well. I am sure she could not abide a man who did not approve of you. She owes you a great deal."

"We are family. There is no debt—"

"I know, I know, you say that enough, but you will have to endure gratitude when it is offered, whether you like it or not. Now, Locke?"

Darcy dropped back into his chair. "He was as

anxious to set the entire incident aside as I."

"How much—"

"Very little, all things considered. The debts of honor are not my concern. A man foolish enough to gamble what he can ill afford to lose deserves what comes to him. Locke, however, manages his affairs with the same precision he writes contracts and suffered little actual loss by Wickham—inconvenience but not harm."

"And his daughter?"

"He played games with her affections but her father prevented serious damage. The biggest issue is the theft—enough for Wickham to hang for it."

"He has not left the county."

"What?" Darcy's catapulted to his feet.

Fitzwilliam raised his hands. "He did not attempt anything untoward, at least not toward our ladies."

"What happened?"

"Georgiana and the Miss Bennets were at the confectionary—Piper escorted them and went to deal with some business. Wickham entered the shop and Miss Elizabeth led them away and to Piper."

Oh, Elizabeth! How could he have left her to face that bounder again?

"When?"

"This morning."

"Bloody hell!" Darcy fell back in his chair. "Bennet knows?"

"Of course."

"And?"

"He is furious, but has not yet sent out a mob set on lynching Wickham—or you."

"I suppose that is a good thing."

"He and Piper will be here tomorrow morning to

discuss the matter. He left only an hour before you arrived."

Darcy scrubbed his face with his hands. "How fortunate for me."

"So what are you going to do or do you intend to wallow in your despair and flagellate yourself."

"I appreciate your confidence."

The maid entered, placed a tray on the desk and scurried out.

Darcy gritted his teeth. "We will find Wickham and escort him to a ship bound for—frankly, I do not give a tinker's dam where, just an ocean away from here."

"You do not expect him to go willingly?"

"When the option is that or the magistrate and his rope, he will be persuaded."

"And if not?"

"I am certain Piper will be happy to assist me in bringing him to see reason. Be assured, no matter what, I will not offer him succor any longer." Darcy pushed up from the chair and leaned against his desk. Ahh, Mrs. Reynolds did send biscuits. He picked up one with exaggerated care.

"Impressive."

"Do you mind, or have you more with which to spoil my appetite?"

"I am quite satisfied." Fitzwilliam bowed and left.

Darcy watched the door shut and kept staring. Certainly, it would open to permit yet another unwelcome intrusion. He shoved his plate aside.

Bother. Another missed meal would not improve his temper. He grabbed a spoon.

Who knew a simple carrot soup could be so restorative? Little rivaled the food prepared in his own kitchen, by hands that understood his tastes. Whatever waited with Bennet tomorrow morning, it was good to be home.

Tea would be served soon and with it the boys regaling him with all their adventures. Perhaps he might persuade Georgiana to play for him. If that did not set him to rights, nothing would, given he could not see Elizabeth until tomorrow.

Chapter 9

THE NEXT MORNING, the Darcy and Bennet carriages passed on the road, the former bearing George and David to Alston to play with the twins, the later conveying Bennet and Piper to Pemberley to discuss Wickham.

Francis and Philip raced back and forth in front of the house under the watchful eye of Miss Wexley.

"I see their coach!" Francis shouted. "Please, can we run to meet it?"

"Certainly not. You do not need to get in the way of the horses."

"No, I won't! I know better—"

Miss Wexley caught him by the elbow. "Enough, Master Francis. Another word and you shall be confined to your chambers and not join your friends today."

"Lizzy would let me! She would run with us. You ought to be like her!"

"Well, she is not here right now. She is doing her work with Mrs. Hill and does not balk at obeying your father. Moreover, your sisters always go out with Piper to accompany them. Perhaps you should be more like them."

"But they're girls! They require a chaperone anyway. It's different."

"No more on this matter." She tightened her grip on his arm just enough to make her point.

"Yes, ma'am." Francis kicked the dirt and sent pebbles skittering.

A few minutes later, the Darcy coach stopped at the front door, and the driver helped Miss Mallory and the Darcys out. All four boys squealed and talked over one another, clambering over each other like a litter of puppies just let into the sunshine.

David broke away from the pack and approached the governesses, hands clasped behind his back in a solemn reflection of his father. "Miss Wexley." He bowed.

She bit her lip but did not quite contain her laugh. Miss Mallory fared little better.

"Pray, may I ask a favor of you?"

"Of course, Master David." She curtsied.

"May we please go down to the stream? We will be very careful and not get wet—"

"I am sorry, Master David. The Admiral's orders were that no one was to leave the immediate vicinity of the house."

Francis ran up and tugged her skirts. "But Miss Wexley—"

"No sir, you know better than to disobey orders. You do not want him to take the cat after you."

George and David gasped.

"Your friends do not wish to see you in such trouble."

"No, Miss Wexley." Francis hung his head.

"Do not be so downhearted. You will find plenty of amusements inside." She patted his back.

"Besides," Miss Mallory said, "I heard one of the grooms speak of excessively heavy rains in the north these past few days and floods are a possibility."

Miss Wexley's eyebrows rose. "Truly? Perhaps we should alert our people—"

"They're always saying that and it never happens." George stomped. "It would be so exciting to see, but we never do."

Miss Mallory clucked her tongue. "Master Darcy! How can you say such a thing? Do you not know the danger and destruction floods bring?"

"Go into the house now." Miss Wexley pointed. "After luncheon, we will come outside on the lawn, and you can play and take some fresh air."

Francis mumbled under his breath and trudged in ahead of the rest.

The governesses settled them into the nursery, playing with conkers and marbles, and after half an hour, retreated to Miss Wexley's sitting room beside the nursery.

George set aside his conker and sat back on his heels. "Does your father really keep a cat'o'nine tails, or was Miss Wexley just blustering?"

"Yes, he does," Philip said, frowning.

"And it is this big." Francis stretched his arms wide. "You can still see the blood stains on it! It makes the most frightful sound when he swings it."

David covered his mouth and squealed.

"Does he use it on you?" George whispered.

"No! He how can you say such a thing?" Philip jumped to his feet and pulled Francis's arm down.

Francis whirled on him. "But he said he would— he would have Piper do it, if we disobeyed!"

"He did not!"

"Yes he did!" Francis leaned close to Philip's face.

"No—"

David jumped between them. "Can we see it?"

"It is in Papa's study, in his chest. We are not allowed in there without him." Philip crossed his arms firmly.

"I'm not scared of him!" Francis mimicked his brother.

"You should be."

"You are a coward."

"Am not."

"Are too!"

"Am not!"

"Prove it!" Francis tapped his foot.

"How?"

"We're going to Papa's study. You will open his chest."

"No, I will not! He said never to touch his things."

"See, you are a coward just like I said!"

Philip stomped. "I am not!"

"And Piper hates cowards! So does Papa and so do I. If you don't do it, you are a frightful coward, and we shall never speak to you again." Francis turned his back and nodded his head sharply.

"But … but," Philip stammered.

"We won't talk to you … ever." George turned his back and stomped his foot.

"Come with us, Philip. We won't hurt anything. Your father won't know." David pulled Philip's hand.

Francis rushed to the doorway and peeked out. Finger pressed to his lips, he beckoned them to follow.

One by one, they tiptoed out. Alone in the room, Philip sputtered and grumbled and followed them out.

They crept down the stairs and paused at the landing, listening for their governesses. Hushed voices came from the room upstairs, but did not approach. They continued into the study.

Francis pushed the door open just enough to admit them. The Darcy brothers followed, leaving Philip to pull it shut behind him. The four boys crept to the sea chest at the far corner of the room.

"Mr. Wickham?" Francis stopped short.

Wickham crouched near the desk, one arm bound in a sling. He fumbled with a key, trying to force it into the keyhole of the strongbox hidden in the wall.

"Why are you using your left hand? You aren't left-handed like me." Francis asked.

"What is that awful smell?" David pinched his nose.

Philip peered at him. "Are you ill, Mr. Wickham? You don't look very good."

Wickham clutched the desk. "Good morning Masters Bennet and Masters Darcy."

"What are you doing here? Papa said you're not supposed to be here." Philip took a step toward the door.

Wickham grabbed his coat.

"Let me go!" Philip pulled away. "Piper told us we need to get him if we ever see Mr. Wickham anywhere."

"Well, Piper and Papa aren't here. I am the master while they are gone, and I say hear him out." Francis stomped.

"He should not be here! Papa sacked him. Why is he trying to get in the strongbox when he should not even be in the house?"

"How should I know? Ask him. I am certain he has a simple explanation." Francis pointed to Wickham.

"What are you doing here? Why do you have a key when you were dismissed?" Philip asked.

Wickham pushed to his feet, wavering as he straightened. Sweat dripped down the side of his nose. "That is a very good question, Master Philip. You are a very smart boy to be asking."

"So then, why are you here?"

Wickham blotted his face with a dirty handkerchief. He tucked it into his pocket and stroked his chin. "The more pertinent question is, what are you four doing here? I recall you are not permitted in your father's study without him."

"They wanted to see his cat." Francis pointed at George and David.

George leaned forward, lower lip extended. "It was your idea."

"Was not."

"Was too."

"Not only are you in his study without permission, you planned to go through his sea chest as well?" Wickham tapped his foot. "I am quite certain that is explicitly forbidden. Utterly shocking—so much disobedience in his absence."

"I told you we should not." Philip looked up at

Wickham. "I told them we should not come, and we should not touch father's things."

"Why did you come against your convictions?"

"He called me a coward."

Wickham frowned. "Truly, Master Bennet? Master Darcy?"

Francis retreated a step. "No—"

"Yes, you did!"

"Did not!"

"Enough boys, that is quite enough." Wickham slapped the desk, key still in hand. A loud metallic *thunk* resounded.

The boys jumped. "Yes, sir."

"Now, off with you—all of you!" He shooed them toward the door with a weak wave.

"But you are not supposed to be here either." Philip stopped in the middle of the room. "I heard Papa say—"

"Master Philip—it is not fitting for you to eavesdrop." Wickham shook his head.

Francis and George mimicked his motions.

"But he said—"

"Adults often say things children do not understand—that is why you are not to listen in."

Philip pumped his fists at his side. "But I was not—"

"Are you going to tell Papa?" Francis asked.

Wickham's lips worked into a frown. "I should. It would be the right and proper thing since you have all been quite naughty. He will be most displeased with what you have done in his absence."

"He will be frightfully angry and so will Piper …" Francis's head whipped back and forth.

Philip's chin quivered.

"Yes. I know his temper well—quite a frightening sight when he is angry. Is he not?" He dropped shakily to one knee and beckoned the boys closer. "I was once a boy with a difficult-to-please father. I recall the temptations well. Hmmm … Since you actually did no harm, I will forget about everything and take all of you to a secret place I know, the most wonderful place for boys to play."

"Oh, let us do!" David bounced.

Philip rose up on his toes. "But Miss Wexley said—"

"That we were not to go out alone," Francis snapped. "If Mr. Wickham takes us, we will not be alone."

"I am not sure." Philip scuffed his feet. "It does not seem to be the sort of thing Papa would have had in mind. Perhaps we should get Miss Wexley."

"I suppose I will have to tell Admiral Bennet—"

"No!" Francis stamped.

"No, no, do not. I should like to see this place. Is it far?" Philip chewed his lower lip.

"Not very, it is on the border between Pemberley and Alston. It is a place where Mr. Darcy, Colonel Fitzwilliam and I played as children."

"Oh, then Papa knows of it?" David asked.

"He does indeed. I expect he remembers it quite well. Come then, let us make an adventure of it." Wickham pushed himself up, leaning heavily on the corner of the desk.

"What if someone sees us? Grumpy old Mrs. Hill will not allow us out the front." Francis pouted.

"We can go out this way." Wickham shambled toward to the servant's door.

"We have never been in the servants' corridors."

Francis rubbed his hands together. "I always wondered—"

"No, we—our Papa says we should not disturb the servants at their work. A proper master does not disrespect his servants that way." George glanced at Philip who nodded vigorously.

"Well, I promise, we will interfere with no one. No one shall see us at all." Wickham pushed the door open. It protested in a loud screech.

He stepped into the dark corridor and beckoned them into the narrow hall. The dim light and shadows in the tight space only heightened the sense of forbidden adventure as they approached a small door. Wickham opened it with a key and ushered them into an overgrown corner of the garden.

Elizabeth pushed up from the cluttered desk and stretched. Over an hour ago, Jane left complaining of a severe headache. Elizabeth now enjoyed its twin.

Papa insisted on a detailed inventory as well as plans for fall supplies. The task required concerted efforts from all, including the footmen who helped wrestle barrels and crates from the dark corners of the pantries for inspection. Though she could have done without the activity, the footmen seemed to appreciate the respite from their otherwise dreary assignment of guarding the house against the possible intrusions of one George Wickham.

How that man disrupted their lives!

The rest of their work would wait, at least until she stretched her legs and took in a little fresh air, from the safety of the balcony, of course. No sense inviting any more of Papa's ire.

She pushed the French doors open. Cool morning breezes carried in her favorite scents: clean breezes with a hint of sweet flowers and just a touch of the stables' earthiness.

Mr. Darcy was to return today. She chewed her knuckle. Would something in London make him reconsider his offer for her?

An icy tangle tightened in her belly.

Enough!

He did not play the games of the *ton*. No, their reunion—despite Wickham—would be pleasing. Perhaps even tonight.

But after seeing Papa at Pemberley, he might be in no temper to come to Alston. Still, one of her nicest frocks would be ready for this afternoon. She shut the doors behind her.

Halfway down the hall, she paused. It was too quiet, far too quiet for having four young boys confined to the house.

She raced upstairs to the nursery. Toys littered the floor, but no children.

"Philip! Francis! George, David! Come out this moment!" Confound it all! She knelt in the center of the ample room and scanned under the furniture.

No giggles, no shifting of childish bodies, no hushed whispers.

"Now, boys!"

Still nothing.

The dainty clunk of ladies' shoes rushed toward her.

"Miss Elizabeth?" Miss Wexley nearly fell through the doorway.

"Where are the boys?"

Miss Mallory appeared over Miss Wexley's

shoulder. "I saw them not half an hour ago. We told them—"

"Not to leave, yes, yes, I know. We must find them. You, go upstairs to the servants' quarters and attics. They might be playing in the hammocks. Miss Mallory, tell Hill what has happened. Check the kitchens and the pantry. Go out to the laundry—"

"I told them to stay inside—"

"Clearly that meant very little. Now go!" She pointed to the doorway with a quivering hand.

The hall emptied.

Elizabeth chewed the inside of her cheek. Where were the boys forbidden? They were not allowed to race down the corridors or slide down the banister; to play on the stairs or the library ladders; or in Papa's study with his sea chest. She flew downstairs toward the library. Please, let them be hanging off the shelves and the ladders. Trembling hands clasped the doorknob, and she flung the door open.

No! Why were they not here, disobeying Papa's direct orders?

They must be in Papa's office. How much trouble would they be in! But they deserved it for scaring her so! She could not feel sorry for them. Perhaps after Papa and Piper were finished with their remonstrations, but not until then.

She paused at the doorway and caught her breath, heart thundering powerfully enough to drown out any boy-sounds from within. The latch clicked, and the door swung open.

The room was stubbornly, maddeningly, terrifyingly empty. She swallowed a scream and stumbled inside.

A tin soldier and a pair of conkers lay on the floor

near the sea chest. On the desk—no—it could not be—

She crossed the room in a single heartbeat.

Yes it was—her key, the final missing key. Papa had the safe rekeyed. If anyone tried to get in—yes, the trim around the hidden keyhole bore fresh scratches.

Wickham!

The room spun. She clutched the edge of the desk. He must have the boys.

Her feet were in motion before she quite knew her destination. "Jane! Hill!"

A moment later, they and the governesses gathered around her at the base of the stairs. The footmen appeared behind them.

"Mr. Wickham has been in the house this morning." She held out the key and toys. "I am certain he has the boys."

Miss Mallory blanched, and Miss Wexley grabbed the banister. Hill clutched Jane's hands.

"How could he overtake all four of them?" Jane asked.

"He must have duped them into going with him willingly."

"What are we to do? The Admiral and Piper are both to Pemberley today?" Miss Wexley said.

Elizabeth gestured to the nearest footman. "Go to Pemberley. Inform them what has happened and that we are making a thorough search."

He bowed and dashed away.

"In the meantime," she pointed at the other footman, "set the grooms and all the gardeners to scour the grounds: the stables, the garden, the sheds, the still room and laundry—all of it. Hill, gather the staff, and set them to examine the service rooms, everything below stairs."

He dashed off.

"It is unlikely they are in the house," Hill said.

"With his injury, he will not be moving quickly. He might well be trying to hide in some little used room. Jane, you and the governesses go through all the guest rooms and the family quarters, even Papa's room and Piper's."

"We will, but Lizzy—that look, what do you intend?" Jane caught her forearm.

"It is just a guess. Do you remember how he rescued Mr. Darcy from the rockslide when they were boys?"

"The cave where Alston and Pemberley abut?"

"Yes, I feel it in my bones. They are there."

"You do not mean to go alone? What will you do if you find them?" Jane's eyes creased just like Papa's when he was cross.

"I am not sure. I will puzzle out something. If I do not return in three hours, you will know I have found them. Send Piper and Papa."

"No, Lizzy I cannot let you—"

"You cannot stop me."

"You are as stubborn as Papa!"

"I am certain this is the right thing."

"Godspeed, then." Jane squeezed her hand and hurried off.

Elizabeth grabbed her spencer and bonnet off the front table and ran to the barn. She made quick work saddling the chestnut mare and led her to the mounting block.

At least the grooms were off searching for the boys, and no one remained to scandalize as she mounted astride. Blasted side saddle was entirely unsuitable when one required haste.

Did Papa know Piper taught her to ride astride? If not, she would happily allow Piper to share in a little of Papa's displeasure.

She urged the horse into motion and soon achieved a rapid clip. What would Mr. Darcy say to her scampering about the countryside, unaccompanied and astride her own animal? Not that it mattered, now. As long as the children were safe, he could be as displeased as Papa.

The cave lay on the Pemberley side of a tight ravine through which the stream bordering the two estates ran. She would have to cross the watercourse south of the gorge, then follow it north to the cluster of hills.

The woods closed in, leaving the narrow bridle path barely visible. Scrubby branches slapped at her face and tore her bonnet back. She shoved stray locks out of her eyes, grumbling and wiping sweat from her brow with her sleeve.

If only Papa and Mr. Darcy had listened to her. They were both so infuriatingly obstinate!

Papa seldom trusted her warnings anymore. After she marked Lord Alrick, he maintained she willfully misunderstood the intentions of every man in the room, condemning them all as rakes and cads if they so much as glanced her way.

After their latest row, did he trust her at all?

Since the morning Mr. Darcy left for London, they had spoken little, only nods and muttered syllables passing in the corridors. He gave orders; she followed them. Their camaraderie was lost, perhaps irretrievably.

This would not do. Control, she must control her thoughts. All that could be considered after this crisis was passed.

The stream babbled ahead of her. She guided the horse across, its hooves splashing her hems. Stray spray kicked up by the rocks—she was on the Pemberley side now —danced over rocks and kissed her cheeks even as Mr. Darcy had.

If anything happened to the boys, any of them, would he withdraw his offer for her? She had been in charge of the house and called the footmen from their duty in the halls. If the men had remained at their posts, would all this have happened?

Oh great heavens, this was her fault!

Could he, or Papa, forgive her? Could she forgive herself?

A narrow path wove north through the trees beside the brook. She guided the horse to follow it. The forest thinned, and the ravine opened up to her right, growing deeper as it progressed northwards. Soon, very soon, she would be at the cave. But what would she do then? With only her knife, how could she—

"Miss Elizabeth?"

She screamed and nearly lost her seat.

Mr. Darcy, atop a huge black horse, pulled beside her. His hair was disheveled, cravat untied, one end flapping over his shoulder. Leaves and broken twigs clung to his coat amidst a fine coating of dust.

"What are you doing here?" they demanded simultaneously.

"Looking for my—"

" ... brothers."

" ... sons."

They regarded each other a long moment, hardly blinking.

"Where are you going?" Darcy asked.

"The cave—I am certain Wickham has taken them there. Where are—"

"Piper and your father have gone to Wickham's cottage. Fitzwilliam went into town to check the inns Wickham frequents."

"Our servants are searching Alston's grounds. He could not have gotten very far."

"Yet you left your sister to supervise them whilst you—"

"She is fully capable. I—"

"You can go back to Alston now. I will—"

"No! Those are my brothers—"

"What exactly did you expect to do if you found Wickham?"

Oh, maddening man! He wore the irritating, all-knowing look Papa was apt to don just before he said something very, very stupid.

She ground her teeth to keep rein on the sharp words ready to pour out. "I planned to keep watch. Jane knows to send Papa if I did not return by evening. If he moves them, I could leave trail markers to follow. If the situation proved too dangerous, I could draw him away from the boys as I have the advantage of a horse and an able body. I may not possess the strength or skill to challenge him as you would, but—"

"You are not without a well-considered plan." Darcy tipped his head.

"I am glad you approve." She urged her horse into

motion.

He may as well become acquainted with her resolve now, whilst he still had the chance to change his mind.

"Do not mistake my admiration for approval."

"Forgive my error." She dared not look at him. If his disapproving stares bore any resemblance to Papa's, her determination might weaken.

"Neither your father nor Piper will approve."

"So very good of you to tell me. I had no idea that was possible." Enough of meddlesome, all-knowing men lording their superiority over her. She leaned forward in the saddle. As soon as the terrain permitted, she would pick up the pace. "I will deal with what comes after the boys are safe."

"Elizabeth!"

She looked over her shoulder. "Have you further orders for me?"

Darcy growled and maneuvered his horse beside hers. A narrow branch slapped his face. "I am not your father! I do not issue commands. You know that. Why are you so angry with me?"

"I am not angry."

"Yes, you are."

True enough. "I am angry, at Wickham—" She ducked under a low hanging branch.

Darcy swatted it away. "And at me for promoting Wickham to your family."

The path widened and cleared. She pressed her heels into her horse's side.

He matched her speed and pulled half a step ahead.

Fine, if it made him feel better, he could lead all the way there. As long as it took them to the boys, it did not matter.

Now what?

He craned his neck to look at her, brow drawn low over eyes that flashed with intensity she had only seen the day he found her after Wickham's attempted assault. They brooked no argument.

Stubborn, headstrong, difficult man!

"Yes, I am angry over that too." At least he permitted her a gracious defeat.

The path narrowed forcing the horses to slow and move very close together.

"I was wrong not to have recognized his façade sooner and been more attentive to your concerns. It was wrong of me to brush them aside and in doing so, dismiss you. It is not a mistake I will make again—if you will give me the opportunity." Tight lines drew furrows beside his lips.

Her eyes misted. For once, that was exactly the right thing to say. What more could she ask of anyone?

"Will you forgive me?"

"I—I will." If he was courageous enough to confess his flaws, could she do less? Would he hate her for not owning her faults sooner? "In all good conscience, I must offer that perhaps you were not so unwise to ignore my warnings. I have come to believe some of my opinions have been tainted by my experiences in London—I am, perhaps, too apt to willfully misunderstand the motives and intentions of others."

"Perhaps we may be of mutual aid to one another as our shortcomings are most complimentary."

"I find that prospect quite appealing, but I am still going with you."

"Promise to allow me to handle any necessary confrontation with Wickham?"

"And I will manage the boys—agreed."

"Your father will have my hide for this."

"Not likely. He will have no doubt where the blame lies"

Darcy flicked his reins.

The horses continued along the overgrown path beside the ravine. The hills rose in front of them.

"Is that it?" She pointed to a pile of rocks half way up the third hill.

"Yes." Darcy shaded his eyes and squinted into the afternoon sun. "I cannot make out anyone on the hill."

"Nor I." She chewed her lower lip. Oh, for Papa's spy glass.

"If he is there, we should hide our approach. I know of a path on the other side." He rubbed sweat from his face.

"Let us go."

He guided his horse along the left fork of the trail. The way narrowed, forcing the horses into single file. Their paced diminished further as the trail steepened. She leaned low over her horse's neck, stomach clenching each time its hooves slipped and fought for purchase on the rocky ground.

"As ill as he appeared in town, how could Wickham manage all four boys if they did not go with him willingly?" she asked.

"I had the same thought. I fear I did not warn my boys to stay away from him strenuously enough. We never considered the boys might be his target."

"Papa did not see that possibility … I am not sure I did either. I … I called the footmen from their duties in the hall to assist us in the pantries. Perhaps if they had been—"

"I doubt it. He would not have risked being seen in the house and probably kept to the servants' corridors and out of their sight. In all likelihood, your orders spared those footmen their jobs."

"But I—"

"No, this is not your fault." His lips working into an odd frown, hovering between despair and determination.

"If you will not permit me to take the blame, then neither can I permit you."

The path opened up into a sandy clearing. He stopped his horse and tied the reins to a sapling.

"Let me help you dismount." He stepped toward her.

"No, turn around."

"What are you taking about?"

"I need to dismount—it is an indelicate sight at best. You must not—"

"You cannot possibly be serious."

"I am entirely serious."

"I have been riding, alone in the forest, with you in a most indelicate seat for well-nigh an hour and you choose now to become missish about it?" He reached for her waist.

"No, you cannot—"

"My dearest, loveliest, Elizabeth, I have been staring at the exquisite curve of your ankle and calf for all these miles and not once allowed you to recognize my attentions. You will reward my discretion by allowing me to help you." He took her firmly by the waist.

"But my father—"

"What can he do? Accuse me of compromising you and make us marry? I have nothing to fear in that. Our license lies safely tucked in my desk. You are of age, so he cannot deny us the privilege either." He helped her down and steadied her on her feet.

She shook out her skirts. He was right, but she did not have to like it.

He cupped her cheek in his palm. "If our errand were any less urgent, I would kiss you now."

Tempting thought indeed "We must go."

Hand in hand, they made their way to the edge of the clearing. The entrance to the cave lay just behind a sunbeam, bathed in grey shadows and dust.

No, no, no! The dirt at the mouth seemed undisturbed, and all was far too quiet.

He crept toward the dark opening. Three more steps and he would be at the telltale pile of rocks, four more and the entry.

Her fingertips quivered and feet itched to move as he slipped inside.

Why did he not come out? Surely they would appear soon. They had to! Please let them appear soon!

But not alone! No, heavens, not alone. She burst through the trees and ran to him.

"They are not here."

"You might have missed—"

"No, four young boys would leave footprints at least."

Her chest constricted, but now was not the time to cry. Tears were an indulgence for when the boys were safe. "I was certain they would be here."

"Perhaps your father or Fitzwilliam has found them, or they might be still on Alston grounds." He rubbed the back of his hand under his chin.

"You have another idea?"

"There is one place."

"Where?"

"A ramshackle cottage on Alston, not too far from here. Fitzwilliam, Wickham and I built it with the two boys who lived at Alston. We called it our 'hunting lodge.'"

"Then let us go!"

"Wait, I should be able to see it from the top of the hill. Come."

In the eternity it took them to ascend, a thousand terrible images flashed through her mind, nearly blinding her with acrid tears. She gasped for breath, her lungs demanding air, but her throat did not deign it passage.

He pulled ahead and clambered the last few yards over the rise. She clutched his hands, and he dragged her over the edge. The broad, flat hilltop, dropped off in into a gaping ravine, a hungry maw threatening any who ventured too close. She shaded her eyes and peered in the direction he pointed.

"I cannot make out anything!" he growled.

Scuffling and murmurings approached from the opposite side of the peak. The voices were pitched too low to be the boys', the footfalls too heavy. Papa and Piper appeared over the hill.

"Damn it all, Missy Lizzy! What—"

"—the bloody hell—"

They ran past Darcy and stopped beside her.

"—be ye doing here?"

Darcy rushed up. "The boys were not at the cave."

Piper hurled invectives into the ravine.

"Have you your spy glass?" Elizabeth said.

"Of course."

She snatched it from Papa and gave it to Darcy. He strode to the edge and sighted through the glass. Thunder rumbled in the distance.

"I see someone. The brush is too dense. I cannot tell if the boys are there, but I believe that is Wickham!"

Papa extended his hand for the glass. "What the devil is he—"

"What be that sound?" Piper searched the horizon.

"Thunder?" Why would there be thunder without a storm cloud in view?

Darcy grabbed the spy glass. "Flood! From the north! Away from the ravine." He dragged Elizabeth back.

A wall of debris barreled through the gully chased by raging torrents that tore away trees and dislodged boulders along the crest of the wave. The roiling waters climbed higher and higher until she was certain they would be licking at their feet. The deluge stopped a foot below the edge of the gorge.

"Bloody hell and damnation!" Piper slammed his fist into his hand.

"Is there any way to the other side?" Papa demanded.

Darcy passed the glass to Papa and pointed.

"Half a mile from here, a bridge Fitzwilliam and I built. He meant to show off skills he learnt in the army. It is well above the flood level."

"We must hurry." Elizabeth turned toward the path.

"Not so fast, Missy." Piper grabbed her arm.

"Take her back to Pemberley and send word to Alston—" Papa glanced at Darcy.

"Send Fitzwilliam to the old hunting lodge. Please, Elizabeth, go with Piper."

"But—"

"No!" All three men shouted.

Piper tightened his grip as Papa and Darcy hurried past.

"Do ya truly think he would let you go with them? Do you now? I always gave ya credit for more smarts than that." He extended his hand and helped her down the narrow path.

His familiar, rough fingers gripped hers painfully—a secure feeling, a solid reassurance all might yet be right with the world. Piper was like that, not a fraction of smoothness or polish, but no surer port in a storm.

"No. I am surprised he left you here with me. I should think he would need you by his side."

"He'll have it yet. I'll set you on the main way, then trust you to get to Pemberley under your own power. Understood, Missy?" He leveled a menacing glare.

It was not an expression to be meddled with. "Yes, sir."

"I need to find Colonel Fitz and get back to them. Get your horse."

She searched for a rock or other bit with which to mount.

"Oh, bloody hell and damnation." Piper bent to boost her up. "Your papa will have my hide for teaching you to ride this way."

"Then he will have less ire to direct at me." She settled into the saddle. "Will they be able to manage together?"

"If not now, not ever, Missy." Piper mounted and

followed her down the hill.

Chapter 10

GIVEN HIS PREFERENCES, Darcy would have urged his steed into a gallop, but the steep, rocky path slowed the horses to barely a walk. Bennet's eyes drilled like cannon fire into the back of his head. He turned over his shoulder and caught Bennet's fiery gaze. Were there any words that might satisfy an angry admiral?

"What the bloody hell was my daughter doing out here?"

Darcy bit his tongue. The appropriate acerbic remark would not be welcome now, no matter how fitting. "Searching for her brothers—and my sons."

"How did she come to be with you?"

"We had the same notion of where Wickham might have taken the boys."

"Why did you not send her home?" Bennet's horse edged closer.

"Have you ever tried to dissuade her when she is

determined? Good Lord above! She is just like you."
That would do it—they would have it out here and
now.

Bennet grumbled but it became something more
resembling a chuckle. "I suppose she is that. I am still
surprised you would permit her—"

"She did not ask my permission—she informed
me of what she was going to do. I had little choice,
unless I tied her to one of these trees. I hardly think
that alternative more to your liking."

Were those laughter-like sounds coming from
Bennet?

"It certainly would not have been to hers."

"Do you consider it an auspicious way to court a
woman—tying her to a tree? As I possess little
experience in the matter, I shall defer to your greater
breadth of knowledge. Do you recommend it as a
sound way to win a lady's affections?"

Bennet threw his head back and cackled. "I have
never tried that approach. I doubt Cathy would
approve."

"Cathy?" Darcy craned to look at Bennet and
nearly lost his seat.

"Cathy."

Something about hypocrisy and audacity bounced
in the back of his mind. He had promised Elizabeth
they would reconcile somehow, but Bennet was not
making it easy. Cathy?

"She is an extraordinary woman."

"I am well aware. You do realize that is my aunt
and mother-in-law you are talking about."

"Quite aware." Bennet rubbed his shoulder.

Darcy coughed to cover his mirth. Undoubtedly,
that shoulder felt the wrath of 'Cathy's' fan. It should

not be so satisfying that she would stand up to him. Perhaps it was better that two women as strong as she and Elizabeth did not attempt to share the household.

"Are you prepared for me to become your father?"

"Certainly not." That may not have been the best way to state that truth.

The trail leveled, and they urged their horses faster. In the distance, flood waters still roared, spitting and shouting along the rocks in the narrow ravine.

"Why?" Bennet shouted over the din.

How could one possibly respond to such a question without inviting wrath? Darcy leaned in and flipped his reins. His horse increased its pace.

"I expect an answer. Out with it, man!" Bennet urged his horse to catch up.

"Now is not the time."

"I asked you a question and expect you to answer. Waiting until after battle to resolve an issue is a foolish maneuver at best. I will not maintain unresolved matters with one whom I may have to entrust my life, or worse, the lives of my sons."

Fitzwilliam had said something similar. He rarely reminisced about his time in facing Napoleon, but one night, after too much port, he gave Darcy a glimpse of the all too gruesome realities of the battlefield. He understood Fitzwilliam's maddening sense of humor in an all new way after that. Perhaps that explained Bennet, too.

"Out with it."

As he wished. "My father was a worthy and admirable man."

"And I am not?"

"You are stubborn, resentful and judgmental—traits I do not relish in any connection."

"You are above rubbing shoulders with a man who has earned his place and connections?"

"I said no such thing, although I am above connecting myself with one who allows his selfishness and bitterness to be poured out upon others and ruin their chance at happiness."

"So you begrudge me—"

"For allowing your possessiveness over Elizabeth to justify blaming me for Wickham's actions." He brought his horse up close to Bennet's. Best keep his voice level lest he spook the animals. "I hold it against you that you have placed your daughter in an impossible position to choose between us."

"You demanded that of her?"

"I promised her I would do whatever I could to reconcile with you, but ultimately the choice was yours."

"What did she say to that—who did she choose?"

Darcy snarled, and his horse took off at a trot.

They raced along an open meadow along the gorge until the bridge came into sight. The wooden structure spanned the ravine at a narrow point and stood only feet above the rushing flood waters. Fitzwilliam assured him that his army engineering skills would keep it steady for a good many years. Hopefully, he was right.

Both men stopped and dismounted.

Darcy handed his reins to Bennet. "I have not crossed here in quite some time." He approached the bridge, grasped the side rails and tested the first boards. The rushing water below cast up spray and a strong breeze. The wooden slats creaked and swayed. Several more steps and he bounced slightly. The structure barely flexed under his weight.

He retrieved his horse and led it across. Bennet followed, but he was off at a trot by the time Bennet landed on the Alston side.

"Where are we headed?" Bennet shouted.

"A grove in the woods—there is a cabin."

They charged along the meadow and into the forest, but had to slow as the path closed with trees crowding to get a view of the interlopers.

"What did she say?" Bennet asked.

"I did not force her to choose."

"Damn it, what did she say?"

"She will be my wife." He would have relished his victory if not for the devastation that crumpled Bennet's face. Poor man, Elizabeth was a difficult treasure to lose. "You cannot stop her any more than I could prevent her searching for the boys."

"True enough."

"For my sake, frankly, I care not. But for hers, do not hold on to your resentment of me and cause an estrangement."

"You have no regard for my opinion of you?"

"I do not give a tinker's dam. But I value her happiness and so, for her sake, I will try to appease you."

"At the expense of your pride?"

"What is my pride compared to her happiness?"

The admiral was speechless, how unusual. Was it a good sign or the calm before the proverbial storm?

Bennet puffed his cheeks and blew a long breath. "You have changed."

"Yes, I believe I have, and your daughter approves. That is all I care about."

A bird called in the distance and was answered by another over the roaring waters.

"You know, she is just like me." Bennet's tone softened. "Stubborn, sometimes resentful."

"I noticed the resemblance. She is, though, far more attractive."

The admiral choked back something between a snort and a laugh. "She is not like Cathy's Anne, but more like Cathy. Can you live with so much fire? I married two fiery women, and I tell you, it is not always peaceful sailing."

"Yet you have chosen a third of the same constitution."

"It is what I am accustomed to, but you are not. I need a woman with backbone, who will stand up to a blustery old sailor, be my anchor, and weather my storms. You are a gentleman farmer. What are storms to you?"

"Life on the land can be just as turbulent, sir. Anne was a good wife to me, but no partner. Anne's weak constitution left her content to stand back and allow me to handle the estate as I saw fit. Aunt Catherine functioned as mistress even then. It was not my desire, but my duty. Elizabeth is what I have always longed for. And I will have her. The only question is upon what terms shall it be?"

Oh, the admiral did not like that. The old sea crab probably never negotiated his own surrender before.

"I will have an answer, sir. Here and now. Do not play games with me."

"Cathy was right. I approve—son. I shall not stand in your way."

"Is that all? I believe Elizabeth would like more than that."

"I expect you are correct. Can you look past a blustery father brooding over the loss of his closest child?"

"There are few reasons I could accept for your behavior, very few indeed. But fatherly feelings mitigate a great number of sins."

Bennet dipped his head.

"I am glad you have come to your senses. But do not expect me to call you father—or uncle."

"Just Bennet will do well enough."

Darcy slowed his horse. "There!" He pointed between the trees.

"That movement, it is them."

Bennet restrained Darcy with an arm across his chest. This was war. He would prefer Piper at his side, not an untried man, but he would make do with who he had. "Do not rush in. Determine what he is about first." He pulled out his spy glass and peered into the trees.

Darcy grumbled, but obeyed.

"I see two of the boys." Bennet tucked the spy glass into his coat.

They crept closer.

"Where are we going?" That was George's voice, just a dozen yards away now.

"Are we almost there?" Francis whined and tugged at Wickham's hand. "How much further?"

"Not too far." Wickham panted, face pale and sweaty.

"I cannot find Philip and David."

"They must be close or George and Francis would not be so calm," Darcy whispered.

Bennet jerked his head and they rushed for the boys.

"Halt!"

"Stop!"

Wickham's head snapped up and he groaned.

"Papa!"

"What are you doing with our sons?" Darcy surged ahead and gathered the children to him. He pushed them at Bennet and stormed toward Wickham.

Bennet grabbed the boys' arms and held them tight. Wickham would not touch them again.

"Mr. Wickham was taking us on a treasure hunt to a secret hideout," Francis mumbled. "It was so boring in the house and Miss Wexley said—"

"We will talk about this later."

Wickham backed away until he hit a tree trunk.

"I repeat, what are you doing with my children? How dare you take them without my permission?" Darcy closed the distance, growing taller and more imposing with each step.

"Take them?" Wickham's voice trembled. "Is that what you think of me? They came with me of their own accord, did you not? Francis, George?"

The boys scuffed their feet in the soft leaves. Francis tried to pull away.

"Answer the question." Bennet squeezed their arms hard. "Did he force you to go with him?"

"No, sir," Francis whispered.

George only stammered and shook his head.

"You see—you falsely accuse me! You should know better than to think I would take anything of yours." Wickham waved his good arm.

Darcy grabbed him by the coat and slammed him into a tree. "Liar! Where are the other two?"

Bennet pulled the boys back. They did not need to

watch—or perhaps they did need to see what a man did to protect his family.

The back of his throat ached. This was the man who would defend his family if anything ever happened to him. Good nib though he was, Fitzwilliam had neither the resources nor the determination to do so much. Cathy and Piper were right; there was none better to care for his Lizzy.

"Where are Philip and David?" Darcy shook Wickham until his eyes crossed and his head wobbled.

He pushed at Darcy's chest. "They did not have the spleen for adventure, so made for Pemberley."

"Is this true?" Bennet rattled Francis's arm.

"Yes sir."

"David got scared that Father would be angry. He wanted to go home," George muttered.

"Philip took him back to Pemberley."

"When did they leave you? Before you traversed the ravine or after?" Darcy growled.

"How should I know ... do I appear to be a governess?" Wickham panted.

Darcy rammed his fist into Wickham's ribs. "That is my son!"

Wickham coughed. "I am not his keeper."

"You took responsibility for them when you led them away from their home. Now, when did they leave you?"

"I don't know. I truly don't know." Wickham just might start to blubbering in a moment.

Coward!

Darcy slammed him against the tree. His head bounced off the trunk. "Think hard and answer me."

Bennet leaned into Francis's face. "What do you remember?"

"They left … they went back … ah … after we crossed. It was after, I am sure, sir."

"What does it matter?" Wickham sputtered. "Surely they are at the house by now."

"Did you not hear the flood?"

Francis gasped. "That was not thunder?"

"Remember Miss Mallory telling us about how there might be a flood?" George covered his mouth with his hands.

Darcy pointed. "The ravine is nearly full."

"David might have convinced Philip to go by way of the stream to look for stones by the creek bed," George said.

"Oh, dear God." Darcy hauled Wickham to his feet. "I've got to find them. You're coming with me."

Wickham's knees buckled. "I can't."

"You did this! Now you must—"

"I can barely stand." He extended his injured hand. Dirty bandages did nothing to mask the stomach churning stench. Angry red lines radiated from the bindings and disappeared up his sleeve. "I cannot hold reins—I am too weak to even stay on a horse."

Bennet grabbed Francis's chin in one hand and George's in the other. "Both of you, go directly to Alston and tell Hill what has happened. Run fast. Once you have talked to Hill, go to the nursery and do not move from there."

"Yes, Papa." Francis tried to salute, but his hand shook.

"Yes, sir."

"Go." Bennet swatted both boys, and they dashed off.

Bennet and Darcy ran for their mounts.

"What of me?" Wickham shouted.

"What of you?" Darcy swung into the saddle.

"You cannot leave me. You owe a duty to me, to save my life as I did yours."

"I paid that debt long ago. Besides, the moment you put my sons in danger, you relinquished all ties with me."

"Where?" Bennet mounted.

"That path leads directly to the ravine."

They urged their horses into a trot. Wickham continued to shout, but the words were lost to the crunching leaves under foot.

"Look!" Bennet pointed at fresh prints in the dirt. He pulled his horse up short and jumped down.

Darcy knelt beside him. "Those are David's boots."

They followed the tracks to the gorge and tied off the horses. Bennet yanked a coil of rope from his saddle and slung it over his shoulder.

The water had receded slightly, but still raged through the narrow crevasse. The footprints trailed off over the ledge and along the remnants of a path, now washed away by the flood.

No! Providence, let it not be!

"Wait." Bennet laid a hand on Darcy's shoulder. "They made it here before the flood. Philip knows the sounds of water. If any of our boys would have the sense to find higher ground quickly, it would be him."

"He is the steadiest of them all."

"Come, I will reconnoiter the far side; you take the near." Bennet pulled him up and they hiked along the jagged chasm. "Philip! David!" His trained voice boomed out over the water.

Darcy followed half a step behind. "Boys!"

Life at sea demanded Bennet disguise fear so many times, the mask came naturally now. No threat to his own life had ever filled him with dread equal to that of losing his son. His feet grew heavier with each step, but he dared not allow Darcy to see. Hope was too fragile to risk.

The ravine angled slightly, obscuring the view ahead.

"Philip Edward Bennet!" Damnit it all boy, answer!

"Sir?"

Yes! Yes!

Darcy pelted around the bend, Bennet on his heels.

"Philip!"

"Here Papa!"

"David?" Darcy cried.

Aching silence.

"With me, sir."

That was his boy!

"There!" Darcy pointed.

They ran fifty yards further. Below them, the boys huddled on a narrow ledge, wet and muddy. Angry water rushed barely two feet below. Sporadic waves splashed up and threatened to sweep them away.

David crowded close to Philip who held the younger boy tightly, shielding him from the deluge with his body. Good lad!

"Are either of you injured?" Bennet called.

"I—I don't think so." Philip's teeth chattered. "We're so cold, I hardly know."

Bennet shook out his rope and wove knots his

fingers knew without thinking.

"You will throw it to them?" Darcy asked.

"No, Philip handles a rope well, but I do not trust his skills enough for this." He stripped off his coat and slipped his legs through the loops he had tied. "Lower me down and I will bring them up myself."

"I should go." Darcy tossed his hat and jacket aside.

"No, this is my bailiwick. I need a sure man on shore." He grabbed Darcy's wrist. Now was not the time for a battle of wills.

Their eyes locked and neither spoke. Darcy took up the free end of the rope and ran it around a ragged tree stump and back.

Bennet leaned over the edge. "Move closer to the wall—I am coming for you."

"Like this?" Philip pushed David close to the wall and flattened them against the rocks.

"Yes, stay like that."

Darcy wrapped the rope around his hands and dug in his heels.

Bennet backed into the abyss, slow and steady. Now was not the time for foolish mistakes. "Tie off. I am with them."

He stood between the boys and the flood. David clung to him, and begged not to be left behind. To his credit, Philip kept a stiff upper lip, though his eyes betrayed his terror.

They were too much to carry together, but how could he leave either behind?

A wave flew up and slapped them. The boys shrieked, but Bennet absorbed most of the blow. Their perch was no sanctuary in the face of such fury.

"I'll send them up together."

"Right."

He adjusted the boys to stand close as he fashioned a harness. "Don't worry, my knots never slip." He patted Philip's shoulder.

"Yes, Papa. I will hold David tight so he won't be scared."

"Of course you will." He tugged on the rope. "Take them up."

"I have you." Darcy called. He hauled them up.

Bennet held his breath until they disappeared over the top. A crushing weight dropped from his chest. They were out of danger.

Darcy leaned over the edge. "I am sending—"

An enormous wave swept Bennet into the raging torrent.

"Papa!" Philip ran into Darcy's back.

He grabbed the boy before he tumbled backward. "Free the rope!"

Both boys dashed to loosen the coil from the tree trunk.

Darcy looped it in his hands. "Go to Alston with the horses. Your brothers are there. Tell Hill what happened. I will get your father."

"Yes, sir." Philip saluted and grabbed David's hand. They ran off.

Darcy sprinted down the ravine, struggling to watch the path with one eye and Bennet with the other. God help him, somehow he would keep his promise and return Bennet to his family.

The roiling waters carried Bennet along like a leaf in a rain driven stream, dragging him under momentarily then releasing him just long enough for him to steal a breath. Twice he grabbed hold of a ledge or tree trunk, only to be torn away again. The waves tossed him high against the side wall and slammed him into the stones with force enough to drag a cry from his lips. Somehow, he managed to cling to the rocks as the roiling waters peeled back.

"Hang on!" Darcy staggered to a halt just above Bennet.

He looked around. Bloody hell! Nothing to tie the rope to. He wedged his foot behind a large rock close to the edge and dug in his heels. "I am sending the line."

"Aye." Bennet's left arm rested at an odd, remotely stomach-churning angle.

"You're hurt?"

"Bloody arm's broken." He took the rope in his uninjured arm and struggled to knot it around his waist.

How much pain did the calm demeanor hide?

"Ready."

Darcy braced his feet. Coarse hempen fibers bit into his hands as the sudden weight wrenched his shoulders.

The rope went slack and a wave splashed up from the chasm.

Blast!

Another swell embraced Bennet and carried him away. The floodwaters peeled back and jerked Darcy off balance. His hip bounced off the rock he braced against. Searing pain lanced through his side as he slipped into churning, frigid water.

The leviathan current grabbed him in its jaws and plunged him into the flood. Swirling sands and debris blinded him. He kicked against it, gaining enough headway to break through the waves. The cord, still tying him to Bennet, took possession of him, like a fish on a line, and dragged him forward.

Air! He clawed to the surface, gasping.

Bennet clung to a bobbing tree trunk, fighting to keep his head up. So close, perhaps—

Hand over hand, Darcy hauled himself along the rope toward Bennet. The log teased and danced out of reach. An errant wave pushed him near the stub of a large branch.

Darcy surged forward and grabbed hold. A new swell slapped his face, blinding him. He shook the murky water away, spitting and sputtering. Bennet's timber spun with the fresh force upon it. Slick wood slipped through his fingers.

"No!" A powerful kick propelled him forward to grab inches of a broken limb.

"That's the way, son!"

The unreserved praise coursed through him like lightening, and he lunged again. He draped his arms around the rugged tree trunk.

"Permission to come aboard, sir."

"Granted."

Bennet's arm slipped. The dark waters hurried to claim him.

Darcy dove over the log and grabbed Bennet's shirt. Their makeshift craft bobbed and spun and skittered away, abandoning them to the hungry currents. Watery jaws snapped over him. The beast would take him today if it could.

But he had too much to fight for—his boys, Pemberley … Elizabeth! He kicked against the monster and shattered the surface for a glorious gulp of air, then another.

Bennet grabbed his wrist and jerked his head toward the chasm wall where the washed out remnants of a foot path offered a tantalizing ledge. "There!"

Darcy maneuvered to Bennet's injured side and caught Bennet's waist in his arm. Several powerful, tandem strokes brought them within reach. Darcy grabbed hold with one hand and propelled Bennet into the side with the other. Bennet dragged himself up and helped Darcy clamber onto the muddy niche.

A sunbeam danced over them, caressing their bruised, scoured limbs. Something trickled down the side of Darcy's face, whether floodwater, sweat or blood he knew not nor did he care. The ground was solid below him—and dry, more or less. His ribs screamed with each gulp of air, but no waves stole them away. He would never have made a seaman.

"Bloody good thing we've got no storm to go with this torrent. A stiff wind would kill quick as those floodwaters." Bennet pushed to his knees. He stifled a moan and hunched over his injured arm. His cheeks drew up tight around his pressed lips. What colorful nautical epithets did he suppress?

Darcy rolled and forced himself up. His left side throbbed, its cries muted by the protests of his rope burned palms. "Can you make it up the path?"

"It's no slicker than a main deck in a storm." Bennet planted one foot down solidly and rose. How was he so steady on his feet after all he had just endured? What sustained him?

Fitzwilliam had not exaggerated the stamina of seamen.

Darcy, feet much less sure, followed him up the slippery trail. A soft patch of grass and clover formed a carpet, calling them. Sunlight blanketed the lawn and demanded they pay homage. They collapsed in its embrace, warmth penetrating numbed limbs. Dry ground never welcomed him so warmly as the blessed patch of grass below them.

"This will make quite the tale." Bennet leaned on his good arm. "The sea would not take me, but a spell on dry land nearly drowned me."

Dear God, it hurt to laugh. "Apparently dry land cares little for you either."

Bennet threw back his head and hooted.

He stared into the face of death and laughed. No wonder Elizabeth admired him.

Pounding hooves approached but it was far too much effort to do more than open his eyes to identify them.

"My God, Darcy!" Fitzwilliam dismounted and pelted toward him before the horse even stopped.

Piper grabbed both horses' reins. "Did you find them?"

"Yes." Bennet staggered to his feet.

"Damnation! You done got yourself broke!" Piper muttered and rushed to Bennet.

"The boys should be at Alston by now." Darcy croaked.

Breathing should not hurt so much, should it?

Fitzwilliam caught Darcy by the elbow. "Were they with—"

"Wickham, yes. We left him on the path … to the old shed in Alston's woods. He won't have gotten far … infection."

"He can rot there and let the weasels feast." Fitzwilliam spat.

Piper snapped a branch over his knee and

smoothed it with his knife. He twisted up his handkerchief and handed it to Bennet who shoved it between his teeth. "Ready?"

Bennet grunted. Piper wedged one hand into Bennet's armpit and pulled until Bennet's injured arm settled into a more natural angle.

"He's quite a useful fellow, Piper." Fitzwilliam elbowed him in the side. "Ought to have him teach you a thing or two. With all the boys we have about these days—"

"Gah!" Darcy spat remnants of flood waters. Would he ever be free from the foul taste? "That old fish is tougher than a pair of worn riding boots. Few men could have survived what he did with two good arms, much less with one."

"The Navy breeds 'em strong or she kills them." Fitzwilliam pulled Darcy to his feet. "He has been an arse to you—"

"He nearly died saving my son."

"And you nearly went west saving him—"

"All is forgotten as far as I am concerned."

Fitzwilliam rolled his eyes. "It only took both of you being carried away in a flood to come to that conclusion. About bloody time."

Darcy spat again—this time grit lodged in his teeth. When had he swallowed that? "Go find the boys—the bridge you and I built stands above the flood. Bring them to Pemberley and notify Alston we are well. Piper will see us to Pemberley."

"Right. Jane must be beside herself—"

"No doubt."

Darcy swayed and Fitzwilliam lodged a hand under his arm. He limped to Piper and Bennet. Getting back to Pemberley might take longer than he anticipated.

Fitzwilliam took to his horse, saluted and rode off.

"He will bring the boys to Pemberley?" Bennet asked.

"Yes, I expect a most memorable conversation with them later this evening."

"You wish to address this matter together?"

"Absolutely, my sons should mind you and Piper as they do me."

Bennet extended his good hand. Darcy took it and shook it firmly.

Elizabeth would be pleased.

Chapter 11

ELIZABETH PACED ACROSS THE FOYER, a falcon confined in a too small cage. If she did not spread her wings soon, she would surely lose her mind. Where were they?

Lady Catherine joined her, matching her step, fan fluttering, an impotent substitute for wings.

Why had she capitulated to Piper so easily? "I should have gone with them—"

"You cannot fix everything." Lady Catherine caught her hand. "While activity is much more satisfying, there are moments in life one can do nothing but trust in Providence."

"How? Are you not—"

"At sixes and sevens?" She tapped her fan in her palm. "Those I love best are in grave danger. Of course I am upset. Yet, worry changes nothing."

"How can you know—"

"I cannot and never will." Lady Catherine tucked

her arm in Elizabeth's and led her outside.

The heat of the day had broken and the sun hovered between afternoon and sunset, between hope and despair. A breeze, tasting faintly of evening, wafted through. Those precious, delicate gusts only fueled the flames of anxiety. She tried to increase her stride to outpace it, but Lady Catherine held her back with measured, controlled steps.

"I do not think lightly of what is at risk. Remember, I lost my husband. I lost my home. I lost my daughter. So many hopes and dreams gone without a possibility of reclaiming them." The waning sun masked her eyes with shadows "If I focused on all the loss and disappointment—no one would fault me for it—but it would leave a bitter old woman."

"How have you borne it?"

"Providence has always made a way for us. The years I managed Rosings, we always found the help we needed, when we needed it. In our most desperate hour, Darcy came upon us. Though I lost Anne, I gained …" Her voice cracked, and she hid her face. "I have my grandsons. Whatever comes to pass, I will be sustained through it, even … even if it is not as I wish it to be."

No wonder Papa esteemed her so. She would be the kind of mother sensitive little Philip needed.

"There!" Elizabeth pointed.

Three men trudged up the path from the stables. Just like Papa to insist they tend the horses first.

Lady Catherine grabbed her hand, and they sprinted toward them.

Blast and bother, gowns were not designed for haste!

Papa and Mr. Darcy, wet, dirty and bedraggled,

hobbled forward, one arm draped over each of Piper's shoulders. Papa's other arm was bound tightly to his side.

"Where—"

"They be well. Col. Fitz be fetching the boys here. Don't be worrying none, Missy Lizzy, Lady Cathy."

"Oh, thank heavens!" Lady Catherine swooned, catching herself on Elizabeth's arm.

"Papa?"

"As you see." He twitched his bound shoulder.

"I shall instruct Mrs. Reynolds to send to town for the—"

"Not on my count." Papa looked at Darcy. "And you?"

"Just, ah, a bit bruised. No need for a surgeon."

Lady Catherine planted her hands firmly on her hips. "I did not ask a question."

"She merely gave you the courtesy of telling you what she intends to do." Elizabeth mirrored her.

"And I will not tolerate you—" Lady Catherine poked Papa's chest.

Elizabeth rose upon tip toe before Darcy. "Ignoring possibly serious wounds—"

"In order to satisfy some manly need—"

Darcy traded glances with Piper and Papa. The three of them snorted and collapsed on each other's shoulders in peals of groan-punctuated laughter.

"Call your surgeon, Lady." Piper rubbed his face with his hands. "I'm quite sure he will find my bone-setting up to scratch."

"At least one among you retains some sense." Lady Catherine positioned herself beside Papa and beckoned Elizabeth to Darcy's side.

Darcy's valet met them with a pile of towels, but

Darcy waved him off and promised to be upstairs directly. He caught Elizabeth's hand and ducked into the parlor, pulling the door shut behind them.

"Papa will—"

"Not notice anything. Aunt Catherine attends him." Darcy pulled her close.

"You are so cold!" She nestled into his chest. The scents of murky water, horse and sweat did nothing to settle her soul.

"Yes, cold and dirty and tired and bruised and sore." He kissed the top of her head.

"But the boys are safe."

"Yes, so all the rest is of little consequence."

The room wavered. She clutched his arm and swallowed back a cry.

"They were thoroughly frightened but unharmed. George is certainly old enough to demonstrate far better judgment. I intend to remind him of it most emphatically."

"So are Francis and especially Philip. I expected more from them." She bit her lip. "What of Wickham?"

"He enticed them away. When Philip and David chose to leave, he did not force them to stay. He did not kidnap them."

"You think him innocent?"

"Hardly. I only said he did not take them by force. Any fool could see, he had them with him without permission."

"Where is he?"

"I do not know."

"What do you mean you do not know? You let him go?" Her words ended in a near shriek.

"We abandoned him in the Alston woods when

we discovered David and Philip missing. He is probably still where we left him. Id doubt he could go far with a septic wound and the ribs I probably broke. Moreover, Fitzwilliam has men combing the woods for him. He will not escape."

"What will you do with him?"

He traced the line of her hair with his fingertips. "I promise you, he will never trouble us again. I will talk to your father—"

"I would rather you talk with me."

"As would I." He pulled her so close there were no secrets.

"Good."

"I am a mess. Do you wish to risk ruining your dress?" He nuzzled her neck.

"I do not care in the slightest. Besides, it is already soaked through."

"If your father—"

"As you pointed out, he is occupied with his lady and I dare say they are far more scandalous than we. If Piper allows it, she will be helping him—"

He kissed her hard. The warmth of his lips melted away all other thoughts and stirred a tantalizing heat within her belly. She tangled her hand in his matted hair. Oh, yes, so much better this. He had been apart from her far too long.

"Please, dearest—" he nibbled at her ear. "There are some images I simply do not want in my mind."

"And Lady Catherine with my father—"

"Is most definitely one of them."

"What of me assisting you—"

He groaned into her neck, fingers clutching her waist and drifting further.

Oh, that he would not stop!

"For the time being, that is another dangerous imagination. Though, it is now there and will haunt me until the day you perform that service for me."

She lifted a brow and tipped her head toward the door.

"Dear God, woman, show a little decorum!" He kissed her jaw. "A man only has so much self-control!"

"You are not marrying me for my great displays of decorum."

"Indeed, I am not." He pulled the pins from her hair and helped it tumble down around her shoulders. "Much better."

So much better—how much freedom did he wish to encourage in her?

He wove his hands in her curls and drew her closer. His tickling, heavy breaths seared her self-control to bare threads.

How could she so crave what she never had? She melted into his embrace, his kiss that stole every breath away.

"My Elizabeth," he murmured into her ear as he nibbled it. "My trip was far too long. I will never be separated from you for so long again."

"I should like that very much." She panted hard.

A door slammed and footsteps echoed in the hall.

They jumped apart.

"The boys will arrive soon and we must—"

"Be a good example for them." She grinned and winked.

"Minx." He kissed the tip of her nose. "Your father and I have resolved our issues. I have no desire to give him grounds to reopen his grievances."

Elizabeth giggled. "If you go upstairs now, you

might find them—"

"I will do no such thing! Whose side are you on? What kind of mischief do you intend to teach my sons?"

"The same variety I have taught Francis and Philip. I have a list you know. They must know how to climb trees and skip rocks and race boats made of paper down the stream—"

"And leave their father alone when he demands their mother's attention." He suckled that lovely spot right behind her ear.

"Mmm, yes. Definitely. I shall be sure to teach them that."

Darcy pulled away. "Yes, yes, but for now, I must attend to these wet clothes. And no, today, my valet will assist."

"I suppose then, it is left to me to wait for the boys' arrival—"

"And to keep them in order until your father and I deal with them."

"Of course. You will not object if I brew some willow bark tea for you and Papa in the meantime?"

"Piper trained you?"

"He and Lady Ellen."

"It took both of them to keep the Admiral hale and hearty, I suppose."

"Quite so."

"Considering the things I saw today ..." his eyes lost all their sparkle, "truthfully, Elizabeth, not one in ten men could have endured what he did and survived. He was swept into the flood because he would not leave ... my son ... behind."

"No doubt he owes a great deal to you as well." She laid her head on his shoulder. "Both of you will be paying for your exploits in the morning. I dare say you will scarcely be able to haul yourself out of bed at your customary hour."

"All the more reason why I must clean up and deal with the children tonight." He kissed her and dragged himself away.

No doubt Papa owed Darcy his life. How close had she been to losing them both? She thumped her head against the wall.

No, no need to dwell upon that now. They were all safe and well.

Mrs. Reynolds's rapid footsteps broke her reverie. The boys must be near. She brushed the moisture from her cheeks and hurried out.

Mrs. Reynolds herded the children into the kitchen whilst Colonel Fitzwilliam trudged upstairs. Elizabeth paused just outside the doorway, watching.

Philip's somber eyes betrayed the weight of his guilt. Francis, dear Francis, talking so fast to cover his anxieties, trying to outdo George who was nearly two years his senior. David huddled close to Philip, apparently still fancying him as his protector. Thank heavens they were safe. Her knees buckled, and she clutched the doorjamb.

Activity, she needed activity. She slipped into the kitchen and set a measure of willow bark to steep in the hot water that stood ready. Just how much water did Mrs. Reynolds have standing ready? That woman was a treasure.

Elizabeth added a dash of ginger to the brew. Papa hated the taste of willow bark. The spice and a generous measure of sugar helped, but not always.

How stubborn would he be this time? She dragged the back of her hand across her forehead.

Not today, no, not today. She had nothing left to deal with his obstinacy. Someone else—anyone else—could do that.

Familiar footsteps shuffled up behind her.

"Missy Lizzy." Weary creases lined Piper's face. "Them boys is in for a pack of trouble."

"I have some willow bark tea nearly ready. Bring it to Papa?"

"You bring it."

"No, he is with Lady Catherine."

"He asked for you and means to see you."

"I will not see him." She loaded a tray with a cup of the tea, a glass of wine and a plate of toast. "Take this up to him."

"No, he called for you, Missy, and only you." He pushed the tray back at her.

"I do not wish to quarrel with him. Not here, with so much company." Now was neither the time nor the place for such feminine foolishness as tears.

"He don't mean to be a'quarreling."

"Still, I … please, I cannot bear—"

"Missy, he's hurting. Go to him. Bring him his tea and yourself." He turned her by the shoulders. "Now go."

One never won an argument with Piper.

Very well, she would bring the medicine in, set it down and leave. Done right, it would be only a matter of seconds in his company, about as much time as she had been in his presence daily since Mr. Darcy's departure.

When had the Pemberley staircase become so short? Surely there had to be more stairs before the first floor. She looked over her shoulder. No, it was as she feared. Papa's room was only a few steps away.

Lady Catherine paced in the hall. "Oh, my dear—"

"Good." She pushed the tray at Lady Catherine. "You may bring this to him."

"No, you must."

"I will not."

"Do not get stubborn with me, Miss Elizabeth, for I assure you, you have not lived enough years to rival my own tenacity. Perhaps in time you might, but not today."

She stared into Lady Catherine's eyes and held them, but the great lady would not back down. Elizabeth had met her match.

"He has called for you, and you will go to him as ordered." Lady Catherine leaned close and kissed Elizabeth's cheek.

Elizabeth gulped and swung the door open. She hurried in. A press stood against the nearest wall. That would do. Three steps took her there. She deposited the tray.

"Lizzy."

Her feet betrayed her and stopped—the force of a lifetime's habit too strong to overcome—but she did not turn.

"Please." His voice lost its commanding tone, flagging like a sail luffing in the sun.

She retrieved the tray and brought it to the chair near the window.

"It tastes foul, despite the ginger and sugar, but drink it anyway. The wine and toast will dull the bitterness." She kept her eyes down as she placed her offerings on his lap. How much fight had the flood left in him?

He downed the bitter brew in a single gulp and chased it with the toast, then the wine. The empty goblet clinked softly against the polished ebony, littered with crumbs. He ran his tongue across his lips, smacking them for good measure.

Cold fingers found hers. She jumped.

"Sit." He pointed at the footstool beside his chair. Her heart would have led the charge out the door, if it could escape the confines of her chest. She perched on the edge of the stool, a bird ready for flight.

He set the tray on the floor and leaned forward. "Look at me."

"No, sir," she whispered, voice shaking as furiously as her hands.

He tipped her chin up and coaxed her to meet his gaze.

All the air of the admiralty had vanished revealing a man so ... so ... vulnerable? This was not the officer who commanded their household. He bore as much likeness to Admiral Bennet as Francis did to Philip. The surface resembled, but underneath was entirely dissimilar.

"I cannot go on like this, Lizzy."

"Like what, sir?"

"As we are."

"And how is that?"

"Blast it all! I will not have you dodging me at every turn, refusing to speak to me."

"Have I somehow failed in my duties, my performance not been to your standards?"

"No, and you know it."

"What more do you require of me?"

"More than three words a day would be a start."

"How many do you require? Five, ten? Tell me

your demands and I shall obey." She focused over his right shoulder, through the window. The gardens below were quite lovely—

"Dash it all, you know what I mean!"

"Do I? I am certain I do not."

He dropped his head back against the chair. "Take pity on me. Cathy already gave me a sound tongue lashing over this."

"Over what?"

"You ... and Darcy."

"Indeed?"

"She did not tell you?"

"Some women are capable of proper behavior like holding their tongues." She pushed up from the stool.

"Stop!" He grunted and stumbled after her.

Curse it! Her feet would not move.

His callused hand tightened around her upper arm, and he slowly pulled her to face him.

She steeled herself to weather his glare, but his eyes, though determined, were full of ... of ... what was that?

"You will listen to me, child." His whisper sliced through her resistance. "I have been—I have been an utter arse to you and I am trying to apologize. Piper and Cathy made it quite clear to me ... Lizzy, it is torture to let you go, even to a man like Darcy. The only way to keep you now is to do exactly that, and I find it difficult to accept."

What had he just said?

"That is better." He held her cheek in his palm. "I am sorry my dear. I should never have declared I was ashamed of you. It was low and bitter and utterly unworthy and nothing could be farther from the truth—do you hear me, nothing."

A little, pained squeak escaped—she hated that sound. It spoke for more poignantly than she wished.

"You are everything I esteem in a woman, and I am very proud of you and the man you have chosen."

"Truly?" She blinked the room back into focus.

"Absolutely. You both made me proud today. Though, I still prefer you ride like a lady." He lifted an eyebrow.

She ducked her head. It would not do to smile, not yet.

"You, my dear, are a force to be reckoned with. Darcy best understand what he is signing on for." He kissed her temple.

"We have your approval?"

"Without reservation. I crossed paths with the true man today, and I would sail with him in any weather."

"High praise from you, indeed." A smile was now entirely appropriate.

His eyes crinkled at the edges and a weight slipped away. "Ah, it is good to hear your voice again."

"I could not have endured any more of your scowls."

He pulled her awkwardly into his chest. "No more silence now. While I would occasionally welcome it from the boys—I cannot tolerate it from you."

"Yes, Papa." She nestled into his good shoulder, tension fading with the reassuring thump of his heart. "I do not much like it myself."

He pressed his cheek to the top of her head. "Will you permit me a few days to recuperate before reviewing the settlement papers with Darcy? You do not need to rush off to Scotland—"

"I never really wanted to do that. We can wait—a whole week if need be." She giggled.

"How I have missed that sound. It does me far more good than that foul tonic-tea of yours." He kissed her hair. "Alas, I must deal with your brothers, soon. Whilst I attend them, would you help Cathy speak with the governesses? I am not of a mind to see them dismissed, despite their less than satisfactory performance today."

"Yes, Papa." She rested against him. "May we wait a just few minutes?"

"Of course. I missed you too, my dear."

Now all was indeed well.

Papa, with Elizabeth on his arm, knocked on Darcy's door. Darcy trudged into the corridor. The poor man actually looked worse for a bath and set of clean clothes.

"Shall we?" Papa asked.

Darcy grunted a sound even wearier than his appearance, and they met Lady Catherine at the stairs.

"He said I should assist you with the governesses." Elizabeth murmured.

"I can manage that well enough." Lady Catherine stopped and scrutinized Elizabeth with that soul-baring look that sent even Papa scurrying for cover. "Go, be with them. You have observed Darcy in every role but this one. He will make you proud."

Elizabeth sniffled and squeezed her eyes shut. "Thank you."

Lady Catherine slid her arm over her shoulders and drew her close. "You will be a fine mother to his boys. They love you already, nearly as much as he does. Go to him. I shall manage quite well." She straightened her back and marched into the parlor, slapping her fan in her palm.

Would he want her with him, though? Elizabeth hurried down the hall, her slippers nearly silent on the marble, and stopped near the study door where stern male voices boomed.

Piper's distinct, shuffling steps approached. The slight drag of his foot, a little heavier than usual, was the only outward sign he offered to hint of the day's trials.

"They are very angry," she whispered

"As well they should be. Every one of thems is old enough to known better. It were just plain folly what they done. Don't you go holding their fathers back from giving them what they earned theyselves. We can't have this be happening again."

"You are right."

"Get yourself in there and stand with them! Them boys need to see you strong, too." Piper opened the door and pushed her in.

She stumbled and caught herself on the bookcase. Papa's commanding voice rang through the room. Her insides snapped to attention and saluted.

"What have you been told regarding my office?" Papa demanded.

Francis mumbled something unintelligible while Philip scraped his still dusty boots along the floor.

Darcy's dark expression mirrored Papa's. The boys would find no quarter from him. "Are you permitted in my study?"

"No, sir." George squeaked.

"Did you have any reason to believe it appropriate to enter the Admiral's private room?"

"No, sir."

Papa loomed over the twins. "Did your governess give you permission to be out of the nursery?"

"No, sir."

"Had you any cause to believe what you did was a right or proper thing?"

"No, sir."

Darcy glanced her way and beckoned her with a nod.

"Did Wickham threaten you? Did he use any devious mean to convince you to follow him?" Papa paced before the boys.

"No, sir."

"Can you give me some means, any means by which to understand your actions as anything other than willful disobedience?"

"No, sir."

"You could have made a different and better choice, but did not?"

"Yes, sir."

"What is to be done with young men who have chosen to be disobedient despite the means to do otherwise?"

Philip squared his shoulders and stepped forward. "We should be punished, sir. I should be, sir. I … I knew better … I should have refused to go and helped David do the same. I should have kept him safe and I did not. For that, I should be held accountable."

Darcy dropped to a knee and looked Philip in the eye. "Why do you feel so strongly about David? He is responsible for his own choices."

"He is my friend and younger than me. It is my duty to be a good example and not lead him into harm because he will follow where I go."

Bennet crouched beside them. "Spoken like an officer and a gentleman. I am proud of you, son."

"Thank you, Papa." Philip turned to Darcy. "I am so sorry for letting you down, sir."

"You have redeemed yourself and are quite forgiven." Darcy extended his hand and shook Philip's firmly.

"Are you prepared to accept your punishment like a man?"

"Yes, Papa." Philip's voice quivered. His bravado has had its limits.

Elizabeth closed her eyes. Had Darcy stood before his father saying the self-same thing? It was not difficult to imagine. Philip was fortunate to have a man like Darcy to understand his intuitive, introspective nature.

Papa led Philip to the far corner of the room, behind a screen that permitted a modicum of privacy. Papa was nothing if not thorough, but he was also just and fair. While his discipline would not soon be forgotten, neither would it leave enduring scars.

Little David's chin quivered and he began to weep. Darcy took his hand and held it. David clung to his father's leg. He lifted David and cuddled the boy into his shoulder.

Elizabeth rubbed the back of her hand across her eyes. Dear, dear man.

Papa and Philip returned, hand in hand. Philip's red eyes and tear-stained cheeks drew a sharp counterpoint to his squared jaw and strong shoulders.

Darcy carried David to the back of the room, behind the screen. Fabric shuffled and boots scraped. Darcy's voice rumbled low to the floor, near David's height.

"Why are we here, David?"

Boyish sniffles and murmurs followed.

"Is that truly what you believe? No? Then tell me why?"

A soft cry and more mutters drifted from behind the divider.

"That is right. Now tell me, why must you be punished? I know you do not want it, but tell me why."

"Because ... it ... it will ... make me remember ... so I won't dare disobey."

"That is right. I love you and will do whatever is necessary to help you to grow up to be a good man. I must make sure you do not forget the danger you put your brother, your friends and your family in by breaking the rules."

Elizabeth bit her knuckle and blinked back the burning in her eyes as Darcy chastised the boy with careful firmness.

He carried David, weeping into his shoulder, back to the rest. Standing beside Elizabeth, he comforted his youngest whilst Papa dealt with a far less compliant Francis. Darcy passed David into Elizabeth's waiting arms and led George away.

Calmer now, David nestled his face into her neck with only an occasion hiccup. George bore his chastisement with far greater dignity than Francis and returned to his place in line. Elizabeth set David on his feet beside his brother and the other watery-eyed, repentant boys.

Papa paced in front of the children. "Do not think this is over. You all shall have additional restrictions until the new year, at which time we will review your conduct and determine if you have proven yourselves worthy of having your liberties restored."

George and Francis immediately protested, but a

glance at the screened corner silenced them.

Mrs. Reynolds tapped at the door. At Papa's signal, she admitted Lady Catherine and the two governesses.

"I believe you all know what is expected of you now." Lady Catherine shot a Papa-like glare at repentant-looking young women.

"Yes, madam," the governesses whispered as meekly as the boys.

"You are all dismissed. See we have no need for another interview like this one ever again." Papa jerked his head toward the door, and they filed out.

Philip stopped at the doorway and ran back to Darcy.

"Yes?"

"Sir … I … I just … I meant what I said."

"Of course you did—as much as I."

Philip blinked up at him. Darcy dropped to his knee and pulled Philip to him in a warm embrace. Philip threw his arms around Darcy's neck while Darcy patted his back.

"There now, go and find Miss Wexley before she frets that you are gone." He gave Philip a gentle push toward the door.

Elizabeth followed and closed the door behind him.

The men's brave facades sloughed away. Papa fell into the nearest chair, face drawn and his injured arm held close to his side. Lady Catherine rushed to him.

Darcy's warm fingers closed around Elizabeth's upper arm. Papa did not need her now, but Darcy, with a face as weary and worn as Papa's, did. He led her into the corner behind the screen.

"What of Papa?"

"He will be glad for a moment of privacy, too, or did you fail to notice she was practically in his lap?" Darcy pulled her to him.

"Did you drink the willow bark tea?"

"I did and it was utterly vile and entirely helpful."

"I am glad to see you are not entirely stubborn. How do you feel?"

"Exhausted and quite certain there is not a single hand span of me that does not ache."

Her eyebrows shot up and she cocked her head.

"Elizabeth! I cannot believe—"

"I said nothing! What are you going on about?"

"You speak quite loudly, even without words." He stroked the top of her head with his cheek. "So, did I pass muster?"

"Excuse me?"

"You came here to be certain of me, did you not?"

She made to protest. He kissed her silent.

Still she would have her say. "I am very proud of you. Thank you for Philip."

"His is a—"

"Darcy, you have thirty seconds to finish kissing my daughter, then I expect you both out here, front and center!"

He kissed her thoroughly and appeared before the admiral with a mere second to spare.

Elizabeth managed to contain her giggles, but only for a moment. Papa's expression, part smug, part amused and all knowing, dissolved her control. She flung herself upon him and wrapped her arms around his neck. "Oh, Papa."

"Dear girl, all is well now, truly." He sighed and embraced her. "Two things further and I am for Bedfordshire."

She released him and slipped back to Darcy.

Papa reached for Lady Catherine's hand. "You have settlement papers for me?"

"In my desk, whenever you wish to review them, sir."

"We may go over them as soon as we are both sufficiently recovered."

"At your earliest convenience, sir." Darcy squeezed her hand. "And the other?"

Papa sagged a bit and leaned against the desk. He brought Lady Catherine's hand to his lips. All levity left his features. "I would ask a favor of you, Darcy. One I would ask of no one else."

"What may I do for you?"

Lady Catherine edged closer, her shoulder brushing Papa's.

"The boys—if anything happens to me before they are of age," he leaned into Lady Catherine, "I—we—want you to be their guardian. Piper will assist you, of course, but they need a gentleman to see them into their inheritance."

"I hardly know what to say."

"Is a simple yes or no so difficult to manage?"

Darcy snickered. "Indeed. I would be honored, sir, though I trust such a contingency will be entirely unnecessary."

"I would prefer that myself. Still, I shall rest easier this way, nonetheless." He yawned, winced and pulled his arm in more tightly. "Right, now I am—"

Three sharp raps sounded from the door. Col. Fitzwilliam poked his head in. "Are you available? Piper and I …"

"Where?"

"The main barn."

"Excuse me." Darcy patted Elizabeth's hand and kissed the top of her head.

Papa tugged his jacket straight and followed Darcy out.

Elizabeth bit her lip. "You do not think—"

"What else would he call them out for, now of all times?"

"Neither of them is in any condition—"

"Richard would not come for them if *he* had any fight left in him."

Elizabeth looked at the door.

"They need to finish this."

"But we only just got them back."

"They are in Richard's and Piper's care. We have nothing to be worried about. Come, let us put the boys to bed." Lady Catherine looped her arm in Elizabeth's.

The nursery did not require their attention, but the activity was preferable to simply waiting.

Bennet caught up with Fitzwilliam in a few long strides. Bloody rank timing. Still, best get this over with.

"Where did you find him?" Darcy asked.

"Near the old shack, as you expected."

Muffled shrieks filtered from the barn.

"Dear god, what is that? Piper?" Darcy's face lost color.

"No. Those aren't the screams of a man under the cat." Why in the name of all that was decent did they do that? He glowered at Fitzwilliam. "You called a surgeon."

"Yes."

"I imagine the man is not as adept with his saw as my ship's surgeon."

Darcy gulped and wiped sweat from his upper lip. Poor man was out of his element.

"What else may be done for a septic wound?"

Darcy winced at another shriek.

"Damn coward'd never last a tour at sea." At least not on one of Bennet's ships.

"The surgeon's taking the arm."

Darcy wavered, and Fitzwilliam grabbed him by the elbow.

"Will he live?" Bennet asked.

"We cannot be sure." Fitzwilliam laid his hand against barn door. "Are you ready, Darce?"

Bennet caught him by the back of the coat. "I will think no less of you for staying out here, son. If you have never seen …"

"Thank you for the warning—but I will join you." Darcy gulped.

Wickham's screams poured from the open door. The stench struck like an open-handed blow—rotting flesh and blood against the less offensive smells of horse and manure.

Wickham writhed on a pile of clean straw. The surgeon, Piper and two grooms knelt at his sides—all spattered with blood and gore. Darcy fumbled for his handkerchief and covered his nose and mouth. He smacked his lips and worked his tongue, clearly fighting not to gag. A hand and part of an arm—Wickham's—bloated and black lay on the floor. The surgeon fixed a tourniquet on the stump.

Piper hauled himself up and wiped his hands on his breeches. "That were a right filthy job." He lumbered toward them. "Took three of us to hold the bugger down."

"I am surprised you did not do it yourself," Fitzwilliam said.

"Settin' bones be one thing, sawing them be quite another."

Bennet leaned close to Fitzwilliam. "Why torture the blackguard with a surgeon?"

"Darcy is not as we are and does not know death as we do. He has not dealt death, nor could he live with himself if he did. This will make no difference to Wickham, one way or the other, but it may keep Darcy's conscience clear. He deserves that much."

Piper grabbed Bennet's upper arm. "Ain't nothing more to be done, and you have seen all you need see. Best get back to the house and to rest a'for you go making yourself ill."

Bennet followed him out. He had seen what he needed. Wickham would die. Darcy deserved a little privacy to find some closure with his former friend.

Darcy knelt by Wickham, shoving aside the empty gin bottle. The stench of cheap alcohol singed his nostrils and brought a bitter tang to the back of his throat.

Wickham's eyes fluttered open. "Darcy—the boys?"

"Philip and David are safe."

"Good."

"You nearly killed Bennet and I, though."

Wickham groaned.

"Why—what were you trying to accomplish?"

"I do not know."

"What the hell do you mean, you do not know?

You took my children for no reason?"

"I did not take them."

"How can you—"

"Would not kidnap … you know better …"

"Why were you in Bennet's house?"

"Needed funds … his strongbox …"

"You broke in—a common burglar—and took the children. What for? Ransom?"

"What else could I do … ask you for the blunt?"

"This is my fault?"

"You made me work for him …"

"Enough!" Darcy started to rise.

"Wait!" Wickham coughed. "Wait … never meant to ransom … to take them. Had to … to get away … they found me. Got them to go with me. So many possibilities … let them think they are lost, lead … lead you to them … rescue them myself … so many ways …"

"To deceive me and Bennet? To extort money from us?"

"You would not give it to me."

So he would make this anyone's fault but his own? Unscrupulous—

"Glad they are safe. Never meant to hurt …"

"You did the same thing to my father so long ago? All these years have been a lie?"

"No, that was real … all of it was real." He panted. "Please, please, take me back to the house. Don't let me die out here, like an animal. Please …" A spasm of coughing tore through him.

Darcy glanced at the surgeon who shook his head.

"Never meant to hurt them … to hurt you. Just wanted … want the life … I deserved."

So many words vied to be spoken, but what point

to say those things to a dying man?

"When the surgeon deems it safe, I will see you moved to the house."

"Thank … you. Always were good … to me." Wickham's head lolled. He drew in three ragged gasps and shuddered. His chest rose no more.

The surgeon felt his neck. "He's gone."

Cold waves, empty of words or feeling, buffeted him. He stood, knees far weaker than he remembered them a moment ago.

"Who would have thought it would come to this?" Fitzwilliam muttered.

"I am shocked and embarrassed I did not see him for what he was."

"I would gladly take a thousand men with too much duty and propensity to see too much good than—"

"Do not minimize my faults."

"Do not over state them! Darce, forgive yourself. Bennet does. I am certain your lady will keep you from making the same mistake again."

"He asked me to be guardian to his sons should anything happen to him."

"You can have no doubt of his approval now."

"After all this, I feel inadequate to parent my own sons."

"I know what their mischief nearly caused, but those are not indicators of flaws in their character, only boyish irresponsibility and poor judgment." Fitzwilliam opened the barn door. "Enough dwelling on this for tonight. You need to rest. I dare say you will not realize how spent you are until you try to get up in the morning. Let Piper and I see to the arrangements."

"I am grateful to leave it to you." He rubbed his eyes.

Bennet met them half way to the house.

"It is over. We can put it all to rest now," Darcy said.

"Yes, we can." Bennet slapped Darcy's back.

Chapter 12

The next morning, Piper brought the surgeon around. Try as he might, he could not muster any suggestions that would improve upon the care both men had already received. He admonished them to keep to their beds for the rest of the day.

Darcy bit his tongue and refrained from reminding the ladies this was exactly what he and Bennet had told them. Better to simply obey the surgeon and allow the ladies their victory. Only on the third day after the flood did the household regain some semblance of normalcy.

The fourth morning, the men and boys attended Wickham's burial in the parish church yard. The grave still needed a headstone. One matching Old Wickham's would be most appropriate. They had at one time been friends.

After a somber breakfast, Darcy and Bennet sat on either side of Darcy's desk, a stack of papers between them. Darcy settled into the comfortably worn spots of his chair. Perhaps now, finally, their lives could proceed on course.

"You must introduce me to this Locke fellow." Bennet tapped the papers before him. "Ever since my solicitor died, I have been trying to find a practice to patronize for the long haul. The man in Lambton is good enough, I suppose, but your green bag far exceeds him."

"Locke is excellent at what he does. Be warned though, he is a … peculiar man. His bag, if he has one at all, is certainly not green." Darcy scratched behind his ear. "I have been asked more than once why I use his service."

"Peculiar is no issue to me, if he draws up clear and straight-forward documents. After what my brother—"

"I had these prepared with that in mind." He pushed several documents toward Bennet. "Elizabeth and her children will always be cared for properly."

"Few men have so much to give their offspring."

"Elizabeth's dowry is very generous and is in no small part helpful."

"So, apparently, is Anne's inheritance. Are you not concerned, setting so much of that aside for other than her sons?"

His father used to lay eyes on him the same way and he hated it then, too. Darcy shifted in his seat and looked away.

"Anne would approve?"

"Yes. If you doubt me, ask Aunt Catherine. She approves."

"Do you miss her?"

Darcy harrumphed and fought to look anywhere

but at the admiral. He quickly lost the skirmish.

Bennet's expression held no animosity, only chronicles of loss etched deep into the weathered lines of the seaman's face.

The tightness in Darcy's chest faded. "I do at times. She was a dear friend. And you? Do you still think of Fanny and Lady Ellen?"

"I always will. My marriages were happy, and I have grieved their loss." Bennet rubbed his chin. "That I loved them takes nothing from Cathy, nor will it."

Darcy tapped the papers in front of him. "Your settlement on her is most generous."

"You expected something else from me?"

"No, not at all. Still this exceeds all I anticipated."

Bennet leaned back and crossed his legs. "I do not expect any more children—though we might be surprised. I must make amends for the two I will inflict upon her."

"She has plenty of practice with mine."

"As grandmother, not mother. It is different."

"Philip quite adores her."

"He does. The boy is a bit of a mystery to me." Bennet scratched behind his left ear. "I am grateful he has you nearby."

"He and David are kindred spirits." As were he and Darcy. "I am pleased that Aunt Catherine's settlement from Sir Lewis includes an estate you may bestow upon him. He will be an excellent master when his time comes."

"That came as a surprise, I confess. I believed you when you said she had nothing."

"You well know, it is a far less dangerous thing to underestimate a lady's fortune to a suitor than to overestimate. Has Aunt Catherine seen the settlement?"

"Seen and signed it." He leafed through the pages and tapped the signatures. "She insisted you sign and approve it too."

"More for the sake of our resolution than anything else, I assume." Darcy chuckled. "She cannot quite rest on my assurances."

"Do not doubt Lizzy is similarly anxious."

Darcy signed the document and pushed it to the side.

"What do you think of the property your cousin considers purchasing? Do you know it?"

"I do. It is not the estate I recommended."

"Will it suffice?"

"It will be a challenging property to manage well. I expect him at my door, though, seeking advice on how to manage the fields. He has a sharp mind but has not been taught land management from his father's knee. The learning will come. It will just take time."

"Still, it is a good thing he is making a decision for himself."

Darcy laughed loudly. "Perhaps you are right. Your daughter has already improved him."

"A week then?" Bennet asked.

"With the settlements prepared, I see no need to wait—unless you believe it would please Elizabeth. She did not seem intent upon waiting for wedding clothes to be purchased."

"I think her content. If anything, she is motivated to act whilst our truce holds. It will be good to see her well settled—"

"And such an easy distance from Alston." Darcy

lifted an eyebrow.

"I cannot deny the appeal."

"Are you prepared for your home to be managed by a new mistress?"

Bennet stroked his chin. "Getting Ellen settled in was a challenge. She trained Jane and Elizabeth, so we still do things her way. Cathy and I will likely have a few heated conversations as we learn to accommodate one another."

"Her temper is a fitting match for yours."

"A certain degree of high spirits in a woman bodes well for—marital felicity."

Darcy rolled his eyes and squirmed in his seat. Only Bennet made him do that, and twice in one conversation was entirely too much.

"Do not give me that. You are a man, no matter how proper you attempt to appear. Remember, I have already witnessed your unguarded moments with my daughter."

One thing of which he did not need to be reminded. Darcy dragged his hand down his face.

"Yes, I am rather enjoying watching you writhe." Bennet smirked. "All joking aside, after your 'amiable' marriage, it is a relief to see you have a bit of passion left in you."

"Sir!"

"I would not have my daughter consigned to mere amicability. She is her mother's daughter. Fanny was quite—high spirited."

Darcy sprang to his feet and stalked to the window. "This is not a conversation I wish to have now—or ever."

"I imagine not, though it matters little to me."

What would make Bennet stop?

"There is no greater comfort to a man than the arms of his wife—but few experience that because they are inconsiderate, selfish, petty louts in the bed chamber and out. Treat my daughter well—in every room of the house—and she will delight you, body and soul, for all the days you shall have on this earth."

"And if I do not, you and Piper will hunt me down and make me wish I had never been born."

"That captures it rather effectively."

"That will not be necessary."

"I count on it."

"I would say the same to you, sir."

Bennet flinched.

Ah ha! Time to turn the man's tactic around—see how Bennet enjoyed it. He stomped to the admiral and towered over him. "My aunt has suffered a lifetime of unhappiness already. I shall not sit by and allow you to add to it. Fitzwilliam and I, and, I dare say, Piper as well, will see to it you are only a source of happiness to her."

Bennet slapped Darcy's shoulder a mite too firmly. "Well spoken. I will see to my end of the bargain."

"Shall we go tell them all has been settled?"

"I imagine they are pacing the hall waiting for raised voices." Bennet led the way to the door.

The corridor was empty. How odd. They shrugged at each other. Perhaps their ladies trusted them more than they thought. After some time searching, they heard voices coming from the housekeeper's room.

Mrs. Reynolds hunched over a book, writing furiously while Aunt Catherine and Jane ticked off points on their fingers. Elizabeth caught his gaze.

"Excuse me." She rose and hurried to him, kissing her father's cheek as she sidled past.

Bennet winked.

Darcy offered his arm and guided her outside into the garden. Bright sun welcomed them, while the path's deep shade path invited them to amble farther.

"Should you not be resting?" She leaned her head on his shoulder.

He breathed in deeply. Honeysuckle or orange blossom? Whichever the fragrance, the effect was intoxicating. "This is resting."

"Your meeting with Papa?"

"Went well and easily—no disputes in any matters of the settlement. You would think us the best of friends had you been there."

She stopped and looked up at him, hands on her hips. "No disputes on business matters … but he wished to discuss other topics less comfortable to you."

Great heavens, she was as bad as her father! "There are some issues one does not converse on—"

"With one's father-in-law?"

"With anyone."

"Anyone?"

He pulled her close. "Well, perhaps one might—with one's wife."

"Might one?" She ran her tongue across her lips. Teasing, vexing woman—she knew how that particular expression invited him.

"He might."

She tipped up her face with a look that dared him to kiss her. Oh, the tempting little minx!

"One week, if that is agreeable."

"For what?" She blinked a mite more rapidly than the bright sun would excuse.

"A wedding."

"That is very soon, you know."

"What? I thought you said—"

"Well yes, but I underestimated the amount needing to be done and how long wedding clothes—"

"Clothes? You told me they were of no matter to you, and they could be ordered later."

"I did. Perhaps I was wrong."

"Gah!" He threw up his hands.

She laughed, a merry bell-like sound that made his heart beat in time with its music, and ran down the path and into the woods.

He dashed after her, dodging the stray branches slapping his face. There she was, in the same clearing where she had sparred with Fitzwilliam, holding her ground with a stout stick held like a sword. A similar stick lay close to his feet, a bit too convenient, but who was he to question his fortune?

He scooped it up and cried, "En garde!"

She parried his first thrust and danced out of range. Her makeshift sword appeared at his side so fast, he barely dodged its advance.

"What kind of swordsman are you, sir?" She ducked behind a tree.

He leapt over a fallen log. "One much better practiced with actual steel than this bit of oak."

Thwack—crack—smack. Their 'blades' crossed.

"Your swordsmanship is quite accomplished, m'lady." He spun away from a blow aimed at his shoulder.

"Yours is improving." She jumped back. Her foot snagged on a rock and she fell. "Oh!"

Darcy ran to her only to find her sword thrust into his ribs.

"This is how you would treat your rescuer?" He

threw his stick aside and took hers.

She propped herself on her elbows and he knelt beside her. He pulled her toward him with one arm.

"Careful!" She tumbled and landed on top of him.

His hands at her waist held her fast.

"This is most improper, sir!"

"And entirely delightful." Perhaps a bit too delightful. His ardor could not be disguised in such intimate quarters.

Her eyes grew very wide. "So it would seem."

"Are you frightened?" He cradled her cheek in his palm and held her so she could not dodge his gaze.

She swallowed and bit her lower lip. "My courage only rises with any attempt to intimidate me."

"Indeed." He pulled her down for a kiss her. "You must be prepared to be 'intimidated' quite regularly."

"So it would seem." She cuddled into him.

"You planned this, did you not?"

"Yes."

She shifted against him just so. Five years of self-control were little protection considering the temptation. One week would be a very long time to wait.

"You were quite put out that Fitzwilliam and I had—"

He rolled them over and hovered on his elbows barely above her. "Never play swords with him again." He growled a deep rumble that vibrated his chest against hers. "This must be my privilege alone."

"Yes, my liege."

"Say that again. I like it." He pressed into her, just so.

She gasped. "Yes—"

He growled softly and kissed the spot in her neck

that made her squirm most delightfully. Oh yes, she was pleased—and pleasing. "In a week, we will play this out to its rightful conclusion."

"I will consider that a promise, my liege." She batted her eyes at him.

"Be prepared to be reminded of your promise." What a long week this would be.

A week later, on a morning that glittered and sang, Elizabeth and Lady Catherine stood admiring each other's reflections in the mirror. Jane had just left them to ensure all was in readiness. Of course, it would be. She and Georgiana had already arranged all the flowers and ribbons bedecking the family chapel.

Though she was not supposed to look, Elizabeth took an early morning walk and peeked inside. Ordinarily pretty, Jane and Georgiana's efforts transformed the stone chapel into something truly magical.

Mrs. Reynolds was already stationed at Alston to assist Mrs. Hill with the final preparations for the wedding breakfast. Neither housekeeper would relinquish the honor, so they agreed to do it together on Alston's front lawn.

"You look lovely," Elizabeth straightened a bit of lace on Lady Catherine's pink sarsenet gown. "I am glad you decided to have a new dress made. It suits you and Papa likes the color on you very well."

"Thank you my dear, but it was frivolous. This really is your day. You are the one who should shine. There was no need for you to share it with me."

"There was every need! Next to Jane, there is no one I would rather stand up with."

Lady Catherine turned away from the mirror and strolled to the window. The early morning sun caressed her face and bathed her with a youthful glow. "I still do not feel entirely right about this—all this fuss over me. I am merely a widow—"

"You are a lady, marrying a man who loves you most ardently—" Elizabeth gazed at her intently, "—something you have never done."

Lady Catherine blushed and fluttered her fan. "While I cannot deny that, the fact is, I was married before."

True enough, but not to a man like Admiral Bennet. Elizabeth approached, but Lady Catherine turned aside and dabbed her cheek with the back of her hand.

"Is there anything you have any questions about—regarding married life?"

"I believe I am quite prepared to run Pemberley's household. Lady Ellen made sure I was well versed in the management of servants—"

Lady Catherine swatted her shoulder with the fan.

Elizabeth yelped.

"You well know that is not what I meant. You are rather adept at changing the topic of conversation."

"As are you."

The fan flickered. "Are you nervous about your new duties as mistress—"

"To Mr. Darcy?"

"Yes."

"A little." Heat crept up Elizabeth's neck and she fought the desire to giggle. "Are you concerned about marrying a man as ardent as my father?"

"What would you know of that?"

"He and Lady Ellen were little more discreet than

you and he."

Her fan fluttered faster.

"Lady Ellen used to say physical affections were the glue that held a couple together during the inevitable difficult times. She said it was the surest way to speak of love in a manner a husband understands."

Lady Catherine fanned faster. "What a very singular philosophy."

"If Papa's happiness was any indication, I would say she was quite correct."

"Indeed?"

"Yes. I hope you will make him very happy as well."

Lady Catherine's face grew redder still. Poor woman.

"Perhaps you already have?" A twinge of guilt nipped at Elizabeth's side. Maybe she had gone too far.

The fan snapped shut and slapped Elizabeth's shoulder. "That is quite enough! I am a lady and have conducted myself as such." Her eyes narrowed. "Even as I trust you have."

"Yes, madam, though admittedly a lady in love."

"He deserves you my dear. Such an excellent husband to my Anne, he will be no less to you."

"I was the one who told Papa he should consider you."

"So you set his cap for him! Cheeky girl." She kissed Elizabeth's cheek. "It is a good thing he listened to you—saved me a great deal of trouble."

A soft tap on the door and Jane appeared. "Are you ready?"

"Indeed we are." Elizabeth looped her arm in

Lady Catherine's and Jane's.

The ladies proceeded down the staircase and through the garden, along the short path to the church.

A light breeze carried the fragrance of roses from the chapel. Elizabeth closed her eyes and relished the perfume. Lady Ellen had always smelled of lavender. Lady Catherine would forever be linked with these roses.

Papa, in his finest suit, waited in the doorway. How dashing he looked, even with his arm still tied up in a sling. His brass buttons and his eyes twinkled in the morning sun. When had he been so satisfied, so happy? Not since Lady Ellen's death. What better than sharing a day destined to bring such joy to all?

"You are simply stunning, my dear."

"You are quite smart yourself, Papa." She held her cheek to his. Piper must have sharpened his razor particularly carefully this morning.

The vicar called them to order. Papa escorted her to the front of the church. Lady Catherine, on Darcy's arm, looked as nervous as any young bride.

Darcy placed her arm in Papa's, and Papa placed Elizabeth's in Darcy's.

He pulled her in close. The roses' perfume mixed with his sandalwood and leather scent and left her heart pounding so loudly she nearly missed her cue.

"I will," she stammered.

Darcy's cheek dimpled. Vexing man, he would have laughed had the consequences not been so very serious. Then again, she would have giggled in reversed circumstances. She could not hold it against him.

He slipped the ring on her finger and it seemed

only a moment later he led her from the chapel to their carriage, one of two waiting.

"I think it a very good idea your father had." he slipped into the seat beside her—his first liberty as her husband.

"Which one? Having two carriages attend us or sending the boys away with Piper to your hunting cabin deep in the woods for the week?"

He slid his arm around her. "Both. I am relieved Piper has charge of all the boys. He is one of the few I feel entirely capable of managing their mischief."

"Indeed he is. Although I expect Papa will insist he take a week to himself afterwards."

"Well-earned that will be, just as I have earned this enchanting opportunity to have a few minutes alone with you before we must meet our guests."

"It does seem a little silly though to take a carriage just to the front lawn of Alston."

"Perhaps, if it were our destination."

"We are not going to the wedding breakfast?"

"I did not say that." Delightful dimples appeared in his cheeks.

She would wake to those every morning now. What a satisfying thought. "What are you saying?"

"I have a wee detour in mind."

"Mr. Darcy!"

"No, no, silly girl. That shall wait for just a little while longer."

"Then what?"

"Have you no patience?"

"No, I have not." She squirmed in the seat and leaned toward the window. "Most certainly not with overbearing vexing men who would seek to tease the good humor from me. I am sure my father warned you."

A funny little crease appeared between her brows, the way it always did when she teased—one of his favorite expressions. A thrill shot through his veins. He leaned closer and held her silky cheek.

Her eyes glimmered with just the barest line of worry at the corner. Of course, she would be nervous, but her courage always rose at the most ideal of moments. She licked her lips. Now she must be kissed.

He leaned in and brushed his lips to hers. Though he had meant only warmth and a promise of what was yet to come, passion flamed unbidden as she melted under his caress.

"Mrs. Darcy," his voice more a breathy growl than a whisper. "You are fortunate I am a man of prodigious self-control and purpose lest Mrs. Hill's wedding breakfast would go unseen by her guests of honor."

"I was only making certain I had not already lost your interest."

"Never." He dove for the spot just below her ear that made her squeal and shiver in her oh-so delightful way. Yes, just like that.

"You will leave me most unpresentable if you continue." She slid her hand under his jacket, along the hem of his waistcoat and inches below.

"You seem to be the one intent on disarranging me," he mumbled into the soft, fragrant skin of her neck.

"Oh! Look!" She sat up straight and pointed. "Is that a folly?"

"Do you like it?"

A diminutive cottage on the other side of the pond peeked at them, tucked between rosebushes and half covered in flowering vines.

"It is exquisite."

"My father built it for mother before I was born. What you see though, is not just a folly, but a humble, completely functional structure. He took me here when I came of age, after her death. It had been a private spot for him and mother alone."

"You maintained it?"

"The gardener's wife manages the place. It is quite lovely inside or so she tells me."

"You do not know?"

"I have never been inside."

"Truly?" The most amazing, intuitive smile blossomed across her face, all the way to her eyes.

Dear, dear woman, she understood. She always understood. Most required him to try and struggle through explanations, but dearest, loveliest Elizabeth deduced what he did not have words to explain.

"I hoped you might spend the next few days there with me."

She squealed, face lit with little-girl joy. "How perfect."

"Mrs. Reynolds will have meals delivered and the gardener's wife will tend anything else we need. We will be entirely, completely, and delightfully alone."

"I can think of nothing better." She brushed his lips with a feathery kiss. "Perhaps we should go to breakfast now."

"You are right. It would not do to start the rest of our lives by disappointing your father."

"Certainly not! For this one day, I wish to have

only pleasing memories."

"I will do my best to make it so."

Bennet could not recall a finer table ever spread and he had supped with royalty. Mrs. Reynolds and Mrs. Hill outdid themselves with the wedding breakfast. Individually, the housekeepers were a force of nature, but together, it was hard to imagine something they could not accomplish. Exactly the kind of day his Cathy deserved.

Finally, Darcy and Lizzy rode off and the guests disappeared. The boys were away and well-minded and Jane was visiting Georgiana, much to Fitzwilliam's satisfaction. Perhaps he was becoming too lax in his supervision of his daughters. Then again, the colonel would not tempt his wrath and Jane was far less … free spirited … than Lizzy. It would all be well.

Bennet offered Cathy his arm. "Come, my dear."

She bit her lip and slid her trembling hand into the crook of his elbow. The poor dear, despite her elegant beauty and poise, she was just this side of terrified.

Francis and Ellen had come to him as maidens. With their high spirits and young love, they were excited to embark on their new journey with him. Not so Cathy. She knew what to expect—what she might expect—and it was the worst sort of expectation, one based on harsh reality.

To call Sir Lewis a boorish brute would have been high praise indeed. She had escaped his pox by locking the door to him, but her heart bore the scars of his betrayal.

Today was time for a new course to be charted.

But it must begin carefully.

He guided her upstairs, to the sitting room between their chambers. A tray with selections from breakfast waited for them. He seated her at the small table. A sunbeam grazed her cheek with an ethereal glow that so reflected her soul, his eyes misted.

"You are very lovely today." He sat beside her.

"I am glad you approve." She turned aside.

"No." He placed a finger under her chin and impelled her to look at him. "We shall not begin with you running from me."

She met his gaze, so fragile, so vulnerable, a careless word or even thought would surely shatter her. Doubtless no one else has ever been privileged to see her so. "I am not him."

"I know."

"No, you are willing to accept the possibility, but you do not believe, not yet."

"But—"

He shook his head. "You desire it to be so, but you cannot lie to me."

"I admire Elizabeth's bravery."

"It does much to recommend her, though it is born of foolhardiness."

"How can you say that?"

"She has no idea of the waters she may face. Innocence often begets such courage."

"Darcy would never—"

"Nor would I." He took her hand—cool and soft, and held her palm to his face. "Look at my daughters, Cathy. They are your surest picture of who I truly am and how I will treat you. What do you see in them?"

"You are a man who must be managed with a very strong hand."

He chuckled. "I suppose that is true. What else?"

She blinked rapidly and chewed her lip. "They trust you."

"Why?"

"They know you are an honorable man."

"If I am only honorable, I have failed."

"You are loyal and dependable and would lay down your life to defend them like you did for Philip and David."

"My sons, my grandsons, my daughters—and you Cathy." He kissed her palm.

She sniffled and choked back a mournful cry. "I am sorry. I am a fool."

"Not at all, you are wise to be cautious. But, I will not have the ghost of another man steal from us." He strode to a writing desk in the corner near the window, and removed a stack of papers. "Do you know what these are?"

"No."

He handed them to her.

"Where did you get them?"

"From Darcy. Apparently Anne had saved the scandal sheets reporting Sir Lewis's excesses, though I cannot fathom why."

"I had no idea." Her gaze skimmed the pages, color draining from her face.

"Darcy showed them to me when I asked about him." He carefully pulled the papers from her grasp. "What do you choose from this day forward—him or me?"

"You." Her voice quivered.

"Then let us be through with him." He tugged her to her feet and held the scandal sheets out at arm's length. "This is your chance—say to him now all those things you never gave voice." He pointed his chin at the trembling pages.

"How could you do that, Lewis?" she whispered.

"Go on."

"I loved you. I brought you everything you desired." Color flushed her cheeks "I gave it to you and you threw it all away." Her voice climbed louder and higher.

He placed his hand on her back. "What else?"

"You treated me like some cheap piece of laced mutton that you bought off the street, not even as well as the courtesan you kept. I, who was the source of it all, did not even rate that much courtesy. How dare you, you low born, disgraceful bye-blow. You were not even fit to darken my door yet you flattered my father enough with your lies—" Screaming now, she marched across the room, stomping tiny footprints into the carpet. "Damn you, you worthless piece of … of …"

"Shit?"

"Yes, yes exactly."

"Go on."

"I … I do not know how. I … I know not the words." She covered her mouth and giggled awkwardly.

"Shall I continue for you? I have acquired rather the right vocabulary for it."

"Please do."

He tucked the pages into his sling and extended his hand to her. She clutched it, and he unleashed a blistering storm of invectives some of his sailors might not even have understood.

Cathy mouthed the words just a phrase behind him.

Poor dear, how horrified she would be when they slipped out unbidden in a future heated moment. However, it was well worth the risk now.

"Have you anything else to say?"

"I am done with you, Lewis! I never wish to hear that name again."

He handed her the papers and pointed to the fire place. She crumpled one sheet at a time and threw them into the flames. The last one left her hand and burst into flame.

Tears trickled down her cheeks, landing on her gown and leaving dark spots in their wake. He dropped to his knees and sat on the floor, and she curled up beside him.

"It is done now." He slipped his arm around her.

"Yes it is. And now I shall remember the past only as it gives me pleasure." She sniffled.

"I shall remind you of that, Cathy."

"I love you."

Warmth exploded in his chest. "And I you." He nuzzled the side of her neck until she sighed that pleased little sound he longed to hear. "Let us go and do something about it."

And they did.

Acknowledgments

So many people have helped me along the journey taking this from an idea to a reality.
Abigail, Sandra, Jan, Dave, Linnea and Ruth thank you so much for cold reading, proof reading and being honest!
And my dear friend Cathy, my biggest cheerleader, you have kept me from chickening out more than once! Thank you!

Other Books by
Maria Grace

GIVEN GOOD PRINCIPLES SERIES
Darcy's Decision
THE FUTURE MRS. DARCY
ALL THE APPEARANCE OF GOODNESS
TWELFTH NIGHT AT LONGBOURN

Available in paperback, e-book, and audiobook format at
all online bookstores.

Don't miss special website exclusives:
free e-book BITS OF BOBBIN LACE with bonus
chapters from the series
And deleted scenes from REMEMBER THE PAST

Both available at
RandomBitsofFascination.com

About the Author

Though Maria Grace has been writing fiction since she was ten years old, those early efforts happily reside in a file drawer and are unlikely to see the light of day again, for which many are grateful. After penning five file-drawer novels in high school, she took a break from writing to pursue college and earn her doctorate in Educational Psychology. After 16 years of university teaching, she returned to her first love, fiction writing.

She has one husband, two graduate degrees and two black belts, three sons, four undergraduate majors, five nieces, sown six Regency era costumes, written seven Regency-era fiction projects, and designed eight websites. To round out the list, she cooks for nine in order to accommodate the growing boys and usually makes ten meals at a time so she only cooks twice a month.

She can be contacted at:

author.MariaGrace@gmail.com

Facebook:
http://facebook.com/AuthorMariaGrace

On Amazon.com:
http://amazon.com/author/mariagrace

Random Bits of Fascination
(http://RandomBitsofFascination.com)

Austen Variations (http://AustenVariations.com)

English Historical Fiction Authors
(http://EnglshHistoryAuthors.blogspot.com)

White Soup Press (http://whitesouppress.com/)

On Twitter @WriteMariaGrace

On Pinterest: http://pinterest.com/mariagrace423/